I0578222

GIRL OF FLESH AND METAL

GIRL OF FLESH AND METAL

ALICIA ELLIS

FIGMENTED INK

GIRL OF FLESH AND METAL

This is a work of fiction. All characters, organizations, and events portrayed in this book are products of the imagination or are used fictitiously.

Copyright © 2020 by Alicia Ellis

All rights reserved. No part of this book may be reproduced in any form or by any electronic or mechanical means, including information storage and retrieval systems, without written permission from the author, except for the use of brief quotations in a book review.

Cover design by J Caleb Design

Published by Figmented Ink in Atlanta
First Publication, April 2020
June 2023 Edition
Trade Paperback ISBN: 978-1-939452-54-2

Library of Congress Control Number: 2020905233

*To my mother,
for taking away the television
and turning me into a reader.*

*To my father,
for loving science fiction
and making me love it too.*

1

CyberCorp Tower, and all its evils, stretched seventy-two stories into the sky.

There it stood, beyond the narrow window of the nightclub where I sat. It was a mile away, but still, it dwarfed every other building in the city—a constant reminder that I couldn't escape it.

I kept trying though.

I sucked down half the cocktail in my glass. My boyfriend Jackson sat beside me on a black loveseat. He pulled a flask from his pocket and added more alcohol to my drink.

"You okay, Lena?" He tipped his head toward the tower looming outside the window.

"It's fine." A thrill tiptoed up my spine and burrowed at the base of my neck. Maybe from his touch, which always made me giddy, or maybe from the alcohol. The more I drank, the less I thought about CyberCorp staring down at me, and that could never be a bad thing.

The first semester of our senior year in high school had wrapped today, and my friends insisted we celebrate by hitting the city's hottest new nightclub. *This* nightclub.

Lit from below, the glass floor revealed a hollow space beneath where drinks and food zipped under our feet on white conveyer belts. Flashing red-and-blue tiles formed the ceiling. The colors winked off each black bar top and table.

Jackson fit in perfectly among the bright lights and the black decor, with his deep-blue eyes and night-dark hair. He lounged across the cushions with a liquid grin like he belonged here, like he belonged everywhere.

The club's manager ambled past as Jackson tucked the flask away, but her gaze stayed straight forward. My parents owned CyberCorp. And one of the few perks of being their daughter was that, despite my age, no one questioned my right to be here—or my right to drink. That extended to my friends too.

Melody raised her bright-yellow drink into the air. "Cheers to winter break and being almost done with high school."

We hooted our approval. Melody, her twin sister Harmony, and Jackson clinked their glasses together.

"What are you guys doing with your time off?" I asked.

"Absolutely nothing." Melody reclined back into the couch cushions. "And looking forward to every minute of it."

Harmony glowered down at her now-empty glass. "We

can't go on vacation because Daddy's working on the Model One androids. Lena's father calls every ten minutes."

"It's not my fault," I said. "If I could get my folks to scrap the whole project, I would. Trust me."

In fact, if I heard the term *Model One* one more time, I would scream.

CyberCorp's androids would ship in less than two months. They'd be the first humanoid, artificially intelligent androids for household use. Every other word out of my parents' mouths these days was about their precious creation.

Melody rubbed her sister's back. "Only two more months."

Harmony raised her arms and gestured in the air. Her brown eyes darkened as shadows moved over the irises. The shadows shifted each time she waved a hand. Thanks to her networked contact lenses, she saw a virtual drink menu floating in front of her. I didn't understand the point of seeing things that weren't there, so I'd never bothered to get lenses of my own.

"I don't get your problem with CyberCorp," Harmony said, attention back on me. "I'm mad right now, sure, but when Daddy gets his free time back, that'll change. Tech or no tech—it's where the money comes from."

Jackson chuckled, more to himself than to us. He came from old money that had nothing to do with CyberCorp. The twins' dad and my parents, on the other hand, had made theirs more recently. Specifically, the twins' family had made its money by working for mine.

"Lena's been listening to those anti-tech programs again." He jabbed me in the ribs. He meant it as teasing, but instead, it riled me up.

"Believe it or not, I can form my own opinions. Machines are replacing living, breathing people. We're forgetting how important it is to be human and interact with other living things. Humanity is sacred." I pointed at Harmony, who was still waving through the menu. "Would it be so bad if someone had to come over and take your order?"

"Yes." She swiped to select a menu item and dropped her hands. "It would take longer to get my next drink."

"And we'd spend that time talking to each other. And when the waitress came over, maybe we would talk to her too."

"No fighting," Melody shouted, before Harmony or I could speak another word. "We're celebrating."

"We're not fighting," I said. "We're discussing."

"Call it what you want, but I'm stopping it before the yelling starts. Now, hug it out."

Harmony and I had heard this demand from Melody enough in the past that we didn't argue anymore. We both stood, removed the space between us, and embraced. Harmony squeezed me around the waist, eyes pressed together in mock emotion. I shoved her away, laughing. I had to admit that Melody's peacemaking was effective— necessary or not.

Harmony flopped back onto the couch, and Jackson pulled me onto his lap.

A blond boy came toward us from a nearby table and

stopped in front of Harmony and Melody. He held out a hand to them and cocked his head toward the dance floor. He didn't care which gorgeous redheaded twin he danced with. Either one would do.

Harmony wrinkled her nose.

Melody shrugged and let him pull her to her feet.

Jackson ushered me to the dance floor after them. The techno music beat harder against my eardrums, and as usual he smelled of cinnamon and vanilla and something else I couldn't pinpoint. His fingers pressed into my lower back and moved me to the rhythm. I breathed it all in and let myself drown in it. His mouth moved to make words, but the music swallowed up all other sound, and I was okay with that.

My arms curled under Jackson's shoulders and around to his back, where tight muscles marked his shoulder blades. I let the rhythms and Jackson's arms at my waist transport me somewhere else. Somewhere that tower didn't exist, and my parents didn't exist, and the Model Ones didn't exist.

Three hours later, the four of us stumbled out of the club, well past my curfew. It had rained while we were inside. Shallow puddles in the parking lot reflected the bright colors of digital billboards nearby.

I'd stopped drinking hours ago, but my head still buzzed from the alcohol. It felt light, no longer stuffed with papers and homework and my parents' robots. I danced in a circle before grinning at my friends.

Harmony pouted at a moving display on a building across the street. "Why do the ads always pick you?"

The fifty-foot-high commercial on the building's side showed an image of me dressed in a pair of designer jeans. The other me twisted and flounced to show off every angle of my ass. The jeans' brand logo filled the space to the right of my head.

The ads usually featured me over the twins because my parents made more money than theirs, which made me a better advertising target. I didn't say that to Harmony though.

Harmony slid between me and the ad. She waved her right arm, to force the billboard's sensor to read the identification chip buried in the flesh of her wrist. The girl in the ad morphed into a waify redhead, still pictured in the same pair of jeans. Harmony stuck her hands on her hips, triumphant.

Jackson nodded toward Melody. "How do you know it's not her?"

"Easy. I'm the pretty one." Harmony flashed a smug smile.

Melody stuck up her middle finger.

Jackson propped himself against the glossy wall of the club's exterior. Next to him, the surface blended into another billboard, this one displaying an alcohol ad. None of us appeared in it—because we were all underage. The glowing images illuminated Jackson's drooping eyelids in technicolor.

"You ready to head home?" I asked him.

"Nah, I'm good. I didn't even finish my flask." He pushed himself off the wall, wobbled, then fell back against it. "Oops." He laughed and tried again. This time, he managed to keep his balance. "See. I'm good."

Even wasted, he attracted flirty glances from the twins. I had known him most of my life, and we'd dated for the past three years. My friends knew he was off limits. But with the deep-bronze skin of his mother's family and the bold blue eyes of his father, Jackson had an entrancing effect on people. His broad shoulders from competitive swimming didn't hurt either.

He caught me admiring him and tossed me a grin that could set the polar ice caps sizzling. Inside, I melted.

Melody stumbled toward the wall space next to Jackson. The nose-wrinkling scent of alcohol, flowery perfume, and other people's sweat trailed after her. "I finished my flask," she said. "And I'm going to sleep now."

Harmony grabbed her sister around the waist and held her in place. "Time to go."

My handbag buzzed, and I opened it. Inside, my hand-screen vibrated with a missed call. "I bet that's my mom."

My parents would freak about my missing curfew, and judging from the way my hand-screen was vibrating and blinking its little notification light, the freaking out was already in progress.

I pulled the small metal rectangle from my purse and slid its halves away from each other. The collapsible screen snapped into place between them. The display showed two messages and a missed call, all from my mother. I deleted the messages and touched the screen to call her back.

"Hold on," I told my friends. I took a couple steps away

from them to give myself space to talk without their over-hearing.

As soon as Harmony no longer blocked the line of sight between me and the ad across the street, the image of her switched back to me. A couple inches shorter, more hips, and dark hair.

In the ad, my hair looked perfect, the curls falling into place around my shoulders—in precisely the way they never did in real life. In real life, my dark mass of frizz grew bigger by the minute, thanks to this post-rain humidity.

My mother answered on the first ring. "Lena, you're downtown? It's the middle of the night." She'd tracked me. I scowled down at my wrist—like it had betrayed me by housing my trackable ID chip.

"I'm out with Jackson and the twins." I braced myself for a lecture. I hadn't intended to stay out this late, but my friends hadn't wanted to leave until now, and part of me loved the thought of making my mother squirm. She never had time for me, so why did it matter where I was?

"The Model Ones ship in less than two months, and I need to focus on that. I can't be up worrying about where you are and whether you're safe . . ." With gritted teeth, I let her go on about her greatest creation—the Model Ones.

"I'm fine, Marissa," I said, when she paused for a breath.

"You wouldn't miss my calls if you wore a micro-comm. And don't call me that."

I resisted the urge to tell her that was a reason *not* to get a micro-comm. The tiny electronic device, a quarter inch on each side, adhered to the side of a person's head behind the ear. While people nearby couldn't hear it ring, a comm's owner couldn't escape it.

"I'll think about it," I told her.

"You still have the one I got for your birthday. Why don't we put it on you tomorrow?"

"Sure. And then you can get back to your machines." As soon as I got home, I would have to lose that comm down the bathroom sink. "I'm on my way now. See you soon."

"I want you home in fifteen minutes." She disconnected before I could respond.

"Are you in trouble?" Melody asked, her brows tweaked with concern.

"Didn't you tell her the semester ended today?" Harmony asked. "We spent the last week buried in that English paper. We deserve a break."

"Marissa doesn't believe in breaks," I said. "They're against her religion."

Jackson pulled me toward himself and hooked an arm around my waist. "She just wants you to be successful." His breath smelled of fruit and alcohol, and the heat of it against my neck made my insides simmer.

"Mm-hmm." I leaned into his touch. "Let's talk about it later."

"She's prepping you for the future." His eyelids drifted shut and then open again, and I wondered whether he knew what he was saying. Maybe the alcohol was talking for him. "CyberCorp's going to be all yours one day." He slurred his words.

"What about what *I* want? That doesn't matter?" I

fumbled my efforts to get my hand-screen back into my purse, and it clattered to the pavement. I swept it up and shoved it in the bag.

Oblivious to my mounting discomfort, Jackson went on. "Imagine what it'll be like to have all that power."

No matter how good he looked, or smelled, or felt—if he didn't stop talking, there was going to be an argument. A big one. "I'm not going to work there, Jacks."

"But it will be all yours."

I clamped my mouth shut. It seemed pointless to explain my feelings to a drunk boy—feelings I'd told him a hundred times already, and each time, he nodded and smiled and insisted I would change my mind.

Harmony leaned on the wall next to Jackson. He poked her on the shoulder and laughed when she squirmed away from him. He poked her again.

"Better get home before you two fall asleep," I told both twins.

"I'm good," Harmony said. "Talk to you tomorrow."

She pushed off the wall, yanked Melody upright, and trudged across the parking lot. When they reached their brick-red car, the doors slid upward automatically. Harmony dumped her sister into the passenger seat and climbed in on the driver's side.

They both looked too drunk to drive, but the auto-drive would do all the work. With a loud honk of the horn, the vehicle pulled out of its parking space and sped onto the road.

Jackson somehow managed to support his own weight and trailed behind me to my pale-yellow car. Its hood, top, and trunk formed an uninterrupted arc, with doors flush against the rest of the smooth exterior. Sensing the presence of my ID chip, the door whirred upward. It revealed two rotatable front seats with a small open space between them and the long backseat.

Jackson's usually tan face had gone pale. "I think I need to lie down."

"Are you going to throw up?"

"Not if I lie down. Can I ride in the back?"

I tried to ease Jackson across the floor space, but he flopped into the backseat. His eyes closed before I even slid into the seat in front of him.

"Welcome, Lena," the car said in a silky female voice. The door slammed shut to secure us inside, and the motor started with a low, artificial hum. Despite the natural silence of electric motors, car companies added the hum to alert pedestrians of oncoming traffic. "Your mother instructed me to take you straight home."

The word *AUTO-DRIVE* lit up on the dashboard's display.

I reached for the door handle to get out. I'd planned to go straight home, after dropping Jackson at his place, but that didn't give my mother the right to make decisions for me.

The door didn't budge.

"I'm sorry, Lena. I cannot open. Your mother instructed me to take you straight home."

"Are you kidding me?" I slammed my palm against the steering wheel, as if that might somehow change the car's mind.

"What?" Jackson jerked into a sitting position. "You say something?"

I spun my seat around, so I could confront Jackson face to face. "You really think I would want to own Cyber-Corp?" I couldn't help myself. This conversation would make more sense if we had it tomorrow, when Jackson sobered up and I felt less like killing my car. But my irritation bubbled at the surface, like water in a tea kettle on the verge of screaming. "Do you even listen to me when I talk?"

"Sure, babe. It'll be perfect. You'll see."

"I'll *see?* Anti-technology isn't a phase for me. People aren't connecting anymore."

"Yeah, yeah, I know." His words agreed with me, but his indifference said otherwise.

The conversation struck a familiar chord. He knew the words to this exchange just as well as I did because he *had* listened every time I told him how I felt. But as far as he was concerned, his picture of our future meant more than my feelings. And that wasn't something I could live with.

"I want to break up," I said. The words flew from my mouth on their own. But once they were out there, I meant them.

"No you don't, babe." His eyes drifted shut.

"Go back to sleep." I spun my chair to face forward again. In the morning, we'd have a serious talk.

Obediently, he leaned against the window behind me and, ten seconds later, started snoring.

The car steered itself toward the road, and I figured I'd

try my luck at a detour. I yanked the wheel left at the edge of the parking lot, but it locked.

Groaning, I hung my head while the wheel rotated to the right on its own and pulled onto the street in the direction of the fastest route home. When we hit the highway, the car shot into the night, zooming past the white dashes that marked the lanes to my left and right. The needle on my speedometer inched upward until it pointed straight at the line between sixty and seventy.

Winter break had just begun, but the night held barely any chill. I pressed the control to roll down my window, and the wind whipped across my face so hard it stung.

Outside the window lay a starless sky. When I was small, there had been stars visible overhead, instead of this matte gray covering a city too bright for them. The city's lights hid them now. I missed the stars.

I pressed my foot hard on the accelerator.

"The speed limit is sixty-five miles per hour," came the car's syrupy voice.

"Oh, come on," I muttered.

At the precise speed of sixty-five, the car took me to my side of town, while I sat in the driver's seat with my arms crossed over my chest. I ripped the glove compartment open and extracted my emergency bag of gummy candies. Too frustrated to fumble with the tie, I tore the bag open and stuffed three in my mouth.

A mile from my house, the car stopped at a red light. For the hell of it, I slammed my foot on the accelerator again, but the car ignored me.

There was an emergency manual override somewhere.

My dad had pointed it out on the day he bought this vehicle to replace my older one, only a week ago. I squinted at the controls between the driver and passenger seats. Manual controls for navigation and music, but nothing for switching to manual drive.

My hand brushed against a button under the steering wheel. I slammed it, and the word *AUTO-DRIVE* disappeared from the dash. I pumped my fist into the air in celebration.

The movement tipped the bag of candies off my lap and onto the floor.

"Crap." I ducked beneath the dash to retrieve the bag, muttering a curse for the lost gummies strewn across the vehicle floor.

"Collision imminent," the car said. "In three . . . two . . ."

"What?" I sat straight up.

A silver vehicle streaked along the cross street, angled toward me. My stomach shrank into a tight ball.

This time, when I slammed my foot on the accelerator, the car jumped forward. For an instant, I squealed. But the other vehicle slammed into the side of my car, and my celebration morphed into a throat-tearing roar. Metal crunched and folded against more metal.

Numb.

Time slowed and skipped ahead in tiny blips.

To my left, someone moved in the silver car. A man stumbled out. He stood beside my window, his face painted with concern and panic.

The rush of adrenaline passed, and pain ripped through

my arm. It burned, like it had been ripped apart, seared in two. The crushed car door hid most of the limb from view, and what I could see of it was only the smashed, bloody flesh of my shoulder.

I yanked to free it. Sobs mingled with my screams, and darkness crept inward until nothing else existed.

2

"Lena."

I wasn't dead. I knew that for certain because, if I were, my body wouldn't feel like it was being crushed under a giant boulder.

"Lena." I recognized my mother's voice now. Doused with concern, it sounded hollow and far away. Yet I smelled her rich, flowery scent as if she sat right beside me.

A steady *bip*, *bip*, *bip* sounded from my right. I tore my eyelids open, but squeezed them shut when fluorescent light stung my eyes. Still, I sensed the brightness on the other side.

"Can we lower the lights in here?" My father had a way of making his requests sound like commands.

A moment later, the room dimmed enough that I risked opening my eyes again.

Seated on the side of my white-sheeted bed, my mother stared down at me. Concern swam in eyes the same dark-brown as mine. For once, her tight curls poofed around her head and fell to the top of her shoulders, instead of being tied into a tight knot. An ivory tunic contrasted against her dark-brown skin. Puffy red eyelids surrounded her eyes.

"Mom." My voice came out ragged, rough against my raw throat. My tongue somehow got in the way of speech instead of helping it. I swallowed the saliva in my mouth and tried again. "Where am . . ."

"Shh." She stroked my hair in a vaguely familiar way—something she hadn't done for many years. "You're going to be fine. Your father's here too." She gestured to my right.

With an effort that made me grimace, I turned my head. Clad in a dark-gray suit, Thomas Hayes sat in a leather armchair, one ankle propped up on the other knee. His tan skin looked paler than usual, and tired eyes stared back at me. But he said nothing, only offered an encouraging smile.

I couldn't remember the last time I'd had both my parents' attention, without either of them rushing off to work. And all it took was me almost dying. I would have laughed if I didn't hurt so much.

Details of the accident came spinning back to me. The road twirled around me. The door crushed into my mangled arm. My own screams—and nothing but silence from the backseat.

"Jackson," I said, trying to sit up. "Is he okay?"

My mother covered my right hand with hers. "He's here, in another room. With his own doctors."

"How is he?"

"He's not awake yet. He . . . needed a little more work

than you." She nodded toward my left arm. A white sheet covered the limb from shoulder to fingertips.

"We have a lot to tell you," came an unfamiliar female voice from the doorway.

Its owner stepped into my oversize hospital room—at least I guessed it was a hospital room, or a cross between one and an office. The beep I was hearing belonged to a heart monitor, attached by a clasp to my right forefinger. A metal stand held a bag of liquid, from which a clear solution flowed through the needle stuck into the crook of my right arm.

But most hospital rooms didn't contain so many robotic parts.

What looked like an array of robotic arms and hands littered a long table stretched across the left side of the room. Some were partly disassembled, with wires attaching the hand to the arm or the fingers to the hand.

Something about them struck me as odd—something other than the fact that they were arms with no torsos, legs, or other body parts. But my head felt cloudy, groggy. My thoughts moved slowly. I couldn't figure out what bothered me about them.

The least hospital-like thing about the room was the walls. Four giant vid-screens surrounded me from floor to ceiling. They displayed a panoramic beach scene in such high resolution that I could almost believe I was lying on the sand.

Waves lapped against the shore in a calming rhythm. Whisper-thin clouds drifted across a blue sky. Faint seagull calls sounded, as if from a distance. The images contrasted sharply with the sterile machines and robotic parts around the room.

The woman who'd spoken wore a white lab coat with the name *CyberCorp* stitched on it in blocky red letters. A pen stuck out of her light-blond hair, which was twisted back into a knot. She stood at about six feet, broad-shouldered, with a nice padding around the waist.

She held a tan folder about an inch thick. The folder's cover had my name, Lena Hayes, printed in large letters.

"I'm Dr. Fisher," she said, her tone clipped and businesslike. "I work for CyberCorp."

So it wasn't a hospital after all. I glanced over at my mom, praying she could see the pleading in my eyes. The pleading to escape this place as soon as possible.

"There's nothing to worry about now," my mother said. "You're at CyberCorp."

I groaned, then flinched when the groan bit deep into my chest. "Allie," I said. "Is she here?" It hurt to talk—like gravel rubbing inside my throat.

"Allison's at home. I didn't want her to see you like this."

At four years old, my sister had a way of looking at the world that I envied. She saw the good in everything. And with the grim faces peering down at me, I could use some of that spirit right now.

"These are my college interns, Ron and Simon." Dr. Fisher nodded toward two young men behind her, both brown-haired and dark-eyed, but only one wore glasses. They couldn't have been much older than me. "You were in an accident."

Ron or Simon—I didn't know which was which—hurried to my side to check the readouts on the machine tracking my vitals. The other boy stayed locked to Fisher's side as she moved farther into the room.

"I want to go home," I said. My words stumbled all over each other, flipping and sliding. But somehow, my mother understood them.

"Not yet, honey."

Dr. Fisher cleared her throat and moved to the foot of my bed, where she was impossible to ignore. "Miss Hayes." She cleared her throat loudly.

"Lena," I mumbled.

She continued with barely a pause. "You were in an accident three weeks ago. Your arm was—"

Without thinking, I jerked my body to try to sit upright. Pain shot through me like a blanket of needles shoved into every inch of my body. I lay back against the pillow. "Was I in a coma?" I asked.

"Yes. A medically induced one."

I opened my mouth to ask why they'd induce a coma, but the doctor continued talking without giving me the opportunity.

"We induced the coma to allow us to operate on your arm, and then to give you time to heal after the operation. You might not remember that it was injured in the crash."

Of course, I remembered. Feeling like my arm was being twisted and seared and burned all at once was not something I would forget. For the second time in a span of five minutes, I tried to see my left arm. It wasn't my bedsheet covering the arm. A second sheet lay over one side, and its sole purpose seemed to be hiding the limb.

It suddenly hit me what was odd about the robotic parts in the room: every one of them belonged to a left arm.

"We tried to save your arm at first, but it would never have been the same again," Dr. Fisher said. "At your parents' request"—my parents rarely made *requests*, which explained this woman's distaste at being here—"I fitted you with a cybernetic limb."

"A cyber—what?" My right fist clenched. I'd lived with my parents long enough to be computer savvy, and if that word meant what I thought it meant, I wasn't about to like whatever Dr. Fisher said next.

"A cybernetic limb. It's coupled directly to your nervous system and to the chip we installed in your brain. Once your body becomes accustomed to it, you'll be able to use it just like the arm you were born with. At first, you'll have to explicitly think about it to make it move. But eventually, thanks to advanced AI—artificial intelligence—the arm will learn how your brain works, and it will react more naturally."

I understood each of the words as she spoke them, but it took a moment for me to recognize their meaning when strung together like that. Cybernetic arm. Chip in my brain.

My parents knew how much I valued humanity and human interaction, and despite that, they'd cut off my arm and replaced it with a machine. For the rest of my life, everything I did would involve a computer.

The artificial intelligence only made it worse. *I* wouldn't be operating the arm—a machine would do that job. Part of my body had been replaced by a whole different entity.

"You installed hardware inside my body?"

"Yes," Dr. Fisher said, "and software too, or else the hardware would be rather useless."

"There's a chip in my brain?"

"Yes."

I blinked at her, mutely. I should have had a hundred different questions, but I had none. None that would rip the chip out of my head or reattach my flesh-and-bone arm. I didn't care how destroyed it was. It was mine. It was human, not an artificially intelligent machine.

"I want to see the arm."

My mother shifted in her seat, and in response, I could practically feel my blood pressure catapult through the roof. She'd already seen the arm, and she was nervous.

I resisted the urge to ask her to leave the room. I was wrecked enough without her making it worse.

Without ceremony, the doctor strode to my side and lifted the sheet. My mouth fell open.

The corner of my shoulder—where it began to curve downward—was still me, but scarred. My olive-toned skin wore a mess of raised scars. The flesh there was all ragged patches, still healing, in an array of shades approximating my usual skin tone. Lines of scarred skin extended upward to the top of my shoulder and over my collarbone.

Just below the curve of my shoulder, the flesh stopped abruptly, melded to silver metal with a slight yellow tint.

I had seen the material before, in news reports and in my dad's home office. CyberCorp called it Flexim, a flexible metal. It had just a touch of elasticity, which made it difficult to break, but it could bend over and over again. The elbow and fingers were made of a series of narrow metal pieces layered to slide over one another in joints.

I reached across my body and touched the connection between flesh and metal. The metal extended even beneath the skin, which felt rigid and stiff overtop it. Inching the fingers of my other hand up along the shoulder, I kept pressing until I hit soft flesh near my collarbone. They'd replaced the entire arm and most of the shoulder.

I tried to raise the arm to get a closer look, but it wouldn't move. I tensed my whole body and concentrated on moving it, but it just lay there like the hunk of metal it was. Like the machine it was. Like the lifeless, heartless, inanimate thing it was.

"It's thinner than my right one," I said. The statement sounded ridiculous, even to my own ears. But it seemed strange that CyberCorp would work so hard to make me a new arm, and then make it narrower than the other one. If I was going to be artificial, at least I could be well-proportioned.

"After we're sure it's working okay, we'll add a layer of skin we've grown in the lab," Dr. Fisher said. "It'll look and behave just like skin you've grown yourself. It will even be able to experience pain. And once it's on there, your arms will be the same size."

"Why would I want pain?"

"Pain lets you know something's wrong. Just think. If

you were shot with a bullet and felt nothing, you wouldn't know to go to an emergency room. You'd bleed to death."

"Okay. So when am I going to get the skin?" I cringed at the thought of walking into school with a robotic limb. I'd attract attention, and not in a good way.

"When you're mostly healed from the surgeries and the arm works as well as your other one. Then we'll know everything's operating as it should. I expect that'll happen by the time we send you home." Dr. Fisher reached into her breast pocket and withdrew a clear disc-like container. It held a tiny black chip, no more than a third of an inch on each side. "We recovered your ID chip. There's a slit for it in your new wrist, but it won't stay put there until we install your skin." She passed the chip to one of her assistants—Simon or Ron—I still didn't know which.

In my original arm—the one I'd lost—the chip was surgically installed. Most people had them installed in their right arms, but my left arm was dominant, so that's where they put my ID chip when I was a toddler.

Fisher's assistant reached over my left arm, which lay limp at my side, and pressed a spot between my bicep and shoulder. A small compartment door slid open. He pushed the chip into the compartment, which slid closed again. "For now, let's keep it here. We'll get it properly installed when we put the final touches on your arm." Unlike Dr. Fisher, this guy was grinning like crazy. He walked with an excited bounce.

It was only after the assistant stepped back that I realized I hadn't felt anything when he'd opened my arm.

"How come I didn't feel that?"

"Right now," Dr. Fisher said, "the arm is just metal, programming, and circuitry. It won't feel touch until we add the skin."

For the second time, I tried to lift my hand to my face, but it refused to budge. "I can't move it."

"You're going to need physical therapy, but not nearly as much as you would with a traditional prosthetic. It will react more naturally over time. Eventually, you'll regain full function, which is more than you could ask for with any other prosthetic. Soon, you won't even have to think about moving it to do so—just like your other arm."

"About that physical therapy," my mother said to the doctor. "I realize most of your work on the arm is behind you, but please remain actively involved in Lena's treatment going forward as well."

"My assistants—"

My mother broke in before Fisher could finish. "I'm sure your assistants are very capable, but I want you overseeing every step of her therapy."

"Of course. I'm sure I can find time to spend with both the Model Ones and your daughter. She's a high priority."

"She's your only priority."

Dr. Fisher nodded, but the way her jaw tensed told me she had a lot more to say on the subject.

My father pushed up from his seat. When he stood right next to me, legs brushing the bed, I had to crane my neck back to see his face. At six feet tall, in his impeccable suit with straight dark hair and prematurely gray strands, my dad struck an imposing figure. Even now, with his face ashen instead of its usual tan, his presence commanded respect. I held back the rest of my questions and waited for him to speak.

"You're going to be fine." His voice held so much confidence that, for once, I was grateful he was in control. "You'll work with the doctors here. Soon, you'll be as good as new."

Despite his words, I would never be as good as new. From this point forward, I'd never again be a complete me.

3

"Is it always going to jerk around like that?" I asked Ron.

I'd been awake for a few days, and by now, I had learned which of Dr. Fisher's assistants was which. Ron was the one who wore glasses, black plastic ones that looked simultaneously cool and nerdy. I suspected Dr. Fisher still hadn't figured out that mystery, because I had yet to hear her call either of them by name.

"You're making great progress," Ron said. "Each time you move it, the arm is learning how your brain impulses translate into action. You'll be up and running in no time."

My nose wrinkled at his words—up and running. They made it sound like I was some kind of machine.

I gritted my teeth and bent my elbow. My hand jumped toward me. I dodged to one side to avoid hitting myself in the face. Ron snorted, barely containing his laughter.

When I shot him a glare, the resistance fell, and he let out a loud guffaw.

Under Ron's watchful eye, I sat on a cushioned weight bench in CyberCorp's makeshift physical-therapy room. The place looked like a cross between a gym and an office. It held the usual gym equipment: weight benches, free weights lining a mirrored wall, and a few adjustable workout machines. A desk occupied one corner of the room, and a small vid-screen faced the chair behind it.

Just like in my assigned room, vid-screens covered every wall. Today, the screens showed a snowy terrain with tall mountains in the distance. I didn't think it was the best choice to create a calming atmosphere. Mostly, it made me feel cold.

I'd spent the first hour of this physical-therapy session staring down at my arm and willing it to move, only to have it ignore me. At first, my elbow wouldn't bend, and the fingers wouldn't curl. As thanks for all my hard work, my shoulder throbbed, but I'd managed to get the arm to move.

My most recent attempt brought the day's total to six bicep curls—meaning six times I had almost hit myself in the face. Lucky for me, I succeeded in actual impact only the first time, and I was too busy celebrating having moved my arm to be upset that I nearly skewered an eye.

"You have my pills?" I let my arm hang at my side. The pain in my shoulder worsened by the second, and a headache was blooming at the base of my neck.

He extracted a bottle of pills from his pocket and tapped one into my right hand. I popped it in my mouth and swallowed without water. The pain never went away, but in a few minutes, it would lessen to a dull ache. I looked forward to that.

"You're doing great." Ron's face lit up with sincerity.

I figured the enthusiasm was meant to keep me motivated. Mostly, it just reminded me that six reps with zero pounds was now a reason for excitement. Lucky me.

"Is your mom still coming by?" He shot a look at the closed door leading into the physical-therapy room. "Weren't you expecting her about ten minutes ago?"

"She wasn't sure she'd be able to make it, so I told her not to worry." Despite my words, I glanced at the door too.

I wiped the sweat from my forehead, and Ron handed me a water bottle. By instinct, I gripped it in my left, my dominant hand. It took me a second to realize what I'd done, and I couldn't help the smile from spreading across my face.

"I'm holding the bottle!" Now it was me who sounded too enthusiastic about minimal progress. My smile withered and died when I tried to raise the water to my mouth. With a frustrated grunt, I passed it to my right hand and took a swig.

"I promise you," Ron said, "this will get better. Everything's going to be fine."

"What about Jackson? Is he going to be fine too?" My chest constricted every time I thought of him stuck in that coma—where I'd put him.

"I checked on him for you this morning. Still asleep. Sorry." He patted my shoulder, but his sympathy did nothing to ease the guilt.

I took another gulp of water. "Can't we just modify my arm's programming to make this easier?"

"Yes, but we're not going to. It's calibrated based on your height, weight, and muscle mass. Once it learns how you operate, it will be just as strong as your right arm. If we change the strength specs, eventually the arm will get too strong. This is a learning process. Be patient."

I hated patience. "How often does CyberCorp do this medical-type stuff?"

"It used to be pretty rare, but they're doing it more and more often now. Mostly charity cases because low-income patients are happy to try out early models. It's more aggressive treatment than their insurance would cover, but from us, it's free."

"So you guys have done a lot of arms like mine?"

"Not that I know of. Up until now, we've dealt with smaller medical devices. Replacement joints—that kind of thing, none of them artificially intelligent." Ron paused and licked his lips. "My mother had treatment here four years ago. Cancer. They used nanobots—incredibly tiny devices—to attack the cancerous cells."

"Really?" I leaned forward in my seat. "Is she . . . How did the surgery go?"

His jaw tightened. "Not well. She died soon after."

My eyes widened.

He gave an awkward laugh and a smile that looked like the edges were glued upright. "The bots didn't kill her. Cancer did."

"I'm so sorry."

"Me too. My dad took her death really hard. The nanobots got his hopes up."

The sound of a door opening came from behind me. I twisted in my seat, expecting to find my mother there. Instead, Dr. Fisher stood in the doorway. She waved Ron toward her. Her other assistant, Simon, stood at her side, his hand-screen open at his fingertips and tilted toward the doctor. Her gaze settled on me briefly before shifting back to Ron, without even a nod of recognition.

"I'll be right back." Ron hurried toward Dr. Fisher and Simon.

While I waited for him to return, I picked up my own hand-screen. An alert blinked in the corner, informing me that Philip Pollock had posted a new audio program online. An anti-technology activist, Pollock kept his listeners in the know about happenings at CyberCorp and other tech companies.

I pressed a button on the side of the device, and an earpiece popped out. I stuck it in my ear, so I could hear the program without subjecting everyone in the room to the noise.

". . . contrary to nature. Not only is technology in direct opposition with nature, but it has evolved to bring out the worst in us. It makes us greedy and selfish, makes us tear down natural forests, build atop natural deserts. We are the destroyers of this world. I'm not saying we should get rid of it completely and return to the dark ages. But a medium needs to be found—a balance between progress and nature . . ."

I found myself nodding along with Pollock's words.

Historically, I didn't agree with everything he said. He'd introduced me to issues that came along with advancing technology, and I respected the man—idolized him, really. But these days, he seemed just as concerned with smearing tech enthusiasts as he did with promoting his cause.

Today, though, his words hit the mark. *We are the destroyers of this world.* CyberCorp had certainly managed to destroy *my* world, first with its auto-drive technology and now with my atrocity of an arm. Sure, I'd played a role in the accident too, but it would never have happened without CyberCorp's tech.

"My sources have confirmed that Lena Hayes, daughter of CyberCorp moguls Tom and Marissa Hayes, was in a serious car accident several weeks ago . . ."

My breath caught as I waited for him to tell the world about my cybernetic arm. He would make me an outcast, a target of the anti-tech community I respected so much.

"I want to know why the Model One rollout has not been postponed in light of this accident. Lena Hayes was in a coma for weeks, presumably on the edge of life and death. Yet her parents carry on business as usual. Why? Because technology is more important than humanity, more important than their own child. When I tell you, time after time, that one of the many evils of technology is its ability to push us farther and farther apart, this is what I mean: technology over humanity."

I exhaled. He hadn't mentioned my arm, and it didn't sound like he knew. CyberCorp employees all signed strict confidentiality agreements, and it looked like the staff I worked with kept their word. No one would know about my arm—until I rejoined the world outside this building.

When this got out, Pollock would have a lot more to say about my accident and how my parents were handling it. He would make me a target of anti-tech fanatics just to make my parents look bad. As a girl who was now part machine, I represented everything Pollock—and I—hated about technology.

The conversation between Ron, Dr. Fisher, and Simon went on longer than I expected, still in progress when the audio program ended five minutes later. The doctor was now pointing back and forth between Simon's hand-screen and me. I couldn't hear her words.

Only one other patient shared the gym with us this morning. A boy with longish dark hair, badly in need of a cut. He sat on a weight machine, working his right leg. In long gym shorts, most of the leg remained hidden. And most of it looked human, unlike my new arm. But a small metal square graced the side of his right knee.

Each time the boy kicked his foot to extend the leg, a thirty-pound stack of weights lifted on the machine. Sweat popped out on his forehead.

With each kick, he murmured a number. When he reached fifteen, he stopped, and his body slumped. The leg hung beneath him, and the stack of weights slammed back into place. The boy swiped up a bottle of water from the floor. He took a series of long gulps and then tossed the bottle back on the floor, where it rolled before stopping.

His gaze followed it and then kept going until it landed on me. He caught me staring at him.

He squinted while he examined my left arm. I wished I'd worn long sleeves. I still couldn't imagine going out in the world and showing it off. Part of me wanted to insist they keep me here until they deemed me ready for new skin, but a louder part of me wanted to get as far away from this cursed building as possible.

Undeterred by my scowl, the boy sauntered toward me.

"I'm Hunter," he said.

Despite his dark hair, he had a fair complexion, the kind that probably burned if he got too much sun. A royal blue T-shirt sporting the Superman emblem draped his lean frame. His lopsided smile revealed a dimple on only his right cheek.

I'd lost my arm, and this boy couldn't seem to stop himself from grinning.

I kept my expression placid. "Lena."

"I know who you are." I wouldn't have thought it was possible, but the smile got wider. He had great teeth, straight and white but way too happy.

"Do I know you?"

"I transferred to Hanover on scholarship last semester. I sat in front of you in Calculus." He spun around to offer me a view of the back of his head. "Recognize me now?" he asked after turning to face me again.

My mouth twitched downward. "Still no."

"They fitted you for a new arm?" He pointed at my left hand, which hung motionless at my side.

"Yep." Why did he bother to phrase it like a question when the answer was obvious?

"What happened?"

"Don't you know it's rude to just ask people about their injuries?" I pushed all the scorn I could manage into my tone. If I was lucky, he'd go back to his side of room, and I could get on with my daily torture ritual without his incessant glee making it worse.

No such luck.

"I got a new knee." He pointed—proudly—at the metal plates on the sides of his right knee. "I was hit by a car when I was ten, been through four different surgeries and a couple years in a wheelchair since then. This was my first procedure with CyberCorp." He bounced up and down, flexing his legs. "Feels fantastic. What your parents do is amazing."

"Yeah," I muttered. "Amazing."

I envied his knee. It improved his life without artificial intelligence. His head had no chip in it, eavesdropping on his brain signals and sending signals of its own. I fully supported the use of prosthetics, but I wanted to be the one in control—not artificial intelligence. The AI in my arm changed a useful thing into something unhuman.

"I guess I should get back to my rehab," I added.

"I'm done for the day. But I'm a pro at this rehab thing, so if you want to talk . . ." He withdrew a pen from his pocket and lifted my right arm—the one that was still human. His grip around my palm came with surprising confidence.

I yanked my hand away and clutched it close to my stomach. "What are you doing?"

"Sorry." He mumbled something unintelligible and then added, "I was just going to write my phone number."

He finally dropped the silly smile, and somehow, I preferred him with it. So I stuck my hand back out toward him. "It's fine."

He touched my wrist more lightly this time, like he feared he'd spook me. On my palm, he wrote out the digits while I ransacked my head for words to shatter the silence.

"Call me if you want to talk," he said as he returned my hand. "See you around."

He ambled toward the door, his steps deliberate, favoring his right leg. Just before he exited, he glanced over his shoulder at me. I silently cursed myself that he caught me staring for a second time. He gave me that tilted grin again, then limped out of view.

Ron finished his conversation with Dr. Fisher, who nodded her goodbye and escaped the room with Simon. Before returning to our torture session, Ron pulled a hand-screen from his pocket and stretched the display to its full size.

"How are you doing?" he asked.

With my right index finger, I pointed at my left shoulder. "Missing an arm."

He ignored my snark. "Dr. Fisher suggested we make a few tweaks to your programming."

He reached to the interior side of my bicep and pressed the small button there. The compartment slid open below it. Ron gestured for me to lift my arm, so he could access it. My ID chip still sat in the interior storage space. Next to it was a small outlet for a rectangular plug.

"Dr. Fisher said your mom's not going to make it

down." He slid a cable from his hand-screen into the outlet.

"Yeah, of course." I bit my lip and bobbed my head up and down, so he'd know I was fine. Of course, I couldn't have expected my mom to drop everything to check on me. I'd see her late tonight, when she wrapped up her work for the day.

Now connected to my arm, Ron's hand-screen displayed bold letters reading *PROTOTYPE INTERFACE*, with the smaller words *Enter Password* below them. He angled the device away from me while he typed the password. The image on the screen changed to a list of file names. They filled the screen, and Ron scrolled down to find the one he was looking for.

"What are you doing?" I asked.

"Dr. Fisher agrees with you that your arm should be stronger than it is. Since we've never produced anything like this before, there's going to be a little trial and error. It'll still take hard work from you to get it to full strength. But since your left is your dominant side, we can up the power a little and see how that goes."

"So it'll be easier to lift things after you do this?"

"After this modification, I think we can bump you up from no weight to two-pound free weights."

"Oh wow," I mumbled. "Lucky me."

He pressed the surface of the hand-screen to open one of the files. The display filled with program code that made my arm operate—or *not* operate given how useless it was at the moment. He changed a few lines in that file, paused, and then deleted several lines in another.

The word *COMPILING* popped onto the screen with a progress bar beneath it. A few seconds later, the display switched to *INSTALLING* and a new progress bar.

A small red light lit up on my palm. Surprised, I tried to jerk the arm toward me, but it didn't budge. It had shut down.

Panic tore a path through my insides. As much as I hated having this thing attached to me, the thought of the alternative—having no arm—terrified me.

The hand-screen beeped when the progress bar reached a hundred percent, and the red light went out. I tried to move the arm again. It whipped up toward me and slammed into my left cheekbone. I shrieked and, instinctively, went to cover the spot—succeeding in slamming myself in the face a second time.

"Whoa, whoa." Ron grabbed my wrist to stop me from pummeling myself a third time. "Relax."

I sucked in a deep breath, then let it out slowly. He released the limb, and it dropped to my side.

"Good," he said. "Let's get back to work. Grab those." He pointed to a pair of bright-pink two-pounders that sat atop the row of free weights lining the wall.

I didn't move. "Why does Dr. Fisher hate me so much?"

"She doesn't hate you. And this isn't relevant to your therapy."

"Sure it is. Most of my therapy is mental. You've said that like five times today. You can improve my mental state by telling me why Dr. Fisher looks like I'm wasting her time."

"She doesn't hate you." He gestured toward the weights

a second time. When I still didn't move, he added, "She doesn't appreciate having to work on you when she could be focused on troubleshooting the Model Ones for the upcoming rollout."

"What's she got to do with it? She's a doctor, and the Model Ones are androids. It's not like they need annual physicals."

"She's a medical doctor *and* a PhD. Until you showed up, she spent her time tweaking the psychological programming of the Model Ones. She's been working all her life for this. But your dad insisted on CyberCorp's best scientists being transferred to your case."

"And you?" I asked. "You're her assistant, which means you were pulled off the Model Ones too. Does it bother you?"

"It did, but not anymore. You're just as fascinating. Dr. Fisher can't see your potential." His eyes lit with excitement. "Tech companies have worked for decades to elevate humankind with technology. You're the culmination of that. Man—or girl—plus machine. You're exactly the project I want to work on right now." He passed me one of the pink, two-pound weights. "But I need you to work harder."

I grabbed the weight with my right hand and set it in my left. The hand refused to grip it, but Ron closed my metal fingers around the weight. I clenched my jaw and willed my arm to move.

4

THE CYBERCORP STAFF HAD TRIED TO HELP ME PACK UP my sparse belongings—the textbooks and clothing our housekeeper Marcy had brought, and the things my friends had delivered. Harmony and Melody had both tried to visit, but I'd refused. I didn't want them to see me like this—helpless. So I'd told them CyberCorp didn't allow me to have visitors.

Now, after three weeks in a drug-induced coma and another two of therapy, my new arm worked almost as well as the old one. So when the staff tried to pack me up, I told them—in the nicest way possible—to go to hell. They'd waited on me for the past two weeks, and Lena Hayes didn't need anyone's help.

Ron stood in the doorway watching me, arms folded across his chest.

"Can't we do the skin transplant before I leave?" I glared down at my shining silver arm.

"When you're at full strength and we're sure the programming is perfect, we'll do the transplant. As long as you're still having bad headaches, we have to wait. They should have lessened by now, but since they haven't, it's hard to predict when Fisher will feel comfortable taking that step." I opened my mouth to say something, but he cut me off with a laugh. "And no, you can't stay here until then. Your mother says today's the day you go home, so today's the day."

I scowled but said nothing more. Not that I wanted to spend another minute in this building, but if the alternative was to show the world my cybernetic arm, I couldn't decide which fate was worse.

"Are you sure you don't want to wait for her?" Ron asked. "She said to expect her around noon."

"You mean like how she waited for my approval before attaching a computer to my head?" I'd spent a lifetime obeying my parents, and this was how they repaid me. I took pleasure in this small rebellion.

I knelt to peer under the bed for any stray belongings and grasped—in my right hand—a small, pink Teddy bear Melody had sent me. I placed the bear in the corner of my suitcase and zipped the thing closed.

Although naturally left-handed, I'd resolved to use my right arm as much as possible. I could do nothing about having this metal limb, but I could minimize my use of it. In that small way, I could take back control of my life.

Ron stepped onto one of the moving walkways in the hallway, and I got on behind him. With its glossy white walkways and floors, the halls had an institutional feel, reduced somewhat by the colorful vid-screens. Here, the screens covering the walls didn't stick with a single scene. Their text and images changed constantly.

Part of one wall displayed company announcements, while another section displayed the status of various projects—the Model Ones, several new micro-comms and hand-screens, and a new line of networked contact lenses. A section to my left held a moving image of a creek flowing over rocks in a forest. It was the same image on my room's displays today.

Despite the pain medication, my left shoulder and head still ached. Each glimpse of the constantly moving images across the walls left my head spinning. I kept my gaze locked straight ahead.

Ron led me off the walkway and pointed to one of the white doors interspersed among the screens. I pushed the door open and stepped inside.

Jackson lay shirtless on a twin-sized hospital bed like the one in my room. Also like my room, the walls displayed the moving image of a creek, with a soft bubbling sound filling the background. They'd told me he'd had more extensive surgery than I had, and that he was still asleep, but I wasn't prepared for what I saw.

While only my left arm had been injured, the entire left side of Jackson's body, and some of his right, appeared to have undergone surgery. A sheet and blanket covered him up to the waist, but his arms lay atop the coverings. His left arm had been replaced, up to and including his collar-bone. The flesh of his neck melded into metal, which stretched across the left edge of his chest and over his entire arm.

Metal covered the left side of his ribcage and stomach as well, disappearing under the blankets. The right arm hadn't been spared either, but its work was less extensive. The upper arm remained flesh, changing to metal at the elbow.

I could barely stand to look at his face. His silver cheek and jaw reflected the overhead fluorescent lights. Except for its metallic glow, he looked just like the faces of those fake skeletons they had at the front of Biology class freshman year. The flesh on the left side was gone, leaving his jaw visible all the way to the back teeth.

What remained of his original face was pale now, no longer full of humor and life. Still, on the right, he'd kept one perfect eyelid with long dark lashes and one model-worthy cheekbone.

I swallowed hard to keep myself from getting sick all over the floor. Ron's hand on my back was the only thing keeping me upright. Barely.

I'd been so angry with Jackson the night of the accident, but I didn't want this. I didn't want his body ripped to pieces, turned into some kind of experiment. Regardless of where he and I stood romantically, I loved him. I'd known him most of my life, and I wanted to continue knowing him for the rest of it.

But not like this.

I stepped deeper into the room.

Ron gripped my bicep before I reached Jackson's side. "You can't touch him."

But I wanted to. I wanted to feel his hands at my waist, his breath on my neck, his heart next to mine. "How long is he going to be . . . ?" My voice cracked.

"It's hard to say. They're doing the same healing treatments on him that they did on you, but as you can imagine, those will be a lot more extensive with Jackson. Plus, he has more hardware, and the team working on him is trying to iron out the kinks with the parts being used."

If I could go back five weeks, I'd promise to reconsider working for CyberCorp someday. We could talk about the future he planned for us, but first, he had to wake up. Whatever he wanted—as long as he looked at me with blue eyes that had searched me a thousand times before, held me with arms that had squeezed me a thousand times before.

But first, he had to *wake up*.

My hand-screen vibrated in the pocket of my leather jacket, and I jumped, startled. I opened it and held it to my ear without checking the caller-identification display.

"Hello." If I hadn't moved my lips to make the words, I wouldn't have recognized my own voice, broken as it was.

"Lena," my mother said, "where are you? I'm in your room. We said noon."

"Sorry. I stopped by to see Jackson. Meet me out front."

"Fine. Five minutes. Lionel is outside waiting for us, and it's a madhouse out there. The police have already threatened to arrest some people for attacking my employees. I don't feel comfortable leaving him and the car there for long."

"Mm-hmm." My attention had strayed to Jackson's face again, and I was half listening. It took me a full five seconds before her words registered. "Wait, what? Who's getting arrested?"

"Some protesters outside the building."

"But they're harmless."

"The usual bunch of two or three are harmless, yes. Haven't you been watching the news?"

"Yeah, of course," I lied.

The truth was I'd been otherwise occupied—mostly watching every other kind of television show, when not in physical-therapy sessions or trying to keep up with my schoolwork. Soap operas, prime-time dramas, and even some cartoons. Anything to keep me from self-pity. But I avoided the news.

Every time I flipped it on, they went on and on about the upcoming Model Ones. CyberCorp was about to introduce the first publicly available android. Soon, the whole country would own them and blah, blah, blah.

I'd seen enough of CyberCorp over the past two weeks, every time I opened my eyes. I didn't need to hear about it on the news too.

"Is Allie with you?" I hadn't seen my sister in weeks. The thought of getting home to her had kept me motivated in my physical therapy. I'd talked to her on the phone almost every day, but that wasn't enough. Thanks to their high-profile jobs, my parents were hardly ever home, and I didn't want Allie thinking I'd abandoned her too.

"No, but she can't wait to see you. It's all she's talked about for the last few days."

"The feeling's mutual. See you in a minute."

In the mirror attached to the inside of Jackson's door, I double-checked the left sleeve of my leather jacket to make sure it fully covered my new limb. With my hand in my pocket, I could hide all but a sliver of metal at my wrist.

"Ready to go?" Ron tapped his wrist at the spot where a watch would have been if he wore one.

"No one asked you to walk me out." I nudged past him into the hallway, dragging my roller bag behind me.

"But you want me to." His smile reached up to a pair of striking amber eyes hiding behind his glasses—an odd color I hadn't noticed before. He grabbed the bag handle from me, threw an arm over my shoulder, and led me in the direction of the elevators.

"Maybe a little," I said.

"Have you heard from your so-called friends?"

"I spoke to them last night. And what do you mean by *so-called?*"

"I don't get how they haven't visited you at all. If I were them, you wouldn't have been able to keep me away."

"I didn't know how to explain the whole arm thing to them—so I didn't. They tried to visit, but I told them not to."

He shrugged but said nothing.

"What?" I asked.

"I would have insisted until you agreed to let me."

"They did insist. I insisted harder."

"I would have stopped by unannounced."

"They wouldn't have gotten past security. I told them last night I was going home today, and they're thrilled."

"But *you're* not thrilled." He made it sound like a statement, instead of a question.

I watched the tiles of the floor pass by next to our moving walkway. A minute later, we stepped into the elevator, and the doors closed us inside.

"Lobby," Ron instructed it. The elevator zipped down to the building's main level, and the doors opened to the grand lobby.

I gasped as I stepped onto the matte silver floor. Apparently, in my time here, they'd redecorated. Multiple display stations were scattered throughout the space.

One station showed a few new hand-screens and small vid-screens. Another displayed a set of networked contact lenses, which allowed the wearer to see virtual objects as if they existed in the real world. Most people already had lenses like those, but these were the newest model. The last station displayed what looked like a cross between an oven, a microwave, and a refrigerator.

A robotic puppy leaped around the remaining space. It yipped and wagged its little metal tail. Giggling, a small boy of about five years old ran after it on stubby legs.

Much like the walls on the hospital floor, the walls to my left and right contained vid-screens that covered their entire surfaces. These didn't include calming nature scenes or important CyberCorp announcements. At the left wall, an older man and two small girls stood in front of the screen, waving their arms and touching the display here and there. In response, it flashed vibrant colors. One of the girls jumped up and down and clapped her hands together, thrilled at the reaction.

Some things hadn't changed—the matte silver floor, a wall of windows across from the elevators, and a long, curved black-and-chrome reception desk in front of the windows. Only now, next to the desk stood a Model One android, the first I'd seen in real life. Its dull red eyes stared back at me, sending pinpricks of ice down my back.

The room was so bright with activity that I needed to blink a few times to adjust. The back of my head pulsed.

"You okay?" Ron asked.

"I just wasn't prepared for all the *stuff* in here."

He laughed. "The head of public relations insists we keep the lobby user-friendly. It's a lot though, I admit."

"I'll say." I turned my face toward his, mostly so I wouldn't have look at the bright room anymore. "What does the rest of your day look like? Back to the Model Ones?"

"Yeah. Dr. Fisher actually just left a message on my micro-comm that I'm to report to her office after I see you out. She's psych-testing Model Ones this afternoon, and I'll assist her with that."

"How thrilled is she to get rid of me?" I failed at keeping the bitterness from my voice.

All the frustration I felt over the past weeks came bubbling to the surface. With rare exception, everyone I'd worked with here looked at me as if they blamed me for taking them away from something more important. They spent half the time grunting and scowling. When I passed them in the hallways, they hurried along, as if afraid they would get dragged into the Lena Project.

I wanted to let it go, to step outside those doors and

leave all the bitterness here in this building. But it wasn't that simple, because the worst part of this nightmare was coming with me—attached to my shoulder.

Ron gave me a reassuring pat on the back and handed my roller bag to me. "Call us if you have any trouble with the arm." He strode back to the elevators.

I heard the chaos as soon as I opened the nearly sound-proofed double doors to the outside. Shouts and chants rose up from a picket line standing at the other end of the circular driveway. Now, I saw what my mother was talking about when she'd said this wasn't the usual two or three protesters.

Over the past month, the anti-tech community had grown metaphorical balls, and they were showing them right now. Lucky for me, CyberCorp had a sizable circular driveway, all of which counted as private property on which the protesters couldn't set foot. I had a clear path to my parents' black car, which idled only about twenty yards away.

The protesters continued to shout as I stepped off the curb and onto the driveway. Most hefted signs that vilified the Model Ones and the people who made them: *Intelligence Is Not Artificial. God Created Man Not Android. Humans Are God's Model One. Remember Skynet.*

One sign in particular made me slow and squint, convinced I hadn't read it right, but I had. *Death to the Spawn of CyberCorp.* The man who held that one stood taller than the rest, towering over everyone in his vicinity by at least a couple inches. Long, stringy blond hair hung to his shoulders, matching the beginnings of an unkempt beard.

"To hell with all of you and your spawn," he shouted. "You cannot create intelligence. Repent or be destroyed."

I picked up my pace. Our driver Lionel waited for me beside the open door. I was still twenty feet from the car when the large protester broke through the security line and bolted toward the front doors.

The two guards who'd blocked his path a moment ago were too slow. Two more guards shot out from inside the building. The protester spotted them and hooked a sharp left. He headed straight toward me.

My vision narrowed to a pinpoint. All I saw was the man barreling forward, arms and legs pumping. I froze. Lionel's voice shouted my name. Out of the corner of my eye, I caught a glimpse of Lionel moving toward me. I tore my gaze away from the sweaty, growling protester and toward the car, but too late.

The man hit me hard in the chest, and air whooshed from my lungs. An instant later, I lay on the ground.

White spots danced in my vision. Pain exploded in the back of my head, where it had slammed into the concrete beneath me. It had ached a moment ago, from the surgery, but now my eyes swam with tears, and the world seesawed beneath me.

"We must stop this," the man shouted. He crouched over me, his legs straddling mine. Beefy hands gripped my upper arms and held me firmly to the ground. As he shouted, saliva sprayed across my face. "The Model Ones mean death for humanity!"

I thrashed from side to side to free myself. Together, Lionel and a guard yanked the massive man off me. As soon as he was on his feet, and I no longer feared for my life, my next thought was of my arm. While I was on the ground, my hand had slipped from my pocket, and now the silver metal shone in the sunlight. I stuffed it back into my pocket.

The security guards dragged the man away. It took all four of them to control him, but none of them could stop his mouth. "Intelligence isn't artificial. It evolves. It learns. You cannot control what you've created!" His shouts continued until they dragged him inside the building, and the doors finally muffled the sound.

"Are you okay?" Lionel asked me. Concern filled his blue eyes.

Before I could answer, my mother hurried across the driveway, high heels clacking against the pavement. Lionel stepped aside to make way for her.

"Are you okay?" She straightened my clothing and smoothed my hair—because heaven forbid I not look camera-ready after being tackled to the ground.

I batted her hands away. "I'm fine, Marissa."

Still numb, I allowed her to usher me into the vehicle. She slid into the car after me. Lionel climbed into the front seat, and we pulled out of the driveway.

"Lunatics," my mother muttered. Her gaze followed the line of protesters as we drove away.

But the man's words echoed in my head. *You cannot create intelligence. The Model Ones mean death for humanity.* I couldn't help thinking he might be right.

5

For the sixteenth night in a row, the sounds of wrenching metal and my own screams lingered with me after I woke. My senses returned to me a second later, and I wasn't bleeding to death in a mangled car.

A light headache tapped at the back of my head. Time for another dose of my meds.

My bedroom door flew open as I rubbed the sleep from my eyes, and Allie burst into the room, her face lit by a wide smile. She looked like a miniature version of me. Same nose. Same full, wide mouth. Same dark-brown eyes and wild, curly hair.

Our housekeeper and nanny, Marcy, had pulled Allie's curls into three tight braids, two at the back of her head and one on the top. Pink, purple, and blue ribbons dressed the ends of the braids.

Headfirst like a charging bull, Allie barreled toward me and dove into my bed. She hit my chest with enough force that I grunted to absorb the impact. One braid slapped me in the chin.

She landed a kiss on my eyelid. "Good morning!"

Laughing, I shifted her to one side, so I could cradle her in my right arm. "Good morning, little one."

"Not little." She stuck out her lower lip. Whenever Allie spoke, her words tumbled together, as if she hadn't yet figured out how to separate each from the next one. People who didn't know her couldn't always understand, but to me, her voice was the most beautiful and clearest thing in the world.

"You're smaller than me."

"You're older."

"So you're little because you're four?"

"Not little!" She punched me with her tiny fist. I cringed, and she burst into squeals of laughter.

I tweaked her top braid, and Allie scrunched up her nose. She hated when I messed up her hair. She pushed her face close to mine, leaving only an inch of space between us. Her tone solemn, she asked, "Better?"

Yesterday afternoon, I'd spent a little time with Allie— long enough to show her the arm and assure her I was home for good. But then a headache had hit me so hard that I spent the rest of the day sleeping. This was our first opportunity to hash the whole thing out together.

I leaned toward her to touch my nose to hers. "I'm home, aren't I? That means I'm better."

Without ceremony, Allie yanked the covers down on the left side of my body, revealing my silver arm. She knocked on it, emitting a soft clang. I must have made a face because she added, "You hate it?"

"It's not . . . me. It's wrong. But I don't want to get into that."

"Why?"

"It's going to upset me."

She narrowed her eyes, as if giving great consideration to my words. Then she grinned. "I like it."

"That's fine, little one. Everything you do is okay." I kissed her on the forehead and, at the same time, pulled the blanket back over my left arm.

Marcy poked her head into the room. "Your mother wants to talk to you, Lena." She reached out a hand for Allie, who slid off the bed and grasped it, allowing Marcy to lead her from the room.

As soon as I was alone again, the sense of contentment drained from me, and I knocked my head against the headboard. I flinched as the small contact sent a ripple of pain through my body. My head begged for its next dose of pain meds, so I stumbled into my bathroom.

The medicine cap wouldn't turn under my clumsy right hand, but I refused to use my left. When the top finally twisted loose, pills scattered across the countertop. I grabbed two, popped them in my mouth, and swallowed them dry.

The bedroom door clicked open, and the lights came on. My mother's voice floated in from the next room. "Lena?"

"In the bathroom. What's up?"

"I'm not going to call back and forth with you while you're in there."

"Then feel free to leave," I shouted back, all syrup and honey.

"Would you come here please?" Her words were sharp, her irritation prickling through.

It made me smile. I trudged back into the bedroom, where my mother stood, already dressed in a navy pantsuit. Her lips tugged downward, as if weighted by an anchor, as she scanned the piles of clothing and scattered books and papers throughout the room. I wasn't ashamed to admit I got a kick out of her distaste for my cleaning habits.

"Your father and I are going out of town on business. We'll be back Friday for our party to celebrate the Model Ones. We expect you to be there."

Great. They'd want me to make small talk and pretend I approved of everything CyberCorp did. I climbed back into bed and pulled the purple covers over my face. "You couldn't wait until a decent hour to tell me that?"

"I could have, but you need to get up for school anyway."

"I've been waking myself for school ever since I was ten. I've got at least another fifteen minutes before I have to get up."

"This will be your first day having your new arm at school. And you no longer have a car, thanks to your little accident. I need—"

"By *accident*, you mean how I almost died because you remotely turned on my car's auto-drive? And then you replaced my arm with an android arm without consulting me because you *knew* I'd hate it. Is that what you mean?"

"I'm not arguing with you. Lionel will meet you downstairs in an hour to drive you." My mother knew me too well. If she weren't standing over me right now, I'd have gone back to sleep and slept through first period. I'd planned to skip school today, and I would have gotten away with it because the teachers knew I'd been out sick.

I groaned. "Fine."

With the blanket still covering my face, I couldn't see her, but the mattress moved as she sat beside me. I pulled the blanket down.

"How's your head feeling?" she asked.

"Like someone cut it open and shoved a metal object into it."

Her expression remained neutral, a flawless mask. "Lionel told me you hit your head on the ground yesterday when that man attacked you. You have to be more careful so soon after surgery. You could have damaged your hardware."

"I'll keep that in mind the next time I consider getting tackled by an unwashed stranger." Just in case she didn't capture the full extent of my smartass-ness, I grabbed my hand-screen off the nightstand and touched the button on the side. The device beeped, ready for my instructions. "Remind me not to get tackled by any more lunatics."

"I'll remind you," the hand-screen chirped. I dropped it back on the nightstand.

My mother's lips pursed, and I couldn't hide the smug smile from my face. I'd cracked her mask. "Let's discuss how we're going to handle introducing your arm to the public."

There it was—the real purpose of her morning visit—a talk about how *her* tech would interrupt *my* life. "Easy. I'm going to hide in my bedroom until Dr. Fisher agrees it's time to put the skin on."

"No. You are going to school today. When asked about the accident, you will not mention any issues with the auto-drive. We can't afford to have your name mentioned any more than it has to be in the anti-technology community. They're irrational enough without giving them fresh fodder for their rants. The family will issue a press release about your new arm in about an hour, so you won't have to explain your situation to any of your classmates. They'll already know. If—"

"You're telling everyone?" Something pushed against my thigh, and I looked down. The metal fingers of my hand had curled and now pressed into my leg. I'd gotten to the point where the limb obeyed me. But this was the first movement I'd managed without having to actively think about what I wanted the thing to do. Just like my old arm. I didn't know whether to celebrate or be completely freaked out that this machine imitated real life so well.

"Yes." My mother's voice pulled me back to the conversation. "The arm is an achievement for CyberCorp—a melding of artificial intelligence with a human being. The public will find out sooner or later. If we tell them ourselves, we'll have the advantage. We can spin it however we like."

"How about we don't spin it? We leave it right where it is."

"That's not an option."

Since my mother cared more about appearances than my feelings, I decided to hit her where it hurt. "We keep this private, or I tell everyone the accident was caused by auto-drive." For good measure, I raised the stakes even more. "And I'll throw in the fact that you installed the arm while I was asleep, and I'm opposed to it. I'll be the new spokesmodel of the anti-tech community. I'm pretty sure I can find Philip Pollock's contact info if I look for it. He does this great audio program. Maybe we can arrange an interview."

She blinked at me a few times, mutely, but her expression remained impassive. "Fine."

I flashed her a shameless smile.

"I will give you a week to tell your friends in your own words what happened. Then we're issuing a press release." Without waiting for my response, she stood and padded away across the carpet. The door clicked shut behind her.

Just when I thought things couldn't get any worse, my mother proved me wrong. Soon, I'd be the new poster girl for CyberCorp.

6

WHEN THE CAR ROLLED TO A STOP IN FRONT OF MY school, I made sure the sleeves of my leather jacket extended past the top of my gloves, covering my left arm completely. Not a bit of metal shone through.

I would have to tell my friends the whole truth today—about the monstrosity now attached to my body—but I didn't want them finding out by spotting it. This was definitely an easing-in type of situation. Luckily, it was winter. Even though it was over fifty degrees today, maybe no one would ask about the gloves.

The car door slid upward, and I hopped out. "Thanks for the ride," I shouted to Lionel as the door shut behind me. He waved and drove away.

"Lena!" Harmony's voice hit me before I made it ten feet.

She jogged toward me from where she'd just parked her car in the lot, somehow managing to balance on the pencil-thin heels of her shoes. She wrapped me in a tight hug. I didn't hug her back, afraid I'd get the pressure of my left arm wrong and either break her ribs or at least give away that my arm was no longer flesh.

She didn't seem to notice. "I haven't seen you in forever. What's up, bitch?" She grinned and stepped back to look me up and down.

I angled my body away from her to put my torso between her and my left arm. "I'm good. Except my head . . ." I started to tell her about my everlasting headache, but then she'd want to know what kind of head injury I'd sustained. I sure as hell wasn't telling her CyberCorp had put a chip in there—not quite yet anyway. "I'm good," I said again. "Happy to be back."

Harmony touched her ear to activate her micro-comm. "Message Melody," she said. "Lena's back. We're in front of the school." She touched her ear again to complete the message. Somewhere nearby, Melody's micro relayed the words.

Harmony gestured for me to follow her up the school's wide front steps. "Any word on Jackson?"

"Last I heard, still in a coma."

She glanced over at me.

"I really don't know anything else. I keep calling, but that's all they tell me."

I'd attended this school for the past three and a half years, and these days, I barely paid attention to its facade. But today, the building had changed.

As usual, the steps led up to columns reaching upward two stories. Beyond the columns, brick covered the building's front, with the exception of two rows of windows. But unlike usual, two digital banners hung around the front entrance, one on each side of the double doors. With images of our school pennant fluttering in the wind, the banners advertised an upcoming basketball game.

"When did they install those?" I asked Harmony.

Her brow scrunched. "They've been there forever."

In three and a half years, I would have noticed two banners, each probably spanning a five-foot-by-eight-foot space. "No—" I started, but Harmony cut me off.

"I can't believe you've been in the hospital. You look fantastic." She flashed me a look that said I was being an idiot, so I let the banner thing drop. The school had probably installed them over the winter break, and by now, I was the only student who hadn't seen them. "Speaking of which, what was up with all the secrets, and why were you at CyberCorp instead of a normal hospital?"

"My parents insisted." I already had an answer prepared for this question, and I knew everyone would believe it. "You know how my folks are—always insisting on the best. They figured I'd get better care under their watch, and they wanted to keep things hushed to avoid a media circus."

"Well, you look good as new," she said. "What was it like there?"

"Mostly, I just sat around watching the vid-screens or doing physical therapy. They have this tube they stuck me in a bunch of times that made my scars smooth out." I started to pull back my collar to show her that my left shoulder looked almost the way it used to.

Its scars had flattened and faded after several sessions in the tube. But I dropped my hand when I realized showing her my shoulder meant showing her the top of the cybernetic arm—the one I hadn't told her about yet. I needed to tell both twins at once. Otherwise, Harmony would open her big mouth to tell Melody, and she'd probably butcher the delivery before I could ease her sister into the idea.

Harmony didn't seem to notice the halted movement. "And what was with this no-visitors nonsense? Were they afraid we were going to steal their medical secrets?"

"Who knows?" I changed the subject. "I never thought I'd be happy to be at school, but I am. I missed you guys."

"You say that now. But wait a week, and you'll beg for another car accident."

I forced myself to laugh but, at the same time, tugged my left sleeve down.

She pointed at my hands. "What's up with the gloves?"

I considered telling her right then. We were friends. She would understand this didn't change who I was.

Or she'd be weirded out by the metal contraption now replacing my arm. I could still change my mind and keep the thing under wraps until they had a chance to install new skin. Maybe I could convince my mother to hold off even longer on the press release.

"My arm isn't completely healed."

Harmony's eyes widened. "Oh, so you've got all kinds of scars and stuff. Let me see."

I was preparing to spit out another lie, when she

cocked her head to the side the way people did when listening to their micro-comms.

"Oh crap," she muttered.

"What?"

"My comm just reminded me to meet with Mr. Hinckley before class. I have some questions about something I got wrong on our first quiz. This was the only time he could meet me this week." Despite the flighty impression Harmony showed the world, she was near the top of our class and planned to stay that way.

"Wait." I clutched her wrist.

"Really sorry. I know you just got back and all. I promise I want to catch up, but this is important." She pulled away and hurried into the building.

With her went my chance to tell both twins at once—unless I wanted to wait until lunchtime, and by then I might have lost my nerve.

"Lena!" Melody's voice caught my attention.

I turned and started to raise my left arm to wave—but rethought it halfway through and waved with my right instead.

Melody grasped me in a quick hug. When she released me, she took a huge step back, wide-eyed. "Did I hurt you? I'm sorry. How are you feeling?"

"I'm fine." When her brow remained knitted, I added, "Really. I promise."

"What's up with the gloves?"

I shrugged and tried my best to look nonchalant. "I'm starting a new trend. They say everything comes back in style, you know."

She stared at them for another couple seconds, then nodded. "They're cute."

I exhaled. I'd bought myself a little time until I could get both of them together.

"Where's Harmony?" she asked.

"Studying, as usual," I said.

"I tried to tell her the semester has barely started, and she doesn't need to work so hard. But she's stubborn." She rolled her eyes. "Speaking of which, Lena, she said she was going to email you a copy of her notes from the past couple weeks."

We stepped through the school's front doors into a hallway overflowing with color. The floor tiles, which used to be light gray, now shone like silver. The lockers were dent-free, and vid-screens hung between the locker banks. The screens displayed the school's social media feeds, along with class schedules.

Like the floor, the walls seemed to glow with an other-worldly light. I blinked rapidly as my eyes adjusted to the unexpected stimulus.

"What?" I muttered

Melody didn't seem fazed by the school's recent renova-tions. She kept moving forward, gaze straight ahead.

"There are vid-screens on the walls." I pointed at one that appeared to be playing a video of the school's most recent pep rally.

"You okay? Still feeling a little off?"

"I'm not off," I insisted. "These vid-screens are new, and the floors—why the change from gray to silver?"

"Oh!" Melody let out a peal of laughter. "You finally got some contact lenses. Way to join the civilized world, Lena."

I accepted the congratulations without a word, but inside, I was seething. The school's vid-screens and glowing floors and walls weren't new. They were virtual. I was seeing them for the first time because I normally walked around blind to the virtual world built on top of the physical one, and I liked it that way.

Could I be wearing networked contact lenses without even knowing it? CyberCorp could have put them in my eyes while I was unconscious.

But I would fix that first chance I got. I'd stop by the restroom before first period and remove the damn things.

A nearby locker slammed, and I turned in the direction of the noise. Olivia Harris stood there. We first became friends because she was the only other black kid I knew within a mile of my neighborhood at the time. We were almost inseparable until the beginning of high school, when she fell in with the artsy crowd and Harmony dragged me into her circle.

Usually, when Liv and I ran into each other these days, we nodded and went our separate ways. But today, her face was painted with concern.

"I'll meet you at our lockers," I told Melody, who nodded and hurried ahead.

"How are you?" Liv asked. She'd changed her hair again. She'd darkened it a couple shades, and she now wore it short and jet black with shock-blue tips that fell just below her chin. She made it work.

"Getting better every day. You?"

"I'm good. I was worried." She gave me a one-armed hug and continued down the hall.

She and I hardly spoke anymore, but it warmed my insides to know she still cared. She turned to wave at me before quickening her pace and disappearing around a corner.

I caught up with Melody at our lockers. When I stepped within a couple feet of mine, the door didn't pop open like it usually did. I waved my left arm at it, but nothing happened. The locker couldn't read my ID chip through the metal arm, and I couldn't fish the chip out of the arm in the middle of the hallway without everyone nearby noticing.

Instead, I waited for Melody's attention to shift to her locker contents, and then spun the combination lock on the door. Lucky for me, our lockers occupied the oldest section of the school. They had been converted to react to ID chips, but the combo locks still worked.

I shrugged out of my jacket and stuffed it inside, then checked the sleeves of my blouse to make sure they extended all the way to the gloves. Unlike most other students at Hanover, my locker held more than just my outerwear.

Although a couple of my textbooks were available only in digital format for reading on my hand-screen, I'd managed to track down hardcover copies of most of the others. There was something comforting about the smell and feel of real, physical books. One of the textbooks was for my first class, so I grabbed it and shoved it into my bag.

Now that Melody and I were alone, her gaze pierced

the side of my face. She could tell I was hiding something. Her most admirable—and annoying—quality was her empathy. She always knew when something was wrong.

"I'm so sorry about letting you drive home alone with just Jackson that night," she said. "He was drunk. We should have followed you and made sure you were okay." She was feeling me out, trying to get me to open up.

"You were barely conscious. It wasn't your fault. And I have to tell you something else about the accident." I stalled. I wanted to gauge her reaction before I told her everything.

She stared at me, brown eyes wide.

I changed directions. "You guys are getting a Model One, right?"

"Yep. My dad placed the order even before preorder sales started."

"And . . . how do you feel about that?"

"I don't know. I haven't thought much about it. I guess it'll be cool to have some robot doing my chores. I'd better still get an allowance though. What's this got to do with your accident?"

"So you're okay with artificial intelligence?"

She shrugged. "Sure. Why not? As long as the thing can do the dishes for me, what do I care about whether it's intelligent?"

Her face displayed no distaste for the Model Ones or AI in general—no strong feelings either way. That meant she probably wouldn't give a damn about my arm. I shifted my position to face my locker, putting Melody on my left side, so that she was the only one in the hallway who could see my arm. Then I raised the bottom of my sleeve just enough to display a sliver of silver.

Her eyes went wide. "What is that?"

"*That's* the reason they treated me at CyberCorp, instead of a normal hospital."

"It's a metal prosthetic?"

"More than that. It's artificially intelligent." I couldn't parse her expression. Definitely amazement. I didn't see any disgust there, so that was a good sign.

"Can I touch it?"

I pulled my sleeve up again. Her fingertips stretched toward it until they barely glanced the metal. I didn't feel the touch, since I still didn't have my skin grafts. But I could tell the instant of contact by the way she yanked her hand back. Neither of us spoke, and Melody stared down at the strip of metal where my wrist should have been.

The seconds piled on top of each other, one after another without a word between us. She was going to reject me—call me names, tell me this changed everything. And it did.

How could she accept me with this *thing* where my arm was supposed to be? I didn't even accept me.

Why didn't she say anything?

I turned away and began stuffing books into my backpack.

Melody reached for the bag. "Let me help you."

I snatched it away from her and, in two large yanks, closed the bag's zipper around my belongings. "I'm not an invalid," I snapped.

She didn't deserve that. I almost apologized, but I

didn't. I didn't want to be here. I didn't want to have to confess my new reality to my friends. I didn't want to wait with my heart in a vise while they judged me, one by one. I just wanted to hop into a time machine and go back to that night.

Why couldn't my parents invent one of those?

"I have to go." I spun away and hurried down the hall. "We'll talk later," I called over my shoulder.

Melody's voice followed me, calling my name, calling me back. I hated myself for running like a coward, but that was what I was, so that was what I did.

I headed straight to the restroom. With five minutes left until class—and not wanting to spend that time with Melody—I might as well check into what the hell was happening to my eyes. If nothing else, it would distract me from the scene I'd made with Melody.

In the mirror, I expected to see a silver ring around my irises, or the shadows that danced there when other people's contact lenses displayed virtual objects. But even when I leaned in so my nose almost touched the glass, I saw nothing more than my dark-brown eyes and the white around them. No metallic ring, no shadows.

With one hand, I pulled my lower eyelid downward to keep it open and touched the eyeball. I cringed away from the contact. There was definitely no thin film there to separate my eye from my finger. No contact lens.

Then how could I see virtual objects?

One thing I knew was that, before my accident, I hadn't been able to see the banners, the vid-screens, and the shiny floor. Now, I could.

I pulled out my hand-screen and called CyberCorp.

"Hell—"

"This is Lena Hayes. Get me Ron Franklin, please." Irritation bubbled in my stomach, and I couldn't help letting it seep into my voice.

"Yes, Miss Hayes. Hold please."

Ron came on the line a minute later. "What's wrong?" The receptionist must have told him I'd given her attitude, because he already knew I was upset.

"Why am I seeing virtual objects?"

"Oh, that?" He breathed a relieved sigh. "The chip is downloading objects from the EyeNet, just like networked lenses. Our androids need to be able to see them to interact with the world in the same way humans do—since humans see them. Since you have an android chip, you're on the network too."

"I don't want to be on the network," I said, teeth gritted. "I don't want my head connected to anything without me specifically saying it's okay—and it's not okay."

"Sorry about that. We had to upgrade you by modifying the parts and software we had on hand. Starting from scratch would have taken years. It didn't occur to us that the network connection would be an issue."

"Well, it is!" I realized I'd shouted, so I dialed my volume down a few notches. "Can you turn off the network connection?" I couldn't mask the tremor of anger and annoyance in my voice.

"Yes, but that would mean modifying the chip again, and we can't go back in with another surgery until Dr.

Fisher feels like you've recovered from the ones you already had. You still having those headaches?"

I considered lying, but I didn't fancy dying on a surgical table. "Yes. They're not getting any better."

"Then no surgery for you anytime soon. But we can modify your software, so it won't display the virtual objects. You'll still be networked, but you won't notice."

As much as I hated the idea of a network having access to my brain, I couldn't do anything about that right now. This was at least a temporary solution. "Fine. I'll stop by after school today. That okay?"

"Absolutely. See you later."

For the rest of the day, I would just have to make peace with the fact that, on top of everything else, I didn't have a monopoly on my own brain.

7

MY STOMACH GROWLED AS I LEFT MY LAST MORNING class and headed back to my locker. I tossed my textbooks inside and slammed the door shut with a clang that vibrated in my head. I took a second to try the art of mind over body to calm the throbbing.

I'd postponed telling my friends everything for long enough. Melody already knew the truth, and if I dawdled any longer, she would be the one to tell Harmony. Who knew what she'd say about it after the way I'd run off this morning? If I explained it to her myself, I could control the conversation. And this time, I'd do a better job of it.

I reopened my locker. Before I could talk myself out of it, I yanked off my gloves and tossed them inside on top of my books. No turning back.

A few minutes later, I strode into the cafeteria, head held high.

No one paid attention to my hand as I weaved through

the food stations and paid for my lunch. My pace slowed when I approached my usual spot in the back of the cafeteria. My friends were already sitting around the table, under the wall of plaques honoring the school's major donors—like my parents.

Silently, I practiced how I would explain my metal hand. *You mean you don't have a metal arm? It's all the rage these days.* In the end, I decided to improvise.

"Hey, Lena."

I stopped moving toward my table and turned toward the voice.

The boy I'd met in physical therapy stood there. He had changed his shirt from Superman to some other superhero whose name I couldn't remember, but he still wore that goofy smile. He pointed at his chest. "Hunter."

"I remember."

"You didn't call."

"No." I shot a glance at my lunch table. My friends hadn't noticed me yet, but I needed to join them before I lost my nerve. "No, I didn't."

"That's cool. You don't have to call to talk about physical therapy, if you don't want. We can talk about . . . whatever. Doesn't matter."

I narrowed my eyes at him. Was he flirting with me? *Why* was he flirting with me? When we met, I didn't remember him from school—even though I must have seen him in class a hundred times. I was rude to him in physical therapy. And I didn't call after he offered to help. "What are you doing?"

His smile twitched but solidified again like concrete. Unmovable. "I don't understand the question."

"What are you doing? Why are you being so nice to me?"

He shrugged. "I thought you might need a friend."

I gestured toward the lunch table I'd been aimed at when he caught me. Five people sat there already—Harmony, our friend Claire and her girlfriend, and Melody and her boyfriend.

Hunter started a chuckle low in his chest and then smothered it before it could break loose. "Yeah, I guess I'm not exactly in their league. See you around." He took off in the opposite direction, weaving his way through the tables with a deftness that was impressive given he'd just had a knee replaced.

I closed my eyes and counted to three in my head to restore my resolve. Then, shoulders straightened, I hurried over to my friends and dropped my tray onto the table. Everyone glanced up as the tray clattered down.

Even Melody, who already knew the truth, gaped at the unhidden metal.

Claire flipped her short dark hair out of her eyes, so she could peer closer. "You know Halloween was three months ago, right?"

"That's her arm," Melody said.

The others stared at me, open-mouthed. No judgment. Just confusion. So far, so good.

I slid into my chair and hoped my bright smile would be contagious. "The accident was more serious than I let on. The whole left side of the car was mangled, including

. . ." I waved my left arm in the air. "My folks hid me away at CyberCorp, so they could put me in a medically induced coma while they replaced it."

When I finished talking, my friends still stared with unreadable faces.

My mouth went dry, but I filled up the silence with chatter anyway. "It's artificially intelligent. I have a chip in my head to control it. After only a couple weeks, I barely have to think about moving it. When I first woke up, I had to concentrate so hard, even stare at it . . ." I finally managed to obey the voice in my head that kept telling me to shut up, shut up, shut up.

With a reassuring smile, Melody reached over and clasped my metal hand in hers. Harmony's and Claire's faces pinched with concern.

I let out a long breath and willed myself to relax.

"Does it . . . I mean . . . Are you feeling okay?" Harmony asked.

"Fine mostly. I get bad headaches sometimes and this throbbing in my shoulder." When Melody's eyes widened, I added, "But it's nothing to worry about it. Mostly, I just hate the idea of having tech permanently attached to me." That was putting it lightly.

Harmony squinted at the arm, gaze rolling up and down it.

I took the hint and pushed my sleeve up to the bicep. The fluorescent lights overhead brought out the hint of yellow in the silver metal.

"Killer." Harmony stroked the forearm and then rapped

on it with her knuckles. "You're totally upgraded. Does it do anything?"

I didn't appreciate her word choice—*upgraded*—but I was too thrilled with the positive response to correct her. I'd overreacted. My friends loved tech. Why had I expected them to be as upset about this as I was? "Only the things my natural arm did. I wouldn't want it to do anything—"

Melody's screech cut off my words. She tried to pull from my grasp, and for the first time, I noticed how tightly I was holding her with my metal hand. I released my grip, and she clutched her hand to her chest.

"Did I hurt you? I'm so sorry." I hadn't realized how far I'd come since struggling with two-pound weights back in physical therapy. "I didn't know I was that strong."

Melody flinched away from me when I reached out to comfort her, and I couldn't blame her. She must have realized she'd done it because, a moment later, she offered me a weak smile.

"Let me see." Harmony beckoned her sister to her. "Does it hurt?"

Melody stayed seated beside me but flexed her fingers. "It's fine. No big deal." I could see her trying to look nonchalant, her face devoid of emotion while her hand trembled. I must have hurt her worse than she was letting on.

Everyone else saw it too, because the atmosphere at the table took a flying leap from curious to awkward. Melody looked down at the table, while Harmony stared at her sister. Claire leaned back in her seat, putting more distance between us.

The silence lasted for no less than eight seconds. I know because I counted them, and my stress rose with each beat.

"So . . . what was it like living at CyberCorp?" Melody asked. Her smile became too bright, like a hundred-watt lightbulb held in our faces after pitch darkness, and it took us all a moment to focus.

"Wait," Claire said before I could answer. "Is that why you didn't want us to visit? Because of the new arm?"

"Yeah, sorry about that. I wasn't ready to explain it. Still not sure I'm ready, but my folks are issuing a press release next week, so I'm out of options."

Harmony's eyes flicked from her sister to me. "So you lied to us."

"I omitted."

"How is that different?"

"Don't fight, you guys," Melody said. "Today's supposed to be happy. Lena's back and we're all together."

"We're not fighting," Harmony said. "We're clarifying the situation." She flinched and then glared across the table at her sister.

Melody's expression looked completely angelic, and I got the impression she'd just kicked Harmony under the table. "Come on, guys. Hug it out." She gestured for Harmony and me to stand.

I got to my feet.

Harmony stayed put, arms crossed over her chest. "We're not fighting."

Melody glared at her until she moved.

Harmony stood, kicked back her chair, and met me halfway around the table. She slung her right arm up and over my left shoulder for the embrace. Even though her pressure on my shoulder was light, the pain there and in my head had been blossoming all day.

Now, it burst open like floodgates, and white spots filled my vision.

My left arm reacted as if on autopilot. My shoulder dipped, and I slipped out of Harmony's grasp. My metal hand shot upward and gripped her around the wrist. Before I could stop the motion, I stood at her back, holding her arm behind her, wrenching her shoulder.

Harmony's shriek cut through the other students' chatter in the cafeteria.

The sound shocked me back into control. I pushed all my concentration into a command to my arm: *Let go.* My fingers relaxed.

She jumped away from me. Wet tears smeared her mascara. Claire shot me a glare that cowed me and leaped from her seat to wrap her arms around Harmony.

"I'm sorry." I took a step toward them but thought better of it and stopped. "I didn't mean to. I can't control . . ." The cafeteria was deathly silent except for the sound of my voice.

My friends and I had chosen this particular table three years ago because of its privacy. Teachers and other students had to walk past every other table to get here, and they usually didn't bother. Our voices had to travel that same distance to be heard.

Today, Harmony's shout had spanned that distance. I turned my neck to the right, just an inch, and students' eyes stared back at me like a field of spotlights. All nearby chatter had stopped.

For a moment, I fantasized about crawling out the window. It stood only fifteen feet away, and I could get there without having to pass any other students. But a window exit would make me *more* of a spectacle.

"You should go." Claire didn't look at me as she hugged Harmony to her chest.

Melody opened her mouth to say something, but I'd already reached my breaking point. This day was a disaster. My life was a disaster. I couldn't stay here a second longer.

I ran from the cafeteria.

8

FOR THE REST OF THE DAY, I WENT OVER THE SCENE IN the cafeteria again and again. I didn't know how I could have handled it differently. Twisting Harmony's arm like that—it had been instinctive, a reaction to the pain with tensions running as high as the ceiling.

Why hadn't Harmony just left me alone? Why did she need to argue about everything?

As I sat in my AP Chemistry class, with the clock ticking down the final minutes of the school day, all I could think about was the crowded hallway that would meet me outside.

At the beginning of the school year, my friends and I had chosen lockers nearby one another. Now I regretted that.

Too embarrassed after the lunchtime fiasco, and too annoyed with Harmony, I'd avoided my friends—and my locker—all afternoon. I couldn't avoid them any longer. I needed to grab my books for homework.

A few minutes before the bell that would end this last class of the day, I raised my hand—my left hand, just for good measure. Our instructor was in the middle of describing the properties of a particular molecule—which one I couldn't say, because I'd spent the entire class planning my escape.

A three-dimensional model of the molecule floated above our heads, in the virtual world. The one positive thing about being plugged into the network was that I no longer had to slip on a pair of EyeNet-enabled glasses to see the virtual objects our instructors used for teaching.

When I raised my hand, the metal palm went straight through the bottom of the object, causing the space around my arm to flicker back and forth between empty air and the molecule. Ms. Lincoln paused for a second before calling on me. When she nodded her approval for me to speak, her attention stayed on my hand.

I scrunched up my face into what I hoped looked like pain. It wasn't hard, since the ache in my head never went away. "I'm not feeling well. May I go home early?"

"Of course, Lena."

Before she could change her mind or insist that I go to the school nurse, I tossed my hand-screen into my bag and rushed out the door. The hall lay empty and quiet, and my shoulders relaxed as soon as the door to the classroom closed behind me. I hurried down to the first floor and to my locker.

On the inside of the locker door, a virtual message

informed me I was supposed to be in class. I figured that was another quirk of being networked. My locker had never given me any messages before, and I didn't appreciate it now.

I brushed my fingers across the words, and the notification disappeared, replaced by a list of all my homework assignments for tonight. At least that was useful. I moved books back and forth between my bag and the locker to make sure I would have the textbooks I needed.

I reached the side door of the building before I remembered the novel I was supposed to be reading for English. I could picture the book lying at the bottom of my locker, where I'd stuffed it after my morning English class.

Maybe I could purchase a digital copy. I could finish it on my hand-screen. Only then, I wouldn't have all the notes and highlights I'd already made in my physical copy. With a frustrated grunt, I spun around and headed back to my locker.

Of course, I'd tossed my other textbooks and notebooks on top, so I had to shift all the contents. I grabbed the book just as the final bell rang.

Students trickled into the hallway from their classrooms. With my head down, I wove my way through them to the exit. Whispers chased me. When I was only twenty feet away from the side exit, a small cluster of students blocked my path near the door.

One of them spoke words I couldn't hear from this distance. Her friends—two boys and a girl—stopped talking to stare at me. I had an audience.

The girl who'd originally spotted me slid to her left

until she stood between me and my exit. I didn't know whether she meant to torment me or soothe me, but either way, I wasn't in the mood.

"Lena, I—"

"Move." I sidestepped around the girl.

That left me toe-to-toe with a tall boy with wide shoulders and a mean grin. I elbowed past him—with my left arm. My elbow hit him square in the chest. I barely felt the impact through my shoulder, but at once, I knew I'd hit him too hard.

The boy's feet left the ground, and he flew backward. His back slammed against a row of lockers. A loud clang sounded at the impact.

The boy slid to the ground. He blinked a few times, eyes glassy. His friends froze in shock. For the second time today, I had the attention of everyone in earshot. The last two kids in my way pressed themselves against their lockers to clear a path.

I fled the building.

I didn't stop running for two blocks. When I'd put enough trees between me and the school so that I could no longer see the site of today's disasters, I slowed to a stop.

A light drizzle sprinkled down on me, and I thanked the sky for the cool water on my hot nerves.

By the time I walked the two miles home, my curly hair would grow to twice its size, but it was worth not having to wait in front of the school for Lionel to show up and drive me home. I pulled out my hand-screen and sent him a message, saying I didn't need a ride after all.

"Hey, Lena!"

I turned toward the familiar voice to find Olivia jogging toward me. Trailing behind her was Hunter.

"Liv? What are you doing?"

She stopped next to me and gave me a nervous grin, while smoothing her black-and-blue hair back into place. "What does it look like?"

"I have no idea."

"Walking you home." She pointed to her companion. "This is Hunter. He transferred in last semester, and he's my Physics partner. We're going to study at my place."

"We've met," he said. "Lena makes a great first impression." His grin told me the opposite was true. "The second one isn't bad either."

Lucky for him, I'd reached my quota of slamming people around today. He would have to wait until tomorrow if he wanted some of that.

Liv gestured for me to continue walking in the direction of my house—*our* houses, actually, since we lived near each other. We walked in silence for a few minutes, which gave me time to get my breathing back to normal after my run.

She reached into her backpack and extracted a small bag of gummy candies, which she held out to me.

"Those are my favorite."

She laughed. "I got so used to keeping them around that I never stopped." She undid the twist tie keeping the bag closed and popped a green one into her mouth. "They're pretty great." She pushed the bag toward me again.

Never one to turn down sweets, I accepted and grabbed

a handful. She retied the bag and tucked it back into her backpack.

"I assume you're being nice to me because I'm an outcast now," I blurted out as I put a blue gummy candy into my mouth.

"I'm being nice to you because I like you. A few years of radio silence can't change that."

I shot her a grateful look.

"How's Jackson, by the way?" she asked.

Unless his condition had changed since I checked this morning, he was still lying in a bed at CyberCorp. He should have been on his way home from school right now. I didn't know whether we'd still be together as a couple, but at least he would be conscious if it weren't for me. "Still unconscious."

"Sorry."

"Me too."

"Who's Jackson?" Hunter, who had been lagging behind us, now squeezed between Liv and me and fell into step beside us. "And what's wrong with him?"

"Her boyfriend," Liv said. "He was in the accident with her."

"Ex-boyfriend." I cringed even as I said it. The least I could do for Jackson was to claim him. But the words were out there now, and I couldn't put them back. "We broke up that night." I stuffed three more gummies into my mouth and watched my feet rise and fall along sidewalk—anything not to look at the two of them.

Hunter stared at me for long enough that the side of

my face tingled from the pressure, and I finally looked up again.

"Do you mind if we talk about something else —*anything* besides the accident?" If we talked about Jackson a second longer, the guilt might rip me in two.

Liv chewed her lip for a moment, then gave me a bright smile. "I have a new boyfriend."

Some of the tension and awkwardness flowed out of me. "What's he like?"

Hunter slowed his steps to allow Liv and me to walk side by side again.

"He's older. Mature." She shot me an apologetic glance. "Super into high-tech stuff."

"Don't look at me like that. We've been friends again for all of five minutes. Give me a few days before I start judging your boyfriends."

She laughed, and it was odd how familiar the sound was. Like an old favorite movie that had been tucked away for years before reappearing. More of the awkwardness between us melted away.

"I think you mean *boyfriend*—singular, as in the only one I've ever had. They're not exactly knocking down my door to get to me."

"That's because the boys you like are always stupid and blind."

She gave me a grateful smile. "He's got these amazing eyes that make me want to melt. I introduced him to my family a couple weeks ago. Both my dads love him, but of course they'd prefer I date a high-school boy."

"You're doing parent meetings already? It must be serious."

"I haven't met his family yet. It's just him and his dad, and he's worried about introducing us because his dad's an alcoholic and a mean drunk."

I squeezed Liv's hand briefly and then released it. "How'd you two meet?"

Hunter cleared his throat loudly. "You think we could talk about something other than boyfriends?"

"Fine. No more girl talk." I turned back to Liv. "Now what? We become friends again? A band of outcasts?" My mind flashed back to the scene in the cafeteria, and I couldn't shake the regret from my voice. "And Hunter." I waved a hand toward him.

"Hey, I want to be an outcast too," he said. "Can we get matching T-shirts?"

Liv gave him a playful shove. "We can start with a walk home and go from there."

We walked slowly. It had been a long day, full of emotional ups and downs—mostly downs. The gummy candies helped, but I couldn't wait to get home and curl up in front of the vid-screen with Allie.

Maybe in a few days, if my headaches cleared up, I could convince Dr. Fisher to install the skin she promised me. By next week, no one would care about my arm anymore. I made the mistake of glancing over and caught Liv staring down at my exposed silver hand.

"You want to ask me about that?" I asked.

"Would that be okay?"

I nodded. I desperately needed to vent, and I couldn't think of better company with whom to do that.

"What does it feel like?" she asked.

I held the arm toward her. "You want to touch it?"

Her face lit up. "If you don't mind. But really, I was asking what it feels like for *you*." She reached over and stroked the arm. "It's cold."

I shrugged. "It's metal, and we're outside in winter. As for what it feels like for me, I'm still getting used to it. At first, it was like a remote control that needed new batteries. I had to stare at it and think exactly what I wanted it to do. Then it still wouldn't do a great job if I could get it to move at all. Now, I barely have to think something, and it just reacts—which I guess is how my old arm worked too. Except when I have headaches. Then, I lose control of it all over again."

When Liv released me, I offered the arm to Hunter. He hesitated for only a second but then lifted my hand. Without my thinking about it, my arm bent at the elbow to allow him to raise the fingers to his eye level.

He rotated it at the wrist. "It's beautiful, Lena."

I couldn't feel the pressure of his fingers, but I watched him hold my hand. Hunter traced the metal joints with his fingertips, and while I felt nothing on the outside, a flutter of nervousness kicked up in my stomach. He let go of the hand, and I dropped it back to my side.

Despite the chill afternoon air, my face felt warmer.

"It's stronger than a human arm," Liv said. Her tone made it more of a statement than a question. So she'd seen my little display on my way out the door.

"You saw that?" I stared down at my feet.

"He had it coming," Hunter said before Liv could answer. "Your prosthetic doesn't give other people the right to bully you."

His voice sounded more sincere than I would have expected from him—more serious than the grinning boy in the Superman shirt I'd met at CyberCorp. He still favored his right leg, but he somehow managed to exude confidence with each step.

It was different for him though. After years in and out of a wheelchair, the new knee was salvation. For me, this arm was a life sentence, made a hundred times worse by its artificial intelligence.

Perhaps I'd judged Hunter too quickly. He'd been a little annoying when we first met at CyberCorp, but maybe his positive energy would rub off on me.

By the time we arrived at my house, it was like Liv and I were friends again. She caught me up on her two dads and brother, and I assured her my parents and Allie hadn't changed a bit. Hunter inserted himself into the conversation every few minutes, but he remained so cheery that I wasn't even annoyed.

"I guess we'll see you tomorrow," Liv said.

For the first time in the last forty minutes, it occurred to me that I still had the problem of my eyes to handle. I was supposed to visit CyberCorp after school today, but I already sent Lionel on his way.

Oh well. They couldn't completely turn off my chip's network capability right now anyway, and I could go another day seeing things on the EyeNet.

Right now, all I wanted was to be myself, cling to the remnants of the positive energy from this walk, and pretend everything was how it used to be.

95

9

For the first night since I woke from the coma, my dreams contained no wrenching metal, no screams. No feeling like my arm was being torn from its socket. Tonight, after I drifted into a deep and peaceful sleep, a cool night breeze tickled my face. Light rain drizzled on my skin. I felt relaxed and carefree.

The blaring honk of a car horn spun me back to consciousness.

I woke with a gasp and found my dream was reality. Water pounded down on me, slicking down my face and clothing.

Light assaulted me on all sides. For a long moment, I couldn't tell up from down, left from right. Headlights blended with digital billboards blended with streetlamps. The world was ablaze, and my feet locked to the ground in the midst of it.

Another car barreled past me, horn screaming. Everything slammed into focus.

I ran to the safety of the grass that lined the road. I'd gone to sleep in my bed, snuggled under pink covers. Now, I stood in the pouring-down rain on the side of the street.

I pinched my right forearm to confirm I was awake. The pinch stung the skin and left a red mark. I was definitely awake, and definitely standing outside instead of lying at home in my bed.

The light rain I'd enjoyed in my dream proved more of a pain in my waking state. Although a hooded sweatshirt covered most of my head, the downpour had soaked the hair toward the front of my face. It stuck to my skin in heavy, drenched clumps.

My fleece pajama pants clung to my legs and weighed down each step. I wore my running shoes, without socks, and my feet squished with each movement.

I recognized my surroundings. I'd taken this two-lane road before, and now I was turned toward home, which was over a mile and a half away.

I had walked over a mile in my sleep. And before doing that, I'd somehow managed to get dressed. I reached into the pockets of my pajama pants, but my hopes plummeted when I found no hand-screen there. I had no way to call someone to come get me.

For the first time, I wished I had a micro-comm. With it stuck behind my ear, I couldn't have left home without it.

A digital billboard in front of me spread a multicolored

glow over the road, casting the passing cars in pink, then blue. Pink. Then blue again.

On the billboard, a teenage girl I didn't know—probably someone passing in a nearby vehicle—sported a pair of fuchsia rain boots. The boots covered the bottom of designer jeans. She strutted across the display to show the footwear from every angle.

The display flickered, and a new teenage girl replaced the last one. I guessed that, like my locker, the billboard couldn't read my ID chip inside my arm. Otherwise, I'd be the one on display.

Despite the rain and the ridiculous situation, I grinned up at the billboard. ID chips came with a lot of conveniences—and a lot of privacy invasions. This was perhaps the first good thing to come of my accident.

I stumbled into a puddle and brought my foot out, soaked to the ankle. I wouldn't have minded seeing myself in those boots right now—in real life. I scowled down at my foot and then up at a third teenage girl, flaunting those damn boots.

I ducked my head and trudged forward through the mud on the side of the road. A vehicle slowed, and someone shouted at me from the passenger-side window. I ignored him.

I could have flagged down a ride, maybe. But accepting one from a stranger in the middle of the night seemed an even worse idea than walking home on my own. At least here, the streetlights and billboards dotting the side of the road provided some semblance of safety.

The rain let up when I was about a quarter mile from

home, but the wind still battered against my drenched clothing. Cold clung to me and settled in my bones. I broke into a run.

When I finally reached the front door, it didn't swing open at my touch. I backed up and waved my left arm at the door, listening for the telltale click that meant it had unlocked for me. But it didn't come.

This was the first time since my accident that I'd tried to get through the front door on my own, without Lionel or my mother and without Marcy waiting to greet me after the school day like she had earlier. The door couldn't detect my ID chip, just like my locker and the billboards.

I pressed the hidden button to activate the opening near my bicep, and the compartment door slid open.

No chip.

I stuck my fingers inside the compartment and rooted around in there. They brushed across the outlet where Ron had plugged the arm in to modify the software, but there was nothing else there. It was empty.

It made sense that I wouldn't have my hand-screen on me when I sleepwalked. I'd placed it on the nightstand when I crawled into bed, and I wasn't in my right mind to grab it while unconscious.

But this—having no chip—made no sense. I had toyed with the idea of removing it, going off the grid now that it was no longer buried in the flesh of my arm. But I *hadn't*. I hadn't touched the chip after Simon put it in this compartment.

I rang the doorbell and heard it ding-dong inside the

house. When no one answered, I pressed the button for the bell twice more.

Marcy yanked the door open, her blond hair flattened on one side from sleep. "Lena! What are you doing?" She grabbed my arm and yanked me inside the house. Concern etched her forehead.

"I . . ." I couldn't tell her I'd sleepwalked. She'd tell my parents, and they'd insist that their employees drop everything to focus on me again. CyberCorp would endlessly poke and prod me, and Fisher would glare at me every few minutes. "I couldn't sleep, so I came out here."

"I was wondering why the security was disarmed. You suspended the alarms on your way out?"

I didn't remember doing that, but I grunted in pretend agreement because I must have.

She glanced back and forth between me and the door. "You couldn't get back in?"

"My chip must have been damaged in the accident." My gaze flitted from her face with the lie. She didn't seem to notice.

"You want me to make you some hot tea?"

"No, but thanks. I think I'll be able to sleep now."

I kicked off my shoes. Water spilled from them onto the marble floor of the foyer. Too tired to scoop them up, I trudged up the stairs toward my bedroom. Marcy followed me up. On the second floor, she turned the opposite direction to her own room, right next to Allie's.

In the quiet behind my bedroom door, I peeled off my soaked clothing and climbed into bed. My ID chip lay on the nightstand, right next to my hand-screen.

I didn't remember removing it.

A cold breeze kicked through the room. The window stood open—something else I didn't remember doing. I could almost understand subconsciously grabbing a hoodie and shoes before sleepwalking across town. After all, those were logical things to grab.

But where was the logic in removing my ID chip or opening the window?

Could I have done those things before I went to sleep last night? Sometimes my headaches were so bad that I felt like I was losing my mind. Maybe that was why I didn't remember.

But as I drifted back to sleep, I had the sinking feeling that wasn't true.

10

I didn't get much sleep. The last thing I wanted was to wake up on the side of the road again. So, tossing and turning, I managed no more than ten minutes of sleep at a time.

I'd never sleepwalked before, and throughout the night, my mind twisted around all the reasons for it. Stress from having to live with this arm. Maybe some kind of post-trauma phenomenon due to the accident. Guilt over Jackson, who still lay in that hospital bed being experimented on by my parents' minions.

When my hand-screen finally beeped its alarm at seven in the morning, I grabbed the device from my nightstand, called CyberCorp, and asked to be transferred to Dr. Fisher. I got the impression she worked long hours, so I was betting she'd be awake and maybe even at the office already.

I needed to ask her about the sleepwalking, and maybe I could ease my mind about Jackson too.

"Miss Hayes?" Dr. Fisher answered.

"I sleepwalked last night. Should I be worried about that?"

"Your body has been through a tremendous trauma, so that doesn't surprise me. I suggest you see a therapist if it becomes a problem." She had a point. Most likely, this problem had to do with my human parts, not my artificial ones. "As you might imagine, I have a ton on my plate right now. Are you having issues with your arm?"

"No, it's fine."

"Then if you don't mind, I'm going to return to the Model Ones." She disconnected before I could respond.

I couldn't blame her. After all, she'd made no secret of the fact that she was available to me only when necessary to make my arm work. Sleepwalking fell way outside her purview.

But I hadn't gotten a chance to question her about Jackson, so I called CyberCorp's main line again and, this time, asked for Ron.

"Hey, Lena. What can I do for you?" he asked when a receptionist connected us.

"Sorry to call so early. Do you have any news on Jackson?"

"No, but hold on."

The line went silent and stayed that way for longer than I'd expected. Long enough that I couldn't help picturing what might be happening over there—Ron calling Jackson's doctors, being told that he'd taken a turn for the worse, trying to figure out how to explain to me that the boy I'd known most of my life would never recover. The metal fingers of my left hand balled into a tense fist.

"No news," Ron said when he came back on the line.

"What does that mean?" I fought to keep the frustration out of my voice.

"He's still in a coma. Sorry, that's all I could find out."

"Let me know when you hear something. Okay?"

"You got it."

After we disconnected, I got ready to go and met Lionel downstairs for our drive to school.

Fifteen minutes later, I waved goodbye to him as I stepped from the car. My usual parking space stood empty, front and center to the school's main entrance. In theory, parking spaces at Hanover were assigned by lottery, but the lottery had gone in my favor all four years. Normally, I wouldn't think twice about that. But now, I saw things differently.

My parents had gotten me that spot, either by calling the administration and insisting, or by just existing and making people want to please them. My whole life was like that—a product of my parents.

Even this arm belonged to them.

Today, the virtual banners around the school's front doors showed nothing more than the school name in our official colors, maroon and blue. The images were stationary, but still, the fact that I saw them at all grated on my nerves.

An odd tension crackled in the air in front of Hanover

High. Faces turned toward me, with gazes pinned on the metal hand clearly visible at the end of my sleeve.

I'd expected today to be different from most days. I'd expected the stares. I'd expected students to shy away from me, to avoid me, to whisper and laugh behind my back the way they had yesterday afternoon.

But this was something else.

As I strode past those horrid banners and through the front doors, one group of girls stepped away from me, eyes narrowed. That looked like anger or fear—something I hadn't expected.

"Lena!" A male voice called my name. Hunter limped toward me down the hallway.

I had warmed to him a bit yesterday, but I wouldn't call us friends. Still, he was one of the two people who'd made yesterday bearable.

I gave him the benefit of a doubt and plastered a smile on my face. "What's up?"

"I didn't want you to hear it from someone else."

"Hear what?"

"Everyone thinks you did it." He shifted his weight back and forth between his bad leg and his good one, winding up like a Jack in the Box about to spring.

My eyes narrowed. "Did *what*?"

He let out a long breath. "Killed Harmony."

"What?" I couldn't have heard him right. "Killed Harmony?"

"Harmony Miller is dead."

The loud chatter in the hallway plummeted down to a quiet hum in my ears, and my head swam. The voices continued, but I could no longer understand them. Hunter's words played over and over again. *Harmony Miller is dead.* I held a hand out to touch the wall, to catch myself before I fell over.

Harmony dead. Harmony.

Dead.

I'd seen her just yesterday. I'd cursed at her in my head for causing our argument, for setting off a chain reaction that led to an overall shitty day at school. I'd even wished I never met her. And now, she was no longer my problem.

I had put negative thoughts about Harmony into the universe, and the universe had responded in the worst way possible.

My stomach turned, and I thought I would lose my breakfast all over the floor, all over Hunter. Tears stung my eyes, but I blinked them back.

"How?" My voice came out low pitched and deliberate as I tried to control my emotions, tried not to break down.

"They're not saying."

"Where's Melody?" My mouth felt dry, the words harsh against my throat.

His brow creased. "Who?"

"Her twin sister."

His mouth made an *O*-shape. "I don't know. She probably stayed home from school."

"What about Claire?" I gestured a couple inches taller than me. "About this tall. Short brown hair. Gorgeous and loud."

"I haven't seen any of your friends. Sorry."

"Okay." A long pause stretched between us. What was I

supposed to say? Then I remembered how this conversation had started. "People think I killed her?"

"You got in a fight yesterday. You almost broke her arm. *I* don't think you killed her, but some people have other ideas."

Liv ran up to us, unconcerned with the school's rules against running in the hallways. "Did you hear?" she asked, out of breath.

I nodded but struggled to form my mouth around words. "What if I killed her?" I whispered, so quietly that Hunter and Liv leaned toward me to hear.

"Huh?" Liv said.

"I sleepwalked last night," I said. "I woke up on the side of the road—not far from her house actually. What if I . . ."

"You think you murdered her in your sleep?" Hunter asked.

When Hunter put it that way, it sounded ridiculous. Still, an odd feeling of dread sat like a dumbbell in my stomach.

Since I'd never sleepwalked before, I was doing it now either because of trauma from the accident or because of the damn chip in my head. One of those things I could fix. "I need to get this chip out of my head."

"No." Liv's answer came fast. "The arm won't work without the chip. You'll have no arm. Plus, they can't do surgery again until your headaches go away, right?"

I nodded, even though I couldn't remember telling Liv that immediate surgery wasn't an option.

I couldn't imagine a life with only one arm, but at least

it would be *my* life, one that I controlled. No chip doing who knows what inside my brain. No more communicating with networks, no more sleepwalking. I'd be all flesh and bone and *me*, and I wouldn't have to worry about what my body did while I slept.

That was what I wanted.

Liv grabbed my hand—the metal one—and clasped her fingers around it. "That's a huge decision to make. Just because you sleepwalked doesn't mean you killed someone. People sleepwalk all the time. It doesn't make them killers.

Hunter nodded along with Liv's words. "I bet Harmony's dad has a lot of enemies. The entire anti-tech community, for example, since he's a CyberCorp big shot."

"I'm part of that community," I reminded him.

"But you didn't kill her," Liv said. "It was probably someone he fired—and I hear he's super tough on his employees—or someone *else* in the anti-tech community. Someone with the skills to get past the Millers' home security."

"Imagine how many threats CyberCorp employees get," Hunter said. "This wasn't you. Trust us."

By the time they finished talking, I began to see their point. There were a hundred better suspects for this crime. Only that didn't change the fact that I was still a suspect myself—at least in my mind.

"You're right," I said. "I've got to make a phone call before class. See you guys later." Without waiting for their responses, I sidestepped around them and took off down the hallway.

I walked until I reached the west wing, head ducked

low to avoid the stares and whispers. I climbed the west stairs two at a time to the second floor and then the third.

The third floor held mostly laboratories and teachers' offices. At this time of day, before classes, the hallway up here was usually deserted. I ducked into the nearest restroom, which was empty, and locked myself in the largest stall.

I dropped down onto the toilet seat, and that's when it hit me: Harmony was really dead.

We would never make peace. I would never hang out with her again. I would never hear her laugh again. We were supposed to have more time. More time to mend our differences. More time for prom and graduation and getting together for spring breaks during college.

I could no longer hold back the tears that had been threatening to spill. They flooded over my cheeks. Their salty taste pooled on my lips and seeped into my mouth. They shook my whole body, forcing themselves out from deep in my gut. My chest ached from the effort of expelling them from my insides.

The first bell rang to announce the beginning of classes. I straightened my back, sucked in a deep breath, and considered cleaning myself up and heading to my classroom.

But I couldn't move. I could barely breathe, and each stabbing breath brought only more sobs.

When I'd finally spent all my energy, my whole body felt empty—like I was made of nothing but skin and tears, and I'd used up all of the tears. Nothing was left of me.

So I stared at the floor of restroom.

And stared.

Another school bell jerked me from my trance. I'd been in here for an hour, and first period had come and gone.

I grabbed a handful of toilet paper and wiped away the liquid that hadn't already dried on my face. My eyes would be bloodshot, so I couldn't yet make an appearance outside the door of this stall.

I widened my eyes a few times to try to clear them. If I could make it ten minutes without crying again, I'd be good. Then I would get out of here and go to my second class.

I fished my hand-screen from my backpack. When I pulled the metal sides apart, the screen snapped into place. The display lit up.

"Search Harmony Miller," I told the device.

An instant later, a series of articles and video titles scrolled across the screen. None of the headlines hinted at the method of death, but the top result was a recording of a news report that had aired this morning. I pressed it, and a video filled the screen. I pulled the top of the device upward to increase the size of the display.

A woman with a short bob of blond hair spoke, her tone all business, no emotion. "Harmony Miller, daughter of tech genius Greg Miller of CyberCorp, was found dead in her bedroom early this morning. We're still waiting on the release of further details, but we know that Harmony appears to have been murdered. Given the high security in the Miller household, we speculate that the family will be first on the list of suspects."

The woman stood on a small street just outside Harmony's front lawn. Behind her, other reporters mingled nearby, some talking to cameras of their own.

In the background, the front door opened, and a flood of reporters collapsed toward it. Harmony's father emerged. A tall, thin man with dark-reddish hair, he seemed to slump into himself today. His eyes looked tired as he waved for silence from the small crowd.

"We're not prepared to speak to the press right now." His voice shook, and he stopped to clear his throat and compose himself. "Please leave us in peace to mourn."

Reporters shouted questions at him.

Mr. Miller shook his head and waved for silence again. "If you value your employment, you'll clear this street within the next two minutes." He slammed the door, and the reporters scattered.

They knew better than to question Greg Miller's power. If he said he would get them fired, he could do it. He was one of CyberCorp's top engineers, and he'd joined the company only a few years after my parents formed it. Even though he wasn't management, he had as much power as any other high-ranking CyberCorp employee— which was a lot.

My parents and CyberCorp made hefty donations to the city and to private companies on a quarterly basis. I couldn't keep track of how many buildings had wings named after them or one of our relatives.

If Mr. Miller called a reporter's employer, that reporter would be fired the same day. Even the press couldn't risk withdrawal of CyberCorp funds and partnerships. So much for freedom of speech.

Before signing off, the blonde reporter added, "We'll keep you updated with further developments."

The hand-screen went black and then returned to the list of search results. I subscribed to new updates on the topic, so I'd be alerted.

If the reporter had her facts straight, the police would be investigating the Miller family, since they were the ones who wouldn't have had an issue with the household security system. I couldn't imagine Melody or Mr. or Mrs. Miller doing this to Harmony. Next, law enforcement would branch out and investigate her friends—especially me, since I'd just had a fight with her. When they interviewed me, I wouldn't be able to give them an alibi.

I couldn't prove my innocence—not even to myself.

11

MY HAND-SCREEN BUZZED WITH AN INCOMING CALL JUST as I was shoving it back into my bag in the restroom. The small readout on its side announced it was my mom calling. I debated not answering, but then I'd never hear the end of it later.

"Hey."

"Lena, I need you to meet me in front of the school."

I groaned and made no attempt to hide the sound. "Please tell me you're not here."

"I don't have all day to sit in the parking lot. Come outside please." Despite her use of the word *please*, this was not a request.

I trudged down the stairs and to the front of the school. One of our black cars idled at the curb. The door slid upward, and my mother stepped out. Her ivory pantsuit made her brown skin glow, and her tight coils of

115

hair were gathered into a neat bun. A man I didn't know stepped out of the vehicle after her.

He looked a decade younger than my mother, so probably in his late twenties. A dark suit covered broad, thick shoulders, and his head towered above my mother's. That had to put him at well over six feet tall. He wore his dark hair in a buzz cut. Overall, he had the look of every military man I'd ever seen in movies.

"This is Owen," my mom said. "He's going to be your bodyguard until this whole Harmony mess blows over."

"Harmony *mess?*" I motioned air quotes when I repeated it back. "You mean the mess where my friend Harmony was murdered in her own home?" My mother didn't know about my fight with her, so she couldn't call me out on my dubious use of the term *friend*.

"Yes, dear. That mess." As usual, her face stayed emotionless.

Sometimes, I wanted to tilt back my head and scream —in public—just to see if she'd react to it. I gritted my teeth to keep myself from doing just that. "I don't need a bodyguard."

"I wish you'd be more agreeable, but since you insist on doing this the hard way . . ." She touched her ear to activate her micro-comm, then said, "Transfer file name Threat Letter to Lena Hayes."

My hand-screen buzzed in the front pocket of my backpack. I withdrew it and opened it. The display showed a document with the words *CyberCorp Confidential* digitally stamped across the top. It was an anonymous letter addressed to "the greedy fat cats at CyberCorp." So far, this letter writer and I were on the same page.

The ungodly cannot be permitted to live, the letter read. *This is a warning. The Model Ones mean death for humanity. They are evil incarnate. Stop the rollout, or destruction will follow. Death to the spawn of CyberCorp.*

I pictured the man in the parking lot of CyberCorp, barreling toward me, screaming about how we all deserved to die. He had used some of the same words. Had he written the letter—or maybe someone else who just happened to be on the same train to crazy town?

More importantly, it looked like my mother had a point about the bodyguard. Harmony's murder might not have been an isolated incident. More of CyberCorp's kids could be targeted.

I couldn't have killed Harmony, because whoever wrote this letter had done it.

"You think I'm in danger?" I asked her.

"You're in no danger at all. We get this type of thing all the time, and it's always nothing. Most likely, Harmony's murder has nothing to do with us or this letter." Her eyes flicked up and then down again in her frigid approximation of an eye roll. "But half of my senior staff has hired bodyguards, and your father and I can't look like we don't care about our own."

Of course. She was more concerned about appearances than anything else. But it stung that she'd come here not to protect me, but to make herself look good. "Do you know how Harmony died?" I asked.

She gave her head a firm shake. "I don't think it's a good idea to go into that right now."

"I'm going to find out somehow. If you want me to cooperate with this bodyguard, I need to know what exactly I'm supposed to be worried about."

She cocked one dark eyebrow upward. "If I tell you how your friend died, you'll accept the bodyguard without further argument?"

I nodded. There was no way she would let me go back inside without Owen. I might as well bargain for something.

"She was strangled in her bed."

Reflexively, my hand rose to my throat and touched the soft flesh there. The muscles in my neck moved as I exhaled. I felt most safe in the world when I was lying alone in my bed at night, nestled deep beneath the covers. The thought of struggling for my life—kicking and writhing as some man choked the life from me in my own bed—sent a shudder through me.

"Why didn't their alarms go off? What about the cameras and chip scanners?"

"The entire system was shut down for five minutes during the night. The cameras were off, and the chip scanners got nothing."

"I'll take the bodyguard." I tucked the hand-screen back in my bag.

She nodded and switched her attention to her new favorite topic. "Is everything working out with the arm?"

"Fully operational. All systems go." I lifted it and waved

my metal fingers at her. "Thanks to the massive betrayal from my parents."

"I told Dr. Fisher you'd stop by after school today, just to make sure the arm's adapting as intended. Owen will escort you."

"Fine." I'd planned a visit anyway, so that Ron could stop me from seeing things on the EyeNet.

Without another word, she disappeared back into the black vehicle, leaving Owen standing beside me. The door whirred shut behind her.

Owen stuck out in contrast to the few students moving across the lawn between classes. A couple teachers were out here as well, but they had a studious look in jeans and blazers or business-casual wear.

Owen, on the other hand, wore a dark-gray suit over impossibly large shoulders and long legs. He held his back too straight. Everything about him screamed bodyguard. No one would mistake him for a teacher or a student.

"You're not coming into my classes," I told him after the car pulled away.

"I'll accompany you into your classrooms, check them for security threats, and then wait outside." He spoke with a slight accent I couldn't place.

"What if I have to pee?"

"I'll accompany you into the restroom, check it for security threats, and then wait outside."

"What if *you* have to pee?"

He hesitated for less than a second. "I won't, ma'am."

"How do you know? You don't pee?"

"I won't need to, ma'am."

"But you plan for these things, right? Humor me. What's the plan if you need to pee?"

"I call one of my colleagues to guard you."

"And you just hold it until he gets here?"

"Yes, ma'am."

"Wouldn't it be easier if you waited out here? I could check in between classes, and you could pee whenever you feel like it. Everybody wins."

His lips pressed into a tight line. "No."

I guessed he was done humoring me. Oh well, it was fun while it lasted. I had to find my little joys somewhere.

The second-period bell rang. I repositioned my bag on my back and hurried into the building. Owen trailed six feet behind me. I wouldn't have thought it was possible, but now I received more stares than I had ten minutes ago.

When Debbie Carlyle approached from the opposite end of the hallway, I relaxed a bit. A bodyguard trailed Debbie too, so I wasn't alone in that. Her mother worked at CyberCorp. She was some kind of doctor, whose job I assumed was similar to Fisher's.

As Debbie and I passed each other, our gazes locked. She rolled her eyes, but I could see the tension in her shoulders.

I might hate the additional attention that a bodyguard brought me, but the alternative was a worse fate. If someone was out there hunting the kids of CyberCorp employees, how long would it take him to come after me?

12

MY HAND-SCREEN BUZZED A FEW MINUTES AFTER THE
bell that ended morning classes. A message rolled across
the screen from Liv: *"In the cafeteria."*

I ducked my head and hurried through the halls toward
the lunchroom. Once there, I selected my food as quickly
as possible. The students behind me in line mumbled
under their breaths as I dug into my pocket for a pay card.

The rest of them simply waved their wrists over the
payment scanner, which read ID chips and automatically
withdrew money from students' bank accounts. I'd decided
my chip was useless now that the metal from my arm
would shield it, so I'd left it on my nightstand.

My bodyguard trailed behind me while I strode to Liv's
table, which—thankfully—stood nowhere near the table I
usually shared with my old friends. I dropped my tray and
slid into the seat next to her.

"Liv, this is Owen," I said. "Owen, meet Liv."

He gave a tense nod and went back to surveying the space around me.

"A bodyguard?" Liv asked.

"Yep."

Her eyes went wide. "You think you're in danger? Because of Harmony?"

I pushed aside the empty feeling in the pit of my stomach—the feeling that reminded me Harmony and I had been best friends for three years before the one day we weren't. When I saw her yesterday morning, before our falling out, she'd been so happy to see me.

Even though Harmony and Melody were identical twins, they had their physical differences. Harmony had a dimple on her left cheek, but it only showed when she was truly happy. Her fake smiles—the ones she gave teachers—looked just like Melody's. But her real ones could brighten any room.

I would never see that smile again.

"I'll be okay." I licked my lips and swallowed, trying to remove the lump in my throat. "CyberCorp received a letter this morning. It said something about how the kids of CyberCorp employees will die because of the Model Ones."

Liv's mouth dropped open. "You think it's serious?"

"Maybe. Maybe not. My mom thinks it's just talk. Owen here is for appearances, since some of the other CyberCorp kids have bodyguards." I gestured toward my guard, who stood directly behind me. "Typical Marissa." I paused to chew a forkful of food.

Liv laughed, but then smothered it when I didn't join her.

"Don't you think it's weird," I said, "that someone would kill Harmony instead of her dad? If you want to stop CyberCorp from making Model Ones, you kill the top engineer, not his kid. Right? Without Mr. Miller, the Model One rollout might have to be postponed."

"Maybe. If he's trying to scare CyberCorp employees, killing their kids sounds like the way to go."

"I guess." It didn't make sense. Why take the long way of killing kids to stop their parents? Not that I approved of the killing at all, but if you were going to do it, why not go right for the source?

Someone who hated CyberCorp so much that he'd commit murder had been in Greg Miller's house—and had left Greg Miller untouched. That story was hard to swallow. As much as I hated to admit it, I was beginning to agree with my mother. This murder had nothing to do with CyberCorp or the threatening letter.

"Who do you think killed her?" Liv asked.

Before I could answer, a tray of food landed on the table next to me, and Hunter dropped down into a chair. He smelled minty and fresh, like he'd just stepped out of the shower. An instant later, my bodyguard was standing between my seat and Hunter's, his hand on Hunter's shoulder. Hunter winced at the pressure.

"It's cool," I said. "We're friends."

Owen nodded and returned to the spot behind me.

"We're friends?" Hunter grinned at me.

I waved a dismissive hand. "I'll take what I can get right now."

"I feel like I should be offended."

"Go with your gut." In spite of this awful day, I smiled.

"You were talking about Harmony?" he said.

"Some anti-CyberCorp terrorist might have done it," Liv said. "CyberCorp got a threatening letter."

"Which was a secret." I glared at her.

"I'm not going to tell anyone," Hunter said. "But at least now you know it wasn't you."

I hadn't really looked at him this morning when he hit me with the news about Harmony. Now, with him leaning in to hear our whispers, I couldn't help it.

Although shorter than when we'd first met, his hair still fell a bit too long—an awkward length that let the ends curl in odd directions. Most of it was combed backward, but one piece near the front hung to the side, sticking upward.

His eyes, which I'd thought were brown, were green around the pupils, darkening to brown at the edges of the irises. They stood out sharply against thick, dark eyelashes. Above them, a scar sliced through his left eyebrow. I liked it. It gave his face character.

He wasn't thickly muscled like Jackson and the guys I usually found attractive. But tight muscles defined the forearms he'd laid on the table to lean closer to me.

"Lena doesn't think the person who wrote the letter is the murderer," Liv said.

Apparently, we were going to discuss this with Hunter whether I liked it or not. "If it's the same guy, his strategy sucks. If he wants to stop CyberCorp from making robots, he should have killed Greg Miller. He's either the worst murderer ever when it comes to choosing targets, or it's not him. Harmony's death might have nothing to do with the Model Ones. That makes the most sense."

"Maybe it's you after all." Hunter laughed through his words.

Liv glared at him. "It's not."

I laughed too, but it was noise without feeling. If the letter writer wasn't the murderer, that threw me right back into the suspect pool. What reason would my sleepwalking self have had for removing my chip? Murder seemed like a good reason—the premeditated kind.

I hoped to God I was wrong and the letter writer had killed Harmony. And I hoped they found him soon.

Hunter and Liv changed the subject to their weekend plans, and I dropped out of the conversation. I'd been upset with Harmony, even blamed her for what happened yesterday, but I didn't want her dead.

Plus, the Millers' home had as much security as any house in the city. All the exterior doors locked digitally, and they had both cameras and chip scanners in every room. To shut down the entire system, someone had to have an approved ID chip or a passcode, and I knew for a fact that they changed their passcodes regularly.

I released a slow sigh of relief. I wouldn't have known where to start to commit this crime, especially in my sleep.

". . . but I've seen almost none of it except the physical-therapy room," Hunter was saying. "I bet you've seen the whole building. Right? Lena?"

"Huh?"

"CyberCorp Tower," Liv said. "Hunter has more therapy Saturday morning, but he's itching to see the rest of the building. You've seen it a hundred times."

"Yeah, but it's been years. When I was a kid, it was cool. But now, they care more about profit than improving people's lives."

"But you can get us in?" Hunter asked. "For a tour?"

"They don't do tours. Almost everything above the lobby is confidential."

"They'll do one for you though, right?"

A girl in a passing cluster of students kicked my chair. She stared over her shoulder at me as they walked away, weaving their way between tables. At the table behind me, someone else mumbled, "Freak." To my right, loud whispers called me a murderer.

The cafeteria felt too small.

CyberCorp Tower wasn't my first choice of places to go. In fact, it was probably my last—second to last—after this school. And Jackson was there in the medical ward. I had put him there, so the least I could do was pay him a visit. It would be my penance. Or a decent start, anyway.

I shoved back my chair and jumped to my feet. "Let's go."

Liv's brows shot upward. "Now? What about afternoon classes."

"Tell your teachers I have a medical emergency, and you guys have to accompany me to CyberCorp." I looked at Owen. "We're skipping classes. Is that a problem for you?"

"My instructions are to let your mother know when you leave campus at the end of the school day."

"We're leaving campus *now*."

"Mrs. Hayes won't approve of that."

"Why don't you call and ask her," I said. "While you're at it, we're heading out." I waved at Liv and Hunter to come with me. Owen hurried behind us to the parking lot, speaking softly into his micro-comm. With his long strides, he took only half as many steps as I did to keep up.

At Liv's car, I sat on the passenger side, and Hunter climbed into the backseat. Owen caught the door just as it was sliding shut.

"Mrs. Hayes is unavailable, but her assistant Missy insists you stay at school."

"She wanted me to see Dr. Fisher. I'll make sure to stop by while we're at CyberCorp." I yanked the door downward, but Owen held it firmly.

"You can see the doctor after school."

"That's nice." I turned to Liv. "Drive."

Her gaze shifted from Owen to me, brow furrowed.

"Drive," I insisted.

She pressed her foot to the accelerator, and the car responded vocally. "Door open," the car chirped in a smooth female voice. "Door open."

I reached across Liv's lap to the switch under the steering wheel that swapped the car's control from auto to manual.

With Liv's foot still on the accelerator, the vehicle jerked backward from the parking space, tires squealing. Owen lost his grip on the door, and we took off.

13

We arrived at CyberCorp just as the lunch hour was ending.

At seventy-two floors, CyberCorp Tower stood taller than any other building in the city. Silvery-tinted windows separated by stripes of rose stone marked each story. It was a beautiful building, not all white and black and chrome like most of the more modern structures in the city—and like its interior.

It was as fake as my arm, pretending to be something it wasn't. It imitated a building with heart and soul, when in reality, metal and circuits filled its guts.

A small group of protesters stood on the sidewalk just outside the property. Among them was the man who'd tackled me last time I was here. His voice rang out even through the car's darkened windows.

"This is the end of days. The Model Ones and their

creators are evil incarnate. The ungodly cannot be permitted to live."

Two security guards flanked him. One of them placed a hand on the man's back and guided him away from the driveway. He continued shouting while he moved out of our path. Sweat covered a face reddened with exertion. Dark-blond hair lay plastered to his neck, and wide blue eyes glared at us as we inched by him.

I pointed. "I bet that's the guy who wrote the letter."

Liv slowed the car, her expression a mix of awe mingled with disgust.

If he had killed Harmony, my conscience was clear. I hit the button to roll down the window.

From the seat behind me, Hunter lunged forward, stretching between my seat and the side of the car. He grabbed my arm. "What are you doing?"

"Finding out how he feels about Harmony's death. Maybe he'll give something away."

"He's not going to just confess. Liv, let's go please."

Liv sped the car toward the entrance of the parking garage. She waved her wrist at the scanner, which recorded her ID and beeped. The gate to the underground lot split in the middle and rolled to the sides.

Inside the garage, Liv raised her hands from the wheel and let the car take control. The vehicle glided to the nearest parking space, turned into it, and shut itself off.

"Hold on." As we got out of the car, I pulled out my hand-screen and opened the letter my mother sent me this morning. "There." I pointed to the sentence.

Liv read it aloud. "'The ungodly cannot be permitted to live.' Is this the letter you were talking about?"

Hunter grabbed the hand-screen and read the line himself, before returning the device to me. "He might have written the letter, but I don't think he's your killer."

I nodded. That was what I'd been thinking too, but I couldn't be sure without speaking to him.

"Why not?" Liv asked.

"Did you actually look at the guy?" Hunter said. "He doesn't seem organized enough to get around the Millers' security."

Before I could put my hand-screen away, it buzzed with an incoming call from my mother. I answered it just as we reached the elevators that would lead us up to the main level.

"Hey."

"You ditched your bodyguard." She phrased it like a statement, not a question.

"I'm at CyberCorp. Safe and sound, where all your minions can watch over me."

"That's not the point."

"Right. The point is that you need me to be seen with Owen, so your reputation remains unimpeachable."

"A girl is dead, Lena. People are taking this very seriously."

"So am I. Of course I am. Harmony was my friend . . ." My voice disappeared, and I had to clear my throat to say more. "She died at home while she slept—not at school or at CyberCorp. We don't even know whether her death is connected to that letter. She could be the only target. Like you said this morning, CyberCorp gets threatened all the time."

"That's hardly the point. I need you to—"

"And they always turn out to be nothing. This one is probably nothing too. It just happens to be timed with a murder." *A murder I may or may not have committed.*

"I still need you to stay with Owen." Her voice returned to its usual false cheeriness. "Go see Dr. Fisher while you're there. Owen will escort you home when you're done. Do you understand?"

"Maybe."

"I'm getting in our jet now, but call me if you need anything."

I shielded my eyes as the elevator from the parking garage opened onto the lobby. Although I hadn't noticed it when I came through here last time, I could now see that the display stations featuring CyberCorp tech had that distinctive faint glow that suggested they weren't really there. They were virtual objects on the EyeNet.

I'd thought CyberCorp had remodeled the lobby, but they hadn't changed anything at all. It remained as cold and empty as it always had been.

A woman who appeared to be in her mid-twenties sat behind the large, curved reception desk. Four vid-screens sat on the desk, facing away from us. Like the other three receptionists beside her, the woman wore a white button-down blouse and a false smile.

"Good afternoon, Miss Hayes. What can I do for you?"

I pointed to my friends and then at my own chest. "We'd like to take a tour of some of the facilities."

The woman's smile remained painted on her face, stiff and unmoving. "We stopped giving tours years ago. Security concerns, as I'm sure you'll understand."

I flashed Liv and Hunter an apologetic glance, but Liv nudged me back toward the receptionist.

"Couldn't you make an exception?" I asked. "Could one of the interns show us around? Ron Franklin, perhaps. He works with Dr. Athena Fisher. I bet if you call him, he'll agree."

Still giving me that fake cheer, she made a series of selections on her vid-screen and then touched her ear to activate her comm. "Ron, Miss Lena Hayes and two of her friends are here to see you. They'd like to tour the facilities." After a short pause, she touched her ear to end the call and made more selections on the vid-screen. She spun the screen toward us and pointed at it. "Wave your wrists here, one at a time." She pointed at Liv, then Hunter, then me. "This gives your ID chip access to our less sensitive facilities."

"Will we be able to see the Model Ones?" Liv asked.

The receptionist frowned, made another selection on the screen, and spun it back toward us. "Yes, now you will. IDs please."

Liv waved her wrist at the screen, which beeped and displayed two photos of her, one face forward and one in profile. Below the photos, the screen listed her name, weight, height, and age. She grimaced at the photo, in which her now colorful hair was longer and braided into dark cornrows. "I really need to get that retaken."

"I thought it looked great."

"You never said so."

"I didn't say a lot of things I should have." I hoped she knew I meant all the times I passed her in the halls without saying hello. And all the times in the past two years when I didn't call or text her to say goodnight.

Hunter went next, waving his wrist at the screen just like Liv did. In addition to his name and vital stats, the vidscreen displayed the words *MEDICAL TEST SUBJECT* in red under his photos. The receptionist gave him a discriminating look up and down, probably trying to figure out which of his body parts CyberCorp had replaced.

She turned the screen toward me. When I waved my wrist in front of the screen, nothing happened. Immediately, I felt silly. "I don't have an ID chip." I raised my arm again, so she could get a better view of the metal. "Lost it in an accident."

"Yes, of course." She eyed my arm longer than she'd examined Hunter, before she said, "Unfortunately, I won't be able to add you to the security system as a guest today. The secure rooms and elevators will only open if a verified guest is using them. Just stay with someone else at all times, and you'll be fine. Ron will be down to get you in a moment."

I started to walk toward the elevators, but thought better of it. The only way to convince myself I hadn't killed Harmony was to prove someone else had.

I spun back around and leaned toward the receptionist. "What's your name?"

Her eyes narrowed. "Vanessa. Is there something else I can do for you, Miss Hayes?"

"Have you heard anything about the murder of Greg Miller's daughter?"

Her expression switched from guarded to sympathetic. "The higher-ups are keeping everything under wraps. But poor Mr. Miller. Even he doesn't deserve this."

Her wording piqued my interest. "*Even* he? You don't like the guy?"

She brought her hand to her mouth, as if to conceal the slip-up. "Mr. Miller is a respected member of the Cyber-Corp community." Her tone sounded automatic, and her words too practiced.

"Does he have any enemies? Someone who'd want him to suffer?"

"Mr. Miller isn't exactly . . ." She drummed her fingers on the desk. "Well liked. I feel awful talking bad about a man who just lost his daughter."

"I'm not going to tell anyone." I could see I'd have to give up something to get the information I wanted. "There's a rumor that the children of CyberCorp employees have been threatened." I made my eyes wide, which I hoped she'd read as fear. "I need to know if the threat is serious or if this was an isolated thing directed at the Millers."

"We get a lot of threats." She waved a dismissive hand. "It's hard to believe that's really something to worry about. I'm only saying this because it concerns you . . ." She lowered her voice to a whisper. "Mr. Miller is known for being a jerk. He fired two of his engineers on Christmas Eve. Yelled and cursed at them. One of them was sobbing when security escorted him off the premises."

"Do you know their names?"

"I processed some of their exit paperwork. Mark Hoffman and Kyle Lowry. I don't know either of them personally, although of course I saw them come and go many times." By now, she had crossed the line from hesitant informant to enthusiastic gossip. "You think one of them killed Mr. Miller's daughter?"

"I don't know." Part of me hoped so. "Looks like Ron's here. Thanks so much for the info. You're saving my life here."

She gave me a wide smile and turned back to her vidscreen.

Ron stepped from the elevator and waved us over. His gaze strayed up and down Liv's body before landing on me.

I took a hint and made the introduction. "These are my friends Liv and Hunter. They're the ones who want to see the place."

Ron shook Hunter's hand, then Liv's. He held onto Liv's fingers a second longer than necessary before releasing them.

"How are you feeling?" Ron gestured toward my arm, which I'd hidden in long sleeves.

"I sleepwalked last night. I've never done that before." Although I had already explained this to Dr. Fisher, I might get a different answer from Ron. He lacked Fisher's complete obsession with the androids, so between the two of them, he was more likely to give me a considered response.

"Have you talked to Dr. Fisher?"

"Yeah. She doesn't think it has anything to do with the arm."

"I have to agree with her. Sorry. Any other complaints?"

"Nothing other than the fact that I'm going to be setting off metal detectors for the rest of my life."

He chuckled. "Do you know how many people would give anything to be in your place?"

I gave him a look that I hoped displayed a healthy amount of skepticism.

"Seriously. You're at the forefront of a technological revolution. Next week, a select few will be the first to receive Model Ones. But today—three weeks ago actually—you're already more advanced than those. You represent the ultimate in CyberCorp's goals—the use of technology to enhance human life." He threw both his hands in the air. "You're it. The culmination of everything we work for."

"I'm a human experiment with a chip in my head."

"You're hopeless." Ron ushered Hunter, Liv, and me into the elevator. "Anything in particular you want to see?"

I gestured toward my friends.

"Model Ones," they said in unison.

I suppressed a groan. I'd learned from years of experience that I couldn't convince the people around me that artificial intelligence was a bad idea. Today, though, I would go along with them because Hunter and Liv were supportive friends.

"The Model Ones then," I said.

"Let's make that our last stop," Ron said. "How about we start on one of the draft floors?"

I had no idea what that meant, so I nodded.

"Eighteenth floor," Ron announced to the elevator cab.

The doors slid closed, and the elevator climbed its way upward.

"Floors two through fifteen are all concept floors, filled with offices and small labs. That's where the ideas start. After a concept is approved, additional engineers are assigned to it, and it's moved up to a draft floor. There are thirty-three of them."

The doors opened on the eighteenth floor, and we stepped into a wide-open space. As far as I could tell, no walls divided the level, just an open expanse with a rubberized gray floor and matching padded walls. Dozens of half-built devices filled the space, each surrounded by a small group of people. Some took notes as they observed, while others tinkered with the devices.

"The draft floors are where designs come after the concept phase, and after the inventors have petitioned for a development budget. Let's look at one of my favorites."

Ron led us to the other side of the room, weaving around metal and plastic devices of all sizes and shapes. I slowed as we passed something that looked like a giant metal dinosaur, but then tripped over myself to catch up when its jaws snapped. A young engineer nearby cackled in amusement. We passed a safer device that looked like a large vid-screen. As we walked past, it rotated to continue to face us, until one of its engineers stepped in front of it and blocked the sight path.

"Here we go." Ron stopped only twenty feet or so before we reached the far wall.

In front of us stood an android, a couple inches taller

than my five-foot-five and humanoid. It didn't quite look like a Model One. It had the same powdered, silver-colored metal body with a slight yellow tint. Black plastic accented the joints. But compared to the Model One, this body looked even more human, with natural curves in the shoulders, back, and upper legs. Stamped into its forehead were the words *Model Two prototype 10*.

"Whoa." Liv shuffled toward it until she stood toe-to-toe with the android. It towered a few inches taller than her, but no broader.

"Beautiful, isn't she?" An engineer stepped forward. Young and wearing light-toned jeans and a polo shirt, he looked more like a graduate student than a professional engineer. The right pocket of his lab coat had his name stitched across it: Dr. Jacobs.

Liv jumped and giggled in surprise when the android's face tilted downward at her. Metal eyelids narrowed, as if it examined her in return.

A shudder worked its way through my body. On top of the fact that androids would soon displace people from their jobs, there was something about them that just rubbed me the wrong way.

"As you can see," said Jacobs, "the Model Two will be even more lifelike than the Model One. Their processing includes a range of newly constructed prediction models. Those help them learn new things every second. If they're powered on, they're learning." He patted the machine on the arm. "Betsy here is just an early design."

"When is this one going to be released?" Hunter asked.

"It'll be at least another two years," he said. "We have a lot planned for her."

"Really?" I said. "It looks . . . human." I shuffled away from it.

"Thank you." He stood straighter. "She'll move like it too. We're training her on not just human movements, but also movements of animals in the wild. Cheetahs, tigers, gazelles. She'll be a beauty to watch. We have a long way to go to get her running smoothly, but we're proud of her anyway."

Liv stroked the android's silvery cheek. "It's beautiful. What can it do?"

"Almost anything you can," Jacobs said. "Each Model One is preprogrammed for hundreds of specific everyday jobs, like cleaning, doing the dishes, running errands, and personal protection. We advertise that they can do almost any household task, and that's because they've been programmed with the basic understanding of so many. They only have to learn the layouts and eccentricities of each household."

Across the room, an auburn-haired woman about the same age as Jacobs waved to get his attention.

He nodded at her before continuing. "The Model Two, on the other hand, can learn any job from scratch, simply by watching a human do it. They are highly customizable learning machines."

"So they're not limited to specific tasks."

"Exactly. They can do anything, in theory. Obviously, we're going to add a few limitations into the program-ming—laws to govern how they behave. We don't want them learning to hurt people or rob banks, for example."

The woman on the other side of the room waved a second time, this time taking several steps in our direction.

Jacobs's expression turned regretful. "Duty calls. As much as I love talking about this project, it's more important that we get it working."

We said our goodbyes, and Ron led us back through the maze of half-finished devices to the elevator.

"Are the other draft floors like this one?" Hunter asked.

"Yes and no. Some inventions require different types of support. Like a couple of the floors are for medical inventions, so some of those are stocked with medical equipment and only open to personnel who've been properly cleaned for exposure to those sensitive devices."

That reminded me of the story Ron told me about his mother being treated for cancer with CyberCorp technology. "Are they still working on nanobot surgery?"

His lips turned down at the edges for an instant and then back up into his usual cheery expression. "Yes. Those are on the medical draft floors."

I wondered if he held any bitterness about his mother's failed surgery. It wasn't as if CyberCorp had given her cancer. But maybe Ron was secretly furious with Cyber-Corp and decided to take it out on Mr. Miller by killing Harmony. Of course, that scenario made sense only if Miller had worked on his mother's treatment.

"Is Greg Miller involved with any of the medical technologies?" I asked.

Ron gave me a questioning look.

"Can we see the Model Ones?" Hunter asked, before he could answer.

I gritted my teeth and silently cursed Hunter. But he offered me that goofy grin, and I found myself nodding back at him. Did he know what a great smile he had? Not perfect and confident like Jackson's, but imperfect and real.

Ron touched his ear to activate his comm. "Call Sophie." After a short pause, he added, "Hey, Soph. I've got Lena Hayes down here with a couple of her friends. You mind if we come up to take a look at the Model Ones?" Another pause and then, "Yeah, we're on our way up." He touched his ear again to disconnect. "As you wish," he told us.

14

I FROZE WHEN THE ELEVATOR DOORS OPENED ONTO THE seventieth floor.

As on the eighteenth, a wide expanse greeted us. Only, instead of a disarray of electronic parts scattered around with no clear organization, order ruled everything on this floor.

Row upon row of androids lined the room, from the back wall reaching to only thirty feet in front of us. The overhead fluorescent lighting glinted off their metal bodies. They faced us with eerily perfect posture, soldiers ready for battle.

Like a drill sergeant, a tall man in a sleek gray suit walked back and forth across their front line, shouting commands. He carried what looked like a toy silver gun.

"Right foot forward," he called.

Each one of them stepped forward and then together. I

flinched at the metal thum-thump of their synchronized footsteps.

"This way." Ron's voice was louder than usual and drew my attention from the scene.

Liv jumped at the sound.

From the amusement on Ron's face, I guessed he'd been trying to get our attention for a while. "I'm going to introduce you to Dr. Sophie Kim. She's one of our quality-control specialists."

A single room stood separate from the remainder of the space, marked by glass walls and an open rectangular arch for entry. Inside, a small woman and a tall man stood behind a metal desk. Another of the androids stood across from them, its back facing us. Ron led us toward the room and knocked on the glass next to the entryway.

A vid-screen covered the wall behind the woman, its surface filled with scrawled equations and notes. Beneath it, a small tray attached to the wall held an array of styluses that I assumed Dr. Kim used to interact with the screen. In the top right corner of the display, someone had drawn a picture of what looked like a Model One petting a sleeping baby elephant.

The wall beside me held a virtual bookshelf filled with books. It was rendered in such detail that the spines contained title and author names, but it had a faint glow that told me the bookshelf wasn't really there.

They appeared to be technical texts on robotics and psychology. I guessed these were books Dr. Kim actually owned. I'd heard about virtual bookshelves where, when someone touched a book spine, the digital copy was delivered to the person's hand-screen.

The woman shifted her attention from the man beside her to us. "You got here faster than I expected."

"Sorry about that," Ron said. "We were already on our way up when I called."

The woman gestured for us to come closer. "I assume these are the guests you mentioned."

"This is Lena Hayes and her friends Hunter and Olivia." He pointed us out one by one. "I couldn't let them tour the building without stopping on this floor." Ron gestured toward Dr. Kim and the taller man beside her. "Dr. Kim and Paul Rodriguez. I think his son goes to school with you at Hanover."

"He does," Rodriguez said. "His name's Kevin. Do you know him?"

"We've had a few classes together," Liv said.

"Me too," I added. "He's been the star of all my History classes since freshman year."

Rodriguez beamed, and his chest pushed out farther.

"What do you do here?" Liv asked him.

"I'm the head of marketing."

Dr. Kim slapped him on the back. "He's being too modest. Paul here is a genius. He could convince the ocean it needed more water. He used to pitch our smaller products, but now he's Vice President of Marketing."

"You're too kind, Sophie." Mr. Rodriguez scratched the back of his head, uncomfortable with all the praise. "It was lovely to meet all three of you, but I'm going to get out of your hair now." To Dr. Kim, he added, "We can continue this later. I have a few more questions about some of the more subtle features that I want to incorporate into our campaigns."

"I'll call you when we're done here," Kim said. After Rodriguez strolled from the room, she turned back to us. "What can I do for you three?"

"Maybe you could tell them what you do with the androids," Ron said.

"Of course." Dr. Kim pointed at the single Model One standing across the room. "This is Jane. She was chosen at random from among the androids ready for shipment. I'm doing quality control to make sure she's ready."

"What kind of quality control?" Liv asked.

"I run through all the same drills that Sergeant—that's what we call him, outside those doors there—is going through with the group. Then I assign her some of the sorts of tasks she'll get once she has a home. If she succeeds at those, I tear her down, piece by piece, and test each component to make sure it behaves as expected."

My brows shot upward. I might not appreciate these androids, but it was hard not to admire how much work went into them.

"I do this to multiple Model Ones, and a couple of the Model Two prototypes as well, because some of the parts and software are shared. If I find a problem in a single component of a single one, I pull out a larger sample of androids and test them for the same issue."

"That sounds like a lot."

"It can be," she said. "We take our quality control very seriously."

Her explanation made me feel a little better about these machines being around humans. "Have you found any major issues?"

"Just one, a couple months ago. A security loophole would have allowed malicious data to be downloaded from the EyeNet. It would take an expensive, high-end machine to infiltrate the EyeNet like that, so it's unlikely but still a concern. We developed a patch for the issue about three weeks ago. Part of my job is making sure these babies have the current software, including that fix."

"What's it doing?" I pointed at the Model One's back.

Dr. Kim motioned me toward the android, so I could get a view of its profile. It stood before a small stove. In one silver hand, the android held a sauté pan filled with vegetables and shrimp.

"She's cooking dinner?" Liv asked, her voice filled with awe. "What else can she do?"

I cringed at hearing her call the machine *she*.

"A late lunch, actually." Dr. Kim's smile grew wider. "When she's done, she'll clean up the mess and then organize my desk." She waved her hand toward the multiple stacks of paper covering its surface.

On the edge of the desk lay a silver pistol-shaped device, just like the one the Sergeant held in the main room of this floor. I pointed to the gun. "What's that?"

"An EMP gun—electromagnetic pulse. It shoots a precise pulse that knocks out electronics. We keep them handy during testing, so we can shut down the androids in an emergency."

"It works on all androids?" I asked.

"On all electronics. This one is coded to my ID chip as a precaution. The last thing we need is someone shooting it at someone's pacemaker."

Liv and Hunter both inched closer to the stove, with Liv in the lead. I hung back toward the doorway.

The android shifted the pan back and forth in jerky movements to brown the food on all sides. Although the movements couldn't pass for human, they were impressively close. Its metal arms looked eerily similar to the one attached to my shoulder, except it was more angular where mine had smooth curves—more like a Model Two actually.

"Hold on a moment." Dr. Kim pressed her ear to activate her comm. "Yes? Mm-hmm. I can be there in five." She pressed her ear again. "We have to wrap this up. I have a meeting."

"We should get back to school anyway," I said.

"Oh crap." Hunter offered a quick apology to Dr. Kim for his language, then added, "I have a Calculus quiz at 2:10. We have to go."

"It was lovely to meet you all," Dr. Kim said. Although she used the word *all*, her gaze stayed on me when she spoke. "Do tell your father how accommodating I was."

I gave her a tight smile. "I will."

When we arrived back downstairs, I wasn't quite ready to face the prying eyes of other students. Plus, I was still seeing those damn virtual objects in the lobby.

"You have time to get me off the network now?" I asked Ron. "The EyeNet is driving me insane."

"Sure."

I turned to Hunter and Liv. "You guys go on without me."

"But I'm your ride," Liv said. "How are you going to get back to school, or home?"

"I'll figure it out. Maybe grab an auto-cab if I need to."

"Okay." Liv gave me a quick hug and then headed for the door.

Hunter stood still for a second. His gaze flicked toward the door and back to me. Then he too moved toward me for a hug.

It caught me by surprise, and at first I stood there with my arms at my sides while he wrapped his around me. I was just reaching up to embrace him back when Hunter stepped back, nodded, and followed Liv to the door.

"Bye," I called after him. "I'll see you later."

He walked out the door with a backward wave and barely a limp. My back still tingled where Hunter touched me, as Ron led me up to a large conference room.

Inside, Simon sat at a table that filled most of the space. Opposite the table, a whiteboard took up the whole wall, covered almost entirely in scrawled equations. When I blinked, the formulas wavered and then solidified once again.

The whiteboard was virtual, and probably nothing but a plain wall in real life. Next to it stood a Model One, its red eyes dead since it appeared to be turned off.

"Hey. How are you feeling?" Simon asked.

"As well as can be expected, considering I have a metal device attached to my shoulder and I'm seeing things that aren't actually there."

"The alternative would be to have no arm at all," he said.

That option looked more and more appealing each time I thought about it.

"Plus," Ron added. "Who's to say virtual objects aren't actually there. If you can see them and experience them, does the fact that they're fleeting make them any less real than this desk?" He knocked on the surface of the table to emphasize his point.

Simon grabbed his hand-screen and a cable from the edge of the table, while Ron pressed the button on my arm to open the small compartment containing the outlet. Simon extended the hand-screen display to its full size, then connected the cable between it and the arm. After he entered the password, a flood of file names scrolled onto the display.

Simon selected one of the files, scrolled downward until he found what he was looking for, and typed on the screen to overwrite a couple lines. He saved and exited the file, and as before, the display informed us it was compiling the revised program.

The arm went limp, and a red light on the palm glowed as the software reinstalled.

I blinked, and the room suddenly seemed a lot emptier than it used to. The far wall, now plain white, no longer displayed the scrawled equations it had a moment ago. The Model One that had been in the corner was also gone. I hadn't even realized it was virtual.

"That should do it," Simon said. "What do you see right now?"

"The whiteboard is gone." I pointed at the wall. "And so is the Model One that was next to it."

"Good. That's what we wanted."

"Once you're healed from the surgery," Ron said, "we'll modify the chip to remove network access altogether. Right now, you're still on the network, but we've suppressed all the virtual images."

"How long until you can modify the chip?" I asked.

"It's hard to say. Not until your headaches are gone. That'll be a good indication that you've healed enough." He opened the office door and ushered me out. "I'll walk you downstairs."

I hesitated in the doorway of the elevator. "Can I see Jackson before I go?"

"Sorry, no. They're working on his upgrades right now. Besides, trust me. You won't want to see him again until he's done. You weren't a pretty sight while your new arm was being constructed, and Jackson . . . Well, he was in worse shape than you."

My gut twisted, and I nodded mutely. I tried to push from my head all the images that invaded it. Images of Jackson with more metal than flesh, barely alive. I wished I'd dragged him into the passenger seat that night. Then he'd be fine, sitting in class right now.

When the elevator doors opened into the lobby, all hell broke loose.

Owen and two other men in dark suits stood only a few feet from the elevators, and all three of them turned their intense gazes on me. My first instinct was to scream and shrink back into the elevator, but my mother's assistant, Missy, stepped forward and grabbed my arm.

"What the h—" I started.

"Your mother sent us to collect you."

"I don't need collecting." I tried to yank my arm away from her, but her fingers dug in tighter.

"That's hardly the point." She sounded disturbingly like my mother.

Missy had worked with my mother for so long that, over the years, she'd become a smaller, lighter version of my mother. Instead of curly dark hair, Missy had straight blond hair that she kept tied in a tight bun. Her black skirt suit fit her like a glove, and she held her head high.

She couldn't match my mother in expression though. Her face looked decidedly irritated, where my mother's would have been unreadable.

Surprisingly strong for someone a couple inches shorter than me, Missy clutched my wrist and tugged me toward CyberCorp's front doors. The three security guys pressed close around us as we hurried through the lobby. A small crowd had gathered to see the commotion, and when we emerged from the building, the repeated clicking sounds of hand-screen cameras met us.

My family's black car idled just beyond the exit. Owen circled to the other side of the backseat and got in, while the remaining two security guys pressed closer to me when Missy opened the door. I had no choice but to fall into the backseat. Missy slid in beside me, locking me into place between her and Owen on my other side.

At least I wouldn't have to worry about finding a ride home.

"Let's go," Missy told Lionel.

Lionel caught my eye in the rearview mirror with a sympathetic glance. It didn't help quell the storm brewing inside me.

Owen took up too much space next to me, but I still managed to extract my hand-screen from my backpack, making a point to elbow him and Missy more than necessary. I placed a call to my mother.

"What did you do?" I shouted into the device as soon as the call connected.

"Watch your tone, Lena." My mother's annoyance snapped over the phone line and electrified the air around me.

With the car in auto-drive, Lionel rotated his seat to cock an eyebrow at me, then smoothly rotated to face the front again. Between the two of them, I took the hint and lowered my voice.

"Your minion and three security guards just dragged me out of CyberCorp headquarters."

"I told you I wanted you guarded."

"You could have called CyberCorp, and they would have told you I was fine."

"Of course, I did that. But I gave you a bodyguard for a reason, and I expect you to keep him with you until I say you don't need him anymore."

"You didn't have to send an army to drag me out of the building. Just Missy and Owen could have done the job."

"I thought this would be more persuasive."

"Haven't you made me enough of a spectacle already? First, the arm. Now, a whole team of guards to bring attention to the arm."

"Keep Owen with you, and we won't have any more problems." Her voice had a singsong quality to it. "Hold on a moment."

The line went silent. I itched to scream into the phone, to tell my mother she had no right to run my life, and that she'd done a sucky job of it so far. To tell her I spent every minute being an outcast from technology lovers, because I disagreed with them, and from the anti-tech community, because they didn't trust the CyberCorp princess. To tell her she'd ruined me, ripped apart my soul, and all that was left was a shell.

"Lena, I have to go," she said when she came back on the line. "This conversation is over anyway."

"It's not over!" I shouted, but silence met my outburst. My mother had disconnected.

At eleven that night, I stared at the ceiling above my bed. My anger still simmered at the surface.

I was too worked up to sleep. It wasn't enough that my parents had sentenced me to this arm, but my mother had topped it off by making me a spectacle and dragging me out of CyberCorp. Just in case I forgot for a moment that they ran my life, my mother's cronies were there to remind me.

I grabbed a throw pillow and threw it against the far wall. It hit and tumbled to the floor, harmless. I snatched up a second pillow and did the same. I itched to cause more damage, to blow off some steam.

Instead, I lifted my hand-screen from the nightstand, intending to call Liv, but an alert blinked in the corner of the display. I touched it, and the device notified me that Philip Pollock was streaming a new audio program. It was probably a bad idea to listen to it right now. It would get me further riled up, but that was exactly what my bad mood needed—something to feed on.

I hit the play button. For the first five minutes of the program, I settled back against the headboard, my pillow tucked under my back. Instead of getting me angrier, as I'd suspected it would, the audio calmed my nerves by reminding me there was a whole community out there that shared my feelings.

"The Model One rollout is scheduled for less than two weeks from today, with the first androids being delivered to a limited number of elite customers. It is inevitable that artificial intelligence, if allowed to grow unchecked, will displace humanity. Scientists and scholars have predicted it, but the Hayeses do not care."

This Hayes absolutely cared.

"Unfortunately, we've not been able to block the distribution of these atrocities through legal means, but I urge you to continue writing letters to CyberCorp. Tell whoever will listen that CyberCorp and their androids directly contradict nature. They are ungodly."

There was that word again—ungodly. The same word from the protester and from the letter to CyberCorp.

"Speaking of ungodly," Pollock continued, "it's been confirmed that Tom and Marissa Hayes have upgraded their own daughter. Many of my listeners sent photos today of Lena Hayes, who was at the CyberCorp building wearing what appeared to be a robotic arm."

My ears perked up. I'd never been mentioned in one of Pollock's programs before. I always figured that, if I got a mention, it would be for something good—like congratulations for maintaining my ethics despite having been raised in this house.

No such luck.

As the audio played, I did a quick web search for the so-called photos, and the pictures flooded my display. Those hand-screen cameras had done their jobs earlier today. They had captured me from every angle.

In the bright sunlight, my long sleeves were slightly sheer, and it was clear from the photo that the metal extended from my hand all the way up the arm. In a few of the images, the sun glinted off the thing, emphasizing how unhuman it was.

"As usual, the Hayeses disregard everything that makes us human. By modifying their own child, they send a clear message: humanity is not to be cherished. We are to place machines over flesh and blood—even our own flesh and blood."

I shut off the audio. I couldn't be upset with Pollock. He spoke the truth I'd already recognized—the arm made me less human and more monster, and my parents were to blame.

I couldn't lie in this bed a second longer, so I jumped up and paced the room, anger pulsing in my bones. I started to call Liv, but my fingers had other plans. Before I knew it, the hand-screen was calling Hunter.

"Hey. What's up?" he answered before I could disconnect.

I pulled the hand-screen away from my ear and stared at it. Why had I just called him?

"Lena?" he said.

"Yeah, I'm here. Sorry for calling so late. I have a lot on my mind." I expected him to laugh it off, tell me I was being ridiculous, tell me how great my life was—the way Jackson would have.

"Tell me about it."

I launched into an explanation of everything that happened at CyberCorp after he and Liv left.

"Shit," he said when I finished.

"Exactly. Is it wrong to wish my parents had never founded CyberCorp?" I stared down at my left arm, uncovered in the tank top I wore in the privacy of my room. "I'd probably have both arms." I clenched and unclenched my metal fist. It reacted so easily now, the same way my other one did. I hated it for that, even more than I'd hated it before. The least it could do was behave like the machine it was. Now, it was masquerading as a real, flesh-and-blood limb.

"If your life was totally different, we might not have met."

I searched for the joke in his words but found none. "I guess." I meant to put more enthusiasm into it. After all, Hunter was turning out to be a decent guy.

He'd gone out of his way to make sure he was the one who told me about Harmony. He'd played hooky with me, and even though he claimed it was to see CyberCorp, I suspected it was really because he knew I needed to get away from school. And now, despite that I was rude to him most of the time, he seemed content to listen to my problems.

"Want me to swing by?" he asked. "I could climb

through your window. Just talk until you get too tired to be upset."

My heart did a cartwheel that flopped abruptly, leaving me winded. I wanted to see him, but Jackson was the only boy who ever climbed through my window. Every Monday at midnight, like clockwork. Now, he was in a coma—where I put him. "I don't think that's a good idea."

"Okay."

Silence filled the call line for so long that I thought we might have lost the connection. "Hunter?"

"If I were smarter, I'd take that as a hint and wish you goodnight. But I'm not. So how about a drive instead? It'll get your mind off things."

"You don't have auto-drive, do you?" The words were out there before I could even plan them.

He chuckled. "Nope. Can't afford it."

"Sounds good. I'm sending my address over." I sent a quick message to his hand-screen. "When can you be here?"

"Fifteen minutes."

"I'll meet you on the street. Don't ring the bell or pull into the driveway."

"You sneaking out?" he asked, his voice teasing. "The CyberCorp princess is a rule-breaker?"

"I don't have many options. My mom's gone insane, and I have a bodyguard standing outside my bedroom door."

Fifteen minutes later, I opened the app on my hand-screen that controlled our home security system and suspended the alarms. I pushed up the window next to my bed, thanking the stars that my bodyguard slept on the other side of my bedroom door.

From the window ledge, I grabbed a branch of the tree just outside and climbed down to the ground.

When I jumped into the passenger seat, Hunter gave me a slow once-over. His gaze slid over my long-sleeved T-shirt, partially covered by an unzipped hoodie, and then veered down to the jeans that hugged my hips. I'd spent twelve of the last fifteen minutes choosing something to wear that showed off my curves and also looked casual enough that someone might slip into it for a late-night drive.

Hunter gave a nod of appreciation. A delighted shiver rippled through me, but guilt slammed it to a stop when I imagined Jackson in his hospital bed.

Hunter set the car into motion as soon as I buckled in.

"Where are we going?" I asked.

"I figured we could drive around McCauley Park."

It wasn't until we got to the park that I realized what a great pick it was for a nighttime drive.

Just north of downtown, McCauley was the greenest area in the city because it was a nature preserve. That meant no digital billboards—real or virtual—in or around the park.

The only lights surrounding us were the occasional streetlamps, casting a soft glow over the trees and shrubbery we passed. If I squinted at a spot above the center of the park, I imagined I could make out a single star outside the reach of the city's bright lights.

"What happened to your knee?" I asked him.

"You know that already. They replaced it."

"Yeah, but why?"

"Oh, you want the long version." He paused for a moment, as if sorting out his thoughts. "I was in a bad bike accident when I was a kid. Hit by a car. It wasn't as bad as it could have been, but my knee was basically destroyed. I had a couple surgeries at first, but it never healed right, always needed more surgeries, and each one meant a painful recovery." He glanced quickly down at his knee and then back at the road. "Until CyberCorp."

"So you like the new knee."

"I have my life back. No more surgeries, and no more being afraid anything I do is going to make it worse—which would mean more surgeries. CyberCorp saved me."

I spread my metal fingers across my thigh and tried to think about my arm that way. Without it, I might have needed surgery after surgery to keep my flesh-and-bone limb working, or I would always be in pain, or I would just have no arm. I tried to be grateful, but my anger won out.

The artificial intelligence, and my parents' role in the whole thing, tipped the scales for me. I had a computer in my head, interpreting my brain's activities and deciding what my arm should do—and my parents had put it there. As much as I wanted to believe this arm was *mine* now, part of me felt like I wasn't the one in control.

"But you had a choice. Your knee wasn't working like you wanted, so you *chose* to have it upgraded. Right? Plus, it's all you up there." I tapped his temple. "No artificial intelligence."

"True."

I couldn't imagine having a conversation like this with Jackson. For years, I'd told him how I felt about Cyber-Corp, and for years, he'd listened without actually hearing me. He brushed off my feelings as if they were the product of rebellion. He refused to see who I really was.

And now he lay in a hospital bed, held together by metal parts, and here I was counting all his flaws. I silently cursed myself.

"What's wrong?" Hunter asked.

"Nothing."

"Then why are you doing that thing with your face?" He pointed at my mouth.

I slapped his hand away. "I'm not doing a thing with my face."

He laughed and pointed again, daring me to slap him away a second time. "You scrunch your lips up when you're thinking really hard." He touched my lower lip. "It's adorable."

This time, I didn't move his hand. He left it there a second longer than necessary, and excited tingles spread outward from his touch. My pulse fluttered as my heart tried to make a break for it, right through my ribs.

"Oh, I forgot." He moved his hand from my face and popped open the glove compartment. He extracted a chocolate candy bar and pushed the compartment closed again. "I got this for you."

I stared at it for a second.

"You love sweets, right?"

"Yeah, definitely." I accepted the chocolate and tucked it into the pocket of my hoodie. "Thanks." I didn't like chocolate, but Allie would appreciate it. She'd adopted my bad sweet tooth, but without the dislike of chocolate that came with it.

"Are we done pretending this conversation is about me?" he asked, after he returned his hand to the steering wheel.

I sighed. "Sure."

"It was wrong for your parents to remove your original arm without discussing it with you. But don't you think you would have come to the same conclusion eventually?"

"I'll never know the answer to that. All I'll ever know is that I spent my whole life in CyberCorp's artificial shadow, and then one day, my parents' beliefs were pushed on me without my approval. If I'd had a say, at the very least, I would have insisted they remove the AI from the arm. If that meant waiting longer for a working prosthetic, then so be it. It would have been *my* choice and based on *my* principles." The anger I had felt for weeks ballooned in my stomach and became so large I felt I would burst.

"Take a right up here." I pointed to the intersection ahead of us.

Hunter slowed the car and turned the wheel.

This route would take us past CyberCorp. I wanted to see the building. I needed a target for my hatred right now, or it would explode out of me and paint the car's dashboard red and sticky with my insides.

"Stop," I said when we were right in front of the building.

A prudent driver, Hunter pulled into the roundabout in

front of the driveway rather than stopping in the middle of the street.

"Where are you going?" He grabbed at me as I opened the car door and jumped out.

Before I knew what I was doing, I flipped up my jacket's hood and ran toward the building. Hunter's footsteps pounded the pavement behind me, but I didn't look back.

I slammed my metal fist into the wall of windows leading to the lobby. The window shattered, and glass pieces tinkled to the ground around me. The glass was reinforced, but still no match for the high-tech monstrosity that was my arm.

Shock coated me like ice water as I stared at the broken glass scattered around my feet.

But the cold left a burst of fire in its wake. It felt good. Powerful.

An alarm cut through the night. Its wail pierced my ears. Pain bloomed in my head, focused where they'd installed the chip.

Spots danced in front of my eyes, but I ignored them. I wasn't done yet.

"Stay there!" I shouted to Hunter, without turning to look at him. "They have cameras."

I kicked away a large chunk of glass from the lower frame of the window and stepped inside. The alarm continued to wail. My vision blurred as the pain in my head swelled even further. Guards would be here any second, but I needed to do this.

I knew this lobby like the back of my hand—my old one. So as I ran to the other side of the reception desk, I kept my face tilted down and away from the cameras attached to the back corners of the ceiling.

When I reached the Model One on display beside reception, I pulled back my left hand and swung my fist forward. Metal crunched against metal, and the android's face collapsed.

I grinned until my face ached. I felt alive.

Still angled away from the cameras, I gripped the thing's mangled head and yanked upward. With a screech of metal against metal, the neck broke and the head came free. I crushed the skull in my hand and grinned as it clattered to the ground.

"Lena, let's go!" Hunter shouted from the direction of the car.

I spun on my heel and ran toward him, head still tilted downward, hood pulled low over my face. Before I reached Hunter, two guards barreled toward me, both clad in black uniforms with Tasers at their hips.

The ache in my head rose and sharpened. I clutched at my temples, certain I would pass out. But I went numb instead. My body reacted.

I shot forward and slammed into the nearest guard. We tumbled to the floor.

I scrambled to my feet and pointed the Taser down at him. The guard reached for his hip—but came up empty. My metal hand now held the weapon he'd been going for. Somehow, I had managed to slip it from its holster when we were on the ground.

I didn't know whether to be creeped out or grateful.

"Look what I've got," the other guard called from outside.

I could barely hear him over the sound of my own heartbeat, filling up my ears, speeding my breath until my head went light.

He had Hunter in a bear hug from behind, Hunter's arms pinned to his sides. Hunter squirmed in the larger man's grasp, but even though he matched the guard in height, the guard had him by about fifty pounds of muscle.

My head still dipped low, I shifted the Taser from the man on the ground to the one holding Hunter. "Let him go." He had to be fifty feet away—way out of the weapon's reach.

"Drop it." He squeezed Hunter harder, until he cringed at the pressure.

My heartbeat skipped and then barreled forward, leaving me breathless.

I hoped my hood and the darkness masked my features. Otherwise, even if we got out of this without getting arrested, I was going to be in deep shit.

I did as instructed and raised both my hands in a sign of surrender.

His face relieved, the guard on the ground climbed to his feet and touched his ear to make a call. I leaped back into motion and lunged at him, metal arm extended. I slammed into his chest. The man grunted and hit the ground. He blinked up at me, dazed. I slapped my palm into his ear to deactivate the comm. The man's eyes rolled back into his head, and he went limp beneath me.

The other guard still held Hunter in a tight grip.

I swiped the fallen Taser up from the ground and ran toward them, back through the broken window frame. When I reached them, I leveled the weapon at the guard's face. "If you let him go, we'll leave. We can pretend none of this ever happened."

What would tomorrow's news reports look like if they recognized me? Would the police come for me before or after they reported that Lena Hayes had destroyed part of her parents' pride and joy? Or maybe CyberCorp and my parents would keep it hushed. Best-case scenario, I would be grounded forever, and only a select few CyberCorp employees would know what I'd done.

"Those windows are going to cost thousands to replace." He pointed at the shattered glass littering the ground between us. "There's no walking away. The best you can do for yourself is to drop the Taser and turn yourself in."

Hunter ground his heel into the man's foot. The man flinched, and his arms loosened. Hunter took advantage and dropped to the ground, slipping through his captor's arms. I leaped over Hunter and slammed my palm into the side of the guard's head. He grunted and collapsed to the ground.

I stood frozen outside CyberCorp, with the two guards and my friend on the ground around me.

"A little help here." Hunter reached a hand up.

I grabbed it and hauled him to his feet. I didn't know whether the guard's call for backup had gone through before I disconnected it. But with these alarms blaring, someone had to be on the way.

The two of us ran for Hunter's car and jumped in. He gunned the motor even before I could buckle my seat belt, and we took off in a shriek of rubber tires.

We drove two blocks in tense silence, my fingers clasped around the sides of my thighs, the fingernails of my right hand digging into my legs.

"Lena."

I looked over to find Hunter with one side of his mouth tilted upward and an arched eyebrow to match. He reached over, grabbed my metal hand, and eased my fingers from my legs. "You're going to leave a bruise."

I loosened my other hand on my own and sagged back into my seat. For weeks, my chest had felt tight, like a rubberband pulled taught. Now, the band loosened—not much, but enough so that I could breathe without breaking.

"You're insane. You know that?" he said, grinning full force now.

"You loved every minute of it." Away from the wailing alarm, the pain in my head lessened to a dull ache. I laughed until my heart slowed to its normal pace and my side hurt. I had officially lost my mind—and it felt amazing.

"I spent half my life with a disability," he said when I finally calmed again. "Now that all my body parts work the way I want, it feels good to rebel." He nudged my arm. "Even if it was more your rebellion than mine."

I swallowed the last of my hysterical giggles. "You're not mad at me?"

"I think I might like you even more." Hunter took his

gaze from the road long enough to meet my eyes. "No, I take that back." He turned back to the road. "I like you just as much."

It shouldn't have made me blush, but I ducked my head and stared down at my knees.

A few minutes later, he stopped the car outside my house, and I reached for the door handle. Hunter leaned over, wrapped an arm around my waist, and pulled me toward himself. My feet lost purchase on the car's floor, and I stumbled against him. My forehead tapped against his, but he held me firmly enough to save us from bumping too hard.

"Sorry," I said, more on reflex than anything else.

He went bright red, but his hand stayed at my waist. "No, *I'm* sorry. I didn't mean to . . . Are you okay?"

"Sorry," I said again, and reached out to brush his forehead where we'd bumped. I yanked my hand back when I realized I was touching his face. "Sorry," I said again—because I wasn't sorry for any of it.

"Stop apologizing." The blush had cleared from Hunter's face, and his voice was low and luscious, like a threatening storm in a drought. His breath tickled my nose, and as usual, it smelled of mint.

My mouth was inches from his. Less than inches? If I leaned forward, would they touch? Were his lips as soft as they looked?

They had to be.

"I have to go." I shoved against his chest and scrambled away from him. I couldn't do this. Not with Jackson lying in a hospital bed. Not with his body in pieces. Not like this. "I'll . . . um . . . see you tomorrow."

I slammed the car door behind me and ran around the side of the house to my bedroom window. Inside, I kicked off my shoes, reenabled the home alarms from my handscreen, and climbed into bed without bothering to undress.

I just needed a good night's sleep.

16

IN THE MORNING, LIONEL PULLED UP IN FRONT OF THE school, and I dragged myself out of the vehicle.

I hadn't sleepwalked to the middle of nowhere again— thank God—but I'd sleepwalked down to the kitchen. I'd woken around four-thirty in the morning standing in front of the open refrigerator, once again wearing my hoodie and sneakers. My nightshift bodyguard, Walt, stood nearby in case any of the food decided to attack me. I guessed my unconscious self had decided it was hungry.

After two nights of sleeping without actually being in bed, I could have fallen over from exhaustion at any minute. The dull ache in my head and left shoulder didn't help either.

Not five seconds after Lionel drove away, my hand-screen buzzed with a message from Liv. She wanted me to meet her on the east side of the school.

When I arrived at the spot, she wasn't there yet. I gave

171

in to temptation and texted Hunter. I held my breath while I typed the message inviting him to meet Liv and me.

Hunter showed up first.

His limp could now pass for a swagger. Despite it being January, the air held barely a breeze, so Hunter wore a long-sleeved shirt with no jacket. Although it hung loose around the waist, it defined the lean form of his chest and upper arms. His too-long hair fell into his face, and he brushed it back. When it fell a second time, my fingers itched to tuck it out of the way.

We had been hanging out only a few days, but yesterday felt like a serious bonding experience. I'd bared my soul to him, and he had done the same. We could see each other's wounds now.

When Hunter stood only ten yards from me, I started to raise my arms, and then dropped them. I wanted to hug him, but a week ago, I barely knew his name.

Hugging would be weird. Wouldn't it? My arms hung at my sides like they were glued there.

When he finally reached me, he wrapped his arms around me, and when he squeezed, I squeezed back. His hands on my waist sent a burst of warmth up my spine. I wanted to nestle my face in the crook of his neck and inhale him. I didn't—but the knots that lived in my chest loosened just a little.

"How are you?" he asked after we stepped apart. His voice had a thickness to it, like good-quality honey, deep and dark and delicious.

It took me a moment to collect myself. "If you're

wondering whether I'm still criminally insane, the answer is no."

I wanted to say more, and from the way his lips parted, he probably did too. But Liv rounded the corner and jogged toward us.

Her text message hadn't said anything was wrong, just that she wanted to see me. The look on her face, however, suggested things were far from okay.

"Have you heard?" She sucked in a deep breath.

I couldn't help noticing that Hunter didn't give Liv a hello hug. Only me.

"Breathe," I said. "What's happening?"

She let out her breath in one long stroke. "Kevin Rodriguez is dead. Strangled last night in his bed."

Hunter's eyes went as wide as Liv's, and I felt mine doing the same.

"Just like Harmony?" Hunter asked.

She nodded.

"Rodriguez," he said. "Why does that name sound familiar?"

"It's a common name," Liv said.

My chest knots pulled themselves tight again.

I hadn't made the connection right away, not until Hunter pointed it out. "Kevin's dad is Paul Rodriguez. We met him when we toured CyberCorp. He leads the marketing team for the Model Ones."

Emotions waged war inside me. On one hand, I'd sleep-walked only as far as the kitchen last night. On the other hand, another of my classmates had died. A boy I'd seen in the hallways just a few days ago, laughing with his friends, would no longer wander there between classes. His life had been snuffed out.

I should have been devastated, but instead, relief vibrated through every inch of me.

I hadn't killed Kevin. And since Kevin was killed just like Harmony—the kid of a CyberCorp employee, strangled in bed—I hadn't killed Harmony either. I didn't know whether to dance or cry—or cry because someone was dead and I wanted to dance.

Hunter squeezed my shoulder. "Lena, you look like you're going to be sick."

"I'll be okay." But the knots were so tight now that they blocked my throat. My breath went thin.

He turned his attention on Liv. "You don't look too hot either. Do you need to sit down after that run?"

"No, it's not that," she said. "I'm just a little tired. I got up super early to finish a paper. I actually heard the news report about Kevin at around five this morning, an hour after it happened. I—"

"What?" I held up a hand to stop her. "Kevin died at four in the morning?"

"According to the news report, yeah. The report hit the newswire so soon because a reporter lives right next door to the Rodriguez house."

Numbness spread from my fingertips outward to my entire body. Even though I thought I'd sleepwalked only down to the kitchen, my subconscious wouldn't have dressed me in shoes and a jacket unless I was going outside.

Kevin had died at four, and I woke up in front of the fridge at four-thirty. I could have come and gone by the window, like I had when I met Hunter last night, and I wouldn't have had to deal with not having an ID chip to get through the front door. The bodyguard wouldn't have known I was out of bed until I arrived back home and went down to the kitchen via my bedroom door, which he watched throughout the night.

Assuming I'd sleepwalked from Kevin's house back to mine, I could have killed him if he lived nearby. In thirty minutes, at a jog, I could have made it about three miles.

"Lena?" Liv asked. She and Hunter both stared at me, concern etched across their faces.

"Do you know where Kevin lives—*lived*, I mean?"

Liv shrugged. "What's that got to do with anything?"

"I sleepwalked again last night."

"What's it got to do with where Kevin lives?"

Hunter caught on to my line of thinking faster. "Not this again."

Liv understood a second later. "You didn't kill them!" she said, louder than she must have intended because she took a quick glance around to check for anyone within earshot. The nearest group of students stood about ten yards away, and they didn't react to Liv's outburst. More quietly, she added, "That's crazy."

"Is it? I hate CyberCorp almost as much as anyone, and I don't know where I was during either murder. What if I—"

"You didn't," Liv said. "No way. You're not a killer."

"I destroyed CyberCorp's lobby last night when I was wide awake. Crushed a Model One's skull in my hand like it was an aluminum soda can . . . and it felt amazing. I'm violent. Maybe my subconscious is even more."

"Whoa." Liv held up both hands to stop me. "You did what?"

"Yesterday afternoon, after you left, my mom's goons showed up and dragged me back home. And then my photo was all over the internet—metal arm and all. And I was pissed about the whole thing, and I kind of lost it. I broke the windows and trashed the Model One in the lobby."

Her mouth dropped open. "We need to talk about your anger issues, but first things first. You damaged a robot. So what? That doesn't make you a murderer. Robots weren't people last time I checked."

Hunter held both hands palm up, as if he were placing the two on a scale, measuring their weight. "They're not the same. Not by a long shot."

"That's not my point. I'm out of control. I didn't plan to destroy that property, but I'm happy I did. And part of me hopes these murders will convince my parents to cancel the Model One rollout. Who can say I didn't kill Harmony and Kevin to make that happen?"

"You didn't," Hunter said, "but you need to talk to someone about the sleepwalking."

"You don't know that. All we know is that this started when I got the damn arm." I gripped the metal wrist with my right hand and yanked, as if I could remove the wretched machine from my shoulder just by pulling it. "I'm getting rid of it. As soon as I can make an appointment to remove it, it's gone."

"We've had this conversation already," Liv said. "There are a hundred other people more likely to have committed these murders." She began ticking names off on her fingers. "Philip Pollock. Any former CyberCorp employee. That guy who had to close down his little tech company last month because of the competition from CyberCorp. Or any other business owner who had to shut down—I'm sure there are a bunch of those."

When she paused, I knew she wanted me to respond, to agree with her, but I could manage nothing more than a shrug.

"Hunter." She waved toward him. "Do something with her."

"Why is she my problem?" he asked. "You've known her longer."

"And she's been this stubborn for all that time."

"You guys do see me standing here, right?" I waved my hand in their faces.

They stopped bickering and stared at me, both with arms crossed over their chests.

"I'm going to make an appointment to see Dr. Fisher. That, I can promise you."

For the remaining minutes before class, we continued to argue. By the time the warning bell for class rang, I'd convinced them that I accepted their explanations. In truth, I still had my doubts.

There was too much I didn't know.

The city's metro area was a big one, so it was more likely Kevin lived outside a three-mile range of me rather than inside it. I needed his address. If he lived far away, I could relax. That would prove my innocence.

I spent my morning classes distracted, itching for the chance to call CyberCorp and convince someone there to help me stop sleepwalking. As soon as the lunch bell rang, I ducked into an empty restroom and made the call.

"Hello, Miss Hayes," the receptionist said when she answered. "What can I do for you?"

"I'm calling for Dr. Fisher," I said.

"Hold please."

A few seconds later, Dr. Fisher came on the line, sounding only mildly annoyed. "Lena. What can I do for you? Everything okay with the arm?"

"Not exactly. I'm still sleepwalking . . ." My voice trailed off. I felt like I needed to say more, but I couldn't come out and tell her I suspected myself of murder. Those words didn't exactly roll off the tongue. "I think something with the arm and the chip in my brain is making it happen. I woke up on the side of the road the night before last." It was far from a perfect explanation of why I needed her help, but it was the best I could manage. "I want the arm and the chip removed. I want a traditional prosthetic without artificial intelligence."

"This again?" She breathed an exaggerated sigh. "We've been testing versions of that chip for the past six years. Your sleepwalking is the result of good old-fashioned trauma."

I opened my mouth to respond, but then snapped it shut. She was right. Based on the information I'd given her,

her explanation seemed a lot more likely than a malfunction in high-tech CyberCorp equipment.

Only her theory didn't explain why I'd sleepwalked to exactly the route that would take me to Harmony's house. That kind of activity was too specific, too premeditated to be explained by trauma.

But I couldn't say that to Dr. Fisher—not without offering myself up as a murder suspect.

"You're right," I said. "Sorry to bother you."

As soon as we disconnected the call, I made a new one to the same place. For a second time, I'd failed to convince Dr. Fisher, but maybe one of her assistants would take pity on me.

"Hello, Miss Hayes," came the receptionist's voice again.

"Sorry for calling again. Can you get me Ron Franklin or Simon McQueen this time, please?"

"Yes, Miss Hayes. Please hold."

A few seconds later, Ron picked up the line. "Lena?"

"Hey. Sorry to bother you. I was hoping to talk to you about my arm."

There was a pause on his end, and then, "Did you talk to Dr. Fisher? I pretty much just do what she tells me to do. If you have concerns, they should go to her."

"She's not interested in helping me. And I know for a fact that competition for CyberCorp's college intern spots is insane, and you got one. That means you're a computer prodigy or something. You probably know as much about this arm as she does—more, since you're the one doing all the work while she supervises."

"I find it hard to believe Dr. Fisher blew off her bosses' daughter."

"Not exactly. I didn't give her the whole story, and the half story I told her was lame. She had every reason not to help me."

"What whole story?"

"Can we meet in person?" I had to assume CyberCorp recorded all phone conversations made to the main line. If I told Ron everything right now, I would have a lot to answer for later.

"Sure, but it'll have to wait a few days. Fisher was pissed that I spent an hour touring the building yesterday. She's on my ass today." He lowered his voice. "She's staring at me right now. Tonight, she's got her whole team going out of town until Friday for some kind of public-relations thing. Maybe we can talk Friday night at your folks' party, or you can come into the office on Monday."

Monday felt like a lifetime away, but Hunter and Liv were probably right. I was overreacting. "Monday's fine."

"I'll still see you on Friday at the party. Okay?"

"Sure. See you then."

Just to be on the safe side, I'd have to keep myself from murdering anyone until then—even if that meant staying awake.

17

By Friday night, I'd forgotten all about my parents' party to celebrate the Model One release. But the hubbub at home reminded me even before I walked through the door after school.

Three men and a woman, dressed in the kind of sleek black suits that could only designate security, stood on either side of the front door. They tipped their heads in recognition as I stepped through.

The foyer was clear of its usual decor and outfitted for the celebration. The glass entryway table had disappeared, showing off the wide-open space of our two-story foyer. The chandelier overhead must have been newly polished. Sunlight sought out the large crystals and cast multi-colored rays across the metallic accent wall. To one side, the coat closet stood open and empty, where hired staff would stand to check coats.

The rest of the first floor displayed more of the same.

Tall metal tables replaced the furniture usually in the sitting and family rooms. Guests would stand around them while they ate fancy hors d'oeuvres.

Our king-sized dining room had been repurposed into a small ballroom. A temporary dance floor lay across the hardwood to avoid scuffing my mother's floors. Smaller versions of the tall tables lined the walls.

They could just have easily rented a nearby venue for this purpose, but my mom prided herself on throwing lavish bashes—never mind the fact that her office and home staff together did all the work. She managed the tasks, and that counted for something in her book.

My bodyguard Owen had followed me into the house. Marcy caught up with us as we reached the stairs leading to my bedroom. "Will you join us for the party, Lena? Or should I bring your dinner upstairs?"

I gave her a quick hug, which basically meant I allowed her to hold me up for a few seconds. I hadn't slept well in days—by choice. Better safe than sorry. "Upstairs. Definitely. And would you mind bringing some coffee too?"

I had an appointment with Ron on Monday, so I only had to make it three more nights on the minutes of sleep I stole here and there. Without the coffee, I doubted I would still be awake by the time Marcy brought my food. It had been days since I'd had a good night's sleep.

Marcy gestured toward Owen. "Your mother says no bodyguards tonight. We'll have a big crowd here soon, and security people are all over the place." She turned and headed for the kitchen.

I used the handrail to support my weight as I dragged

my feet up the stairs. Owen followed close behind me, his arms raised as if he'd catch me if I couldn't make it. When we reached the top, he offered an awkward bow and retreated back down the stairs.

In the upstairs hallway, my dad's voice drifted toward me from his office. His door stood a couple inches ajar. Although I didn't understand the words at first, the tone was impossible to miss.

He'd used the same one when he found out I skipped a day of school last year, and that time I was caught shoplifting back in middle school. A soft-but-firm voice that let me know his disappointment ran deep, and I would regret it if there were a repeat event. I preferred it when he shouted, which unfortunately, he almost never did.

I hesitated at the door to my room, but curiosity won out against better judgment. I sneaked closer to his office door and stood just out of view of the interior, straining my ears to hear the discussion.

"I definitely should not be eavesdropping," I muttered to myself—but stayed put. "Or talking to myself." Clearly, stress was getting the better of me.

My father's voice floated into the hallway, barely loud enough for me to overhear. ". . . security that has failed to *secure* the company's premises. What do you expect me to tell the hundreds of elite customers who each paid tens of thousands for a Model One? We can't secure our own lobby from vandals, and they're supposed to trust our androids with all their vital details and tasks. If we have security concerns, our product is worthless. So what should I tell them?" He paused. My dad never asked rhetorical questions. He waited for an answer.

I jumped when another person spoke. I'd assumed he was on the phone, but it looked like the object of his ire sat right there in the room.

"We could tell them . . . our security team is doing everything in its power to ensure this will never happen again. We've doubled our men in the lobby and on the seventy-second floor." His pitch rose at the end as if the statement were actually a question.

"Oh, we've doubled our security," my father said, his tone mocking. "You would like me to call our best customers—the ones who purchased our most expensive product, at full price, without waiting for the discount that will accompany later sales. You want me to tell them our security was lacking to begin with, so that now it must be doubled. Is that right? Perhaps the security of their Model Ones will be lacking as well."

"No," the man said. His voice was little more than a whisper. It was the tone of prey—some poor beast searching for an escape route where none existed. Hoping that if he spoke quietly, perhaps my father would forget about him and find something else to do. No such luck.

Guilt did somersaults in my gut. My dad was chewing out his employee because of what *I* did.

My fingertips itched to push open the door and confess to the vandalism. That man could lose his job, and the worst I would get was being grounded forever. My parents wouldn't let me go to jail.

I reached for the door, but then froze.

I imagined the lecture my dad would give me, and it would be even worse than this one. I wasn't some random guy he'd hired to provide security. I was his flesh and blood. I should have been better. I was worse than a disappointment. I had shamed him.

"You're dismissed for now," my father said.

Before I could make up my mind, a large bald man flew through the doorway. He practically ran down the hall and didn't even notice me pressed against the wall on the other side of the door. My father followed a moment later at a steadier pace, offering me a stiff smile as he passed.

The room now stood wide open. It beckoned to me. I hadn't expected an opportunity like this, but now that I had one, I had to take it.

This was how I could figure out where Kevin lived, and if he was close enough for me to get from his place to mine in half an hour. There was no way I could have made it farther than three miles—probably two and half—without running full out. And if I'd run, I would have been exhausted when I woke at four-thirty.

If Paul Rodriguez valued his privacy as much as other CyberCorp employees did, his address wouldn't be listed publicly. But my father would have it.

To convince myself of my innocence, I needed to know.

I slipped inside the office and headed straight for the floor-to-ceiling window occupying the wall on my right. Right now, it displayed a wide green lawn, bounded on the far side with a row of privacy trees. I placed my right palm against the glass, and the surface went opaque black.

Where I made contact, a small white square appeared with the words "Welcome, Lena Hayes."

I hoped my dad didn't check access records on this vidscreen.

A two-foot-wide rectangle in front of me filled with icons representing files and folders. I opened a file labeled *Contacts* and scanned the contents until I identified a row for Paul Rodriguez.

I held my breath and touched the address to initiate the screen's mapping application.

The map filled the wall, so I had to step back several paces to take it all in. The red flag that marked 432 Nova Road stood near the green flag for my house, but I couldn't tell how near. I pressed the flag, and the screen outlined a route from my house to his.

Just under two miles.

All the air rushed from the room, suffocating me. My mouth went hot. My stomach flipped and threatened to expel everything inside it. I swallowed hard to stop it.

Kevin lived well within the range that would have allowed me to make it back home after murdering him.

I couldn't eliminate myself as a suspect, not by a long shot.

18

BY NINE THAT NIGHT, THE SOLID WOOD OF MY BEDROOM door could only muffle the sounds of music and occasional uproarious laughter of the party downstairs. I played my own music loudly through the speakers built into my walls, and that helped a little.

But it couldn't drown out the possibilities.

At this point, all I had was a suspicion. I had motive and opportunity, but that didn't make me guilty.

I couldn't have done this. Right?

I would have known if I'd killed someone. That was the sort of thing that changed a person, tainted the soul. My soul wasn't tainted. Right?

I popped another gummy candy, cranked up my music another notch, and moved faster to the beat.

"Lena." My mother skipped the part where she was supposed to knock and just barged in.

"What's up?" I shouted, without bothering to turn down my music.

She said nothing until I touched the controls on my hand-screen to lower the volume.

"Your father and I think you should come downstairs and mingle with your guests. It's rude for you to stay up here."

"They're not my guests."

Her lips pursed. "They're our family's guests, and whether you like it or not, you are part of this family."

I didn't like it one little bit. "Fine." I strode toward the door. I knew what I looked like right now, with my hair twisted back into a frizzy ponytail. I had traded the fitted jeans and blouse I wore earlier for sweatpants and a T-shirt almost as soon as I walked in the door this afternoon.

She held up a hand to stop me. "Change first. Why don't you wear that black dress with the sweetheart neck-line? I've always loved that one."

"You've never said a word about that dress. Besides, it has short sleeves." I stared down at my left arm. "You just want me to show this off."

"Lena, I need you with us on this. Three of our employees have quit, and six more refuse to work on the Model Ones. They're scared. They need to be reminded of how important our technology is, how much it helps people. It would do wonders for morale if they could see you looking confident and unafraid."

"And showing off the arm."

"Yes, that too. Could you try not to be so difficult?"

"I didn't realize not wanting to be your poster girl made me difficult."

She opened her lips just enough to let out a stream of air. "I'll make you a deal. You put on a nice dress and come downstairs, and I'll let you skip the next party we have."

"Why don't you let me skip this one, and I'll attend the next one?" By then, I would have skin covering my monstrosity of a limb.

She offered stony silence in response. My mother was in a bind here. She needed me to come downstairs, or else she'd be embarrassed her daughter had played hooky *and* held her new cybernetic arm hostage at the same time.

Heaven forbid my mother allow herself to look bad for any reason. Heaven forbid she put her kid's needs ahead of her company.

"I want a new car," I said.

"Excuse me?"

"A new car. I've been riding with Lionel since I got back home, and I know he's reporting my every move to you. I need space. I want to be able to drive myself."

"I'll think about it."

"Something without auto-drive." I pointed at my arm. "That's what got us into this mess in the first place." We both knew that was an exaggeration, bordering on an outright lie. We'd gotten into this mess because of *my reaction* to the auto-drive. I'd been fumbling with the car's controls instead of watching the road.

But this wasn't all on me. If my mother wasn't so controlling, or if the damn auto-drive didn't exist, none of this would have happened. She deserved a piece of the blame too.

"Fine," she said, her teeth gritted. She straightened her posture and gave me a wide, sweet smile. "I'll see you downstairs in ten minutes."

Had I been in a better mood, I might have gotten dressed right away as instructed. Instead, I made a pit stop at Allie's room. The door stood closed, which meant she was asleep. I swung it open and padded across the carpet to her toddler bed.

Marcy had taken Allie's braids out, and her hair formed a dark halo beneath her head. Her arms lay stretched away from her, one angled up, the other one down. Her mouth yawned open, and loud snores emanated from her tiny nose. I swallowed a laugh.

Allie always swore up and down that she didn't snore, but the noises this little person emitted in her sleep impressed me. Kind of like an elephant had climbed into her nose and was now trumpeting its arrival. My parents refused to admit it, but I suspected they wouldn't let her sleep in the bed with them because she kept them awake all night.

I sat in the window seat and watched her. So carefree and happy. Had I ever been like that? I couldn't imagine getting back to that place. Not now. Everything had changed now.

I reached down and touched Allie's hair, soft beneath my fingertips.

Her eyes opened, the snoring ceased, and she offered

me a weak smile before falling back to sleep. The snores started anew, and louder this time.

I tiptoed from the room and closed the door behind me.

Feeling a little better—almost like I could face a room full of CyberCorp flunkies—I got dressed and fixed my hair. Five minutes after the deadline my mom gave me, I descended the stairs in a long-sleeved blue dress and matching satin gloves.

As if on command, my mother met me at the bottom of the stairs. Her eyes narrowed for only an instant when she spotted my arm, completely covered by the dress and gloves. But she painted a smile on her face and led me around to meet her *friends*—which, apparently, was what we were calling her employees.

They greeted me with fake grins and false laughter while I told them about my college plans—really, my *parents'* college plans for me. All the while, their gazes could have bored a hole in my left glove.

Something solid brushed against my back, and I turned, prepared to glare at the perpetrator. A silver Model One stood there, its head pointed to the side just far enough on its neck to look wrong.

I let out a sharp squeal.

The thing stood a few inches taller than me, its hand holding a tray of mini quiches. The android's head rotated toward me, back to a human angle, and it shifted the tray in my direction, offering me a quiche. Its red eyes glowed down at me, eerily human despite their unnatural color.

What was it thinking? Did it even think?

"Lena, watch where you're going." My mother scolded me as my foot smashed down on hers. She caught my arm and righted me.

I circled to her other side to escape the android. "You didn't tell me there'd be a Model One here."

"The party is *for* them. Why wouldn't they be here?"

"They?"

She gestured toward the kitchen door, where two more androids entered the room. Despite their metal bodies, they glided across the floor as if weightless.

No one else at the party looked shocked to see them—as if machines each worth tens of thousands of bucks always spent their Fridays serving bite-sized eggy pies.

My hands fisted at my sides. I could do this. It wasn't like they were going to destroy humanity in one night. I could get through this party on my best behavior.

As my mother wove us through the crowd to a new mingling target, she whispered to me, "The man I'll introduce to you next is a promising new addition to the company."

I hated when she called CyberCorp *the company*—as if no other companies existed.

"He graduated from MIT at sixteen, got his PhD two years later, then signed on with a small start-up making telecommunications equipment. At his last employment, he developed some of the hardware in your hand-screen and in that micro I bought you for your birthday."

She aimed me toward a man who looked barely older than me. With a shudder, I sidestepped another Model One along the way to him.

Before we reached our target, my mother's gaze flitted over to the swinging door separating the room from the kitchen. I followed her line of sight to find one of the catering staff waving her over, a panicked expression on his face.

"Excuse me for a moment." She spun on her heel and left me in the midst of her CyberCorp flunkies and androids. I would rather have been anywhere else in the world.

Dr. Fisher slid into my path. More accurately, she wobbled into it on high heels that put her well over six feet. From her bloodshot eyes and the unraveling knot of blond hair, it looked like she'd had too much to drink. Way too much.

"Lena!" It was the first genuine smile I'd ever seen from her. "How are you feeling?" She glanced down at my left arm.

"I'm fine, thanks. Fully operational." I shifted my weight from one foot to the other, then back again, while I searched for a mode of escape.

Although I'd spent weeks in Dr. Fisher's care, she'd left most of the talking to her assistants, Ron and Simon. When she was in the room, I always felt like I was wasting her time. But not tonight. Now, she seemed *too* excited to see me.

It worried me.

"You know, your mother is the one who pulled me off the Model Ones to work on your arm. I've been wanting to tell her something." She slung one arm over my shoulder and leaned into it.

I cringed under her considerable weight and ducked away before she took me down to the floor with her.

Dr. Fisher wobbled again but stayed upright.

She turned toward the kitchen, where my mother had disappeared a moment ago. She shouted in that direction. "I have a lot of resentment about being pulled off my life's work to focus on a child's arm!" Dr. Fisher turned back to me. "My therapist helped me see that. *Resentment*." This time, when she said the word, spittle sprayed from her mouth and hit me in the forehead.

If I couldn't escape this conversation, perhaps I could use it to my advantage. Thanks to Kevin's murder—on top of Harmony's—I felt more determined than ever to find a killer who wasn't me. Since it looked like Dr. Fisher was a chatty drunk, now was a good time to ask questions.

"Who do you think killed Harmony Miller and Kevin Rodriguez?" I asked her.

She made a noise that sounded like *pfft*. "When it was just the Miller girl, it could have been anyone." She lowered her voice to a whisper that wasn't nearly as quiet as it should have been. "He's an asshole. It's really too bad that killer went after his daughter—when he was right down the hall." She let out a loud guffaw.

I stepped back.

Dr. Fisher grabbed the collar of my dress and pulled me back into her confidence. The stink of her alcohol-soaked breath wafted over me. "My son Mark worked for him. He applied just like anyone else—no nepotism. On his second day, right before Christmas, that jackass claimed Mark stole equipment from the lab. Fired him, ruined the boy's life. He hasn't been able to get a job since." Bitterness and anger coated every word.

So one of the men fired on Christmas Eve had been her son. Although I'd started questioning her to add others to my list of suspects, now I had no choice but to add Fisher herself to the list. "What about Paul Rodriguez. Do you hate him too?"

"Everyone likes Paul. Always smiling, always positive." The bitterness had not left her voice. "The man's . . ." She wobbled on her feet.

I held out an arm to catch her, but she righted herself and continued where she left off.

"So cheery it makes you want to stick a fork in your eye —or in *his* eye." She stabbed a finger at my chest, and for a second, I thought she would accuse me of the murders. "Be careful. Don't end up dead. Then all my work on your arm would be even more of a waste." She guffawed again, this time snorting along with it.

Of course, she hadn't been about to accuse me. My friends and I were the only ones who knew about the sleepwalking and how it lined up with the murders. I let out a relieved sigh.

My mother returned in enough time to hear Fisher's last few words. "Athena," she hissed. "Control yourself."

"I'm just checking on your precious progeny. Wouldn't want her to have an ouchie that wasn't cared for by half your staff. Would we?" Fisher reached out for me, but I dodged her hand. She stumbled, flailed, and this time managed to clasp onto my left shoulder.

I shrieked as her fingers dug into the flesh just above

my new arm. The constant dull throb in my shoulder flamed into a stabbing pain, and I blinked back tears.

My mother's eyes went wide. For an instant, I thought she would lunge at Dr. Fisher, but Ron arrived in time to prevent that. He gripped the doctor's forearm until she loosened her fingertips. My body sagged with relief as the pressure eased, but my shoulder continued to throb.

Ron nodded at my mother and me, his expression apologetic. "Dr. Fisher, let me see you out."

She yanked her arm loose. "Don't act like you're not upset about having to work on this child. You're just as excited as I am about the Model Ones. But *management*"—she sank as much derision into that word as a drunk person could muster—"would rather we work on an arm that will never be a mainstream CyberCorp product."

"Please." For a second time, he attempted to steer her to the front door.

"You're as bright as any engineer we've got, and we both know it. Don't act like you're okay with having to coddle Lena over the phone on a daily basis."

My mother fixed her gaze on Ron. "Are you not happy with your job? Because we can rectify that."

"No." He raised both arms in surrender. "I love my work, and I love working with Lena."

She raised a hand in a beckoning motion, and out of nowhere, a huge man in a black suit showed up beside us. "Please escort Dr. Fisher and her intern outside and put them in a taxi."

The man shifted to put himself between us and Fisher and gestured toward the door. Ron's shoulders slumped, but he trudged toward the exit and guided Fisher along the way.

As soon as the two of them stepped away, one of the engineers pulled my mother into a deep conversation about the ethics of artificial intelligence. I was relieved to no longer be the center of attention.

The throbbing in my shoulder inched its way up to the back of my head, and each time I blinked, the world spun for an instant.

"Marissa." My tongue felt too thick, and I barely managed to get the word out.

She waved a dismissive hand toward me.

Anger boiled in my stomach, but the pain eclipsed it an instant later. I grabbed a table as I stumbled. The wood crunched under my grip. The two people whose drinks had been on the table shouted as liquid sloshed on me and splattered them.

"Lena?" My mother's voice. Her face appeared between the spots that bounced around my vision.

She wrapped an arm around my shoulders and led me into the kitchen. A small group of caterers, all wearing black button-downs and matching skirts or pants, occupied the room. They turned toward us as we stepped into the kitchen, faces curious.

My mother pushed a bar stool away from the counter and motioned toward it. "Sit."

"I need my medicine," I murmured.

"Troy." My mother snapped her fingers, and a tall man in his mid-thirties appeared. "Run up to Lena's room—left at the top of the stairs, first door on the right—and grab the pills in her medicine cabinet." When he stared at me, brows furrowed, she added, "Now."

Troy jumped into action, racing from the room. A minute later, he returned, and my mother shoved two pills and a glass of water at me. I swallowed the pills dry and then gulped down the water.

My headache began to subside right away, and I noticed the room was now empty except for my mother, Troy, and me. All the caterers had gone. I wondered whether she had cleared it to give me space—or because she didn't want me embarrassing her.

I sat straighter in my chair. "I'm fine. Can I have a moment alone please? To recover."

She gestured to the empty room.

"I mean *alone*. Please."

With an exaggerated sigh, she led Troy from the kitchen.

Only seconds later, Hunter popped his head through the other door, the one leading to outside. "You okay?"

"Hey. What are you doing here?" Despite the ache in my head, I sat up straighter and grinned.

He stepped inside, bringing with him a burst of refreshingly cool air from outside before he closed the door behind him. "My mom's your caterer."

"Not my caterer," I corrected. "My parents'."

"Whatever. Are you okay? You looked a little green a moment ago."

"Oh, you caught that? No big deal. I just needed to take my pain meds."

"And before that?" he asked, grinning at a private joke.

I gave him a questioning shrug.

He pointed toward the family room, where I'd been before the headache attacked. "You looked like you were two seconds away from grabbing one of those little hors d'oeuvre forks and sticking it in your eye."

I laughed. "That would have been more enjoyable." I couldn't remember the last time I'd let out such a genuine laugh, not just to fit in or to make the people around me feel comfortable. I liked the feeling.

His fingertips brushed my right arm. Even through the fabric of my dress, the warmth of his skin sent tingles through my body. He stood near me, his face less than a foot from mine. The fresh mint that always danced on his breath floated over me. His lips were so close. The upper one had barely a hint of a dip in the top of it. I bet they'd be soft against mine.

My gaze rose back up to his eyes, which looked amused. I angled my face away, so he wouldn't see me blush.

"Like what you see?" he asked.

"I don't know what you're talking about."

His hand moved from my arm around to my lower back and pulled. I leaned closer, without even meaning to. He smiled.

I leapt up from the chair and away from him. "No." Not with Jackson lying unconscious in the hospital bed, and not when I'd put him there.

Just like that, he slid away from me. The space around me felt cold. We stood in silence for a few seconds, staring at each other, my arms wrapped tightly around myself. Hunter reached out and unwrapped one of my arms, then grabbed my hand and pulled me toward the side exit.

We didn't need to speak, so I followed him without words.

As if they had a mind of their own, my fingers intertwined with his. His rough hands were firmer than I would have expected. Confident and comfortable. I breathed into the chill evening air as we stepped out onto a walkway. It led to the front of the house in one direction and to the back in the other. From the front, soft chatter drifted toward us. Still holding my hand, Hunter pulled me around to the back.

A sound caught my attention in the thick trees separating our yard from the next. A low rustling of leaves. A movement. There shouldn't have been any guests on this side of the house, especially not hiding in the greenery.

A man burst from the trees and barreled toward us.

19

Massive and red-faced, the man ran at us. In my shock, my legs locked.

Hunter jumped into his path, but he didn't slow. His shoulder slammed into Hunter's chest, and Hunter went down. His head thumped against the ground.

I screamed—until the man slammed into me next. Air exploded from my lungs, and my scream died in my throat.

Déjà vu washed over me, as the huge guy with the stringy hair and unshaven face—the same one from back at CyberCorp—pressed me into the ground. I'd been wrong to assume he wasn't the killer, and now he'd come to murder me.

"Death to the spawn of CyberCorp. The ungodly cannot live!"

He shook my shoulders so hard that I felt like my brain bounced against my skull. My vision blurred, and panic rose in my chest.

With both arms, I shoved his chest. He flew off me and landed hard on his back. The yelling stopped abruptly.

I glanced over at Hunter. He lay still, and my world slowed for instant. But he groaned and rolled over. He'd be fine—he had to be fine. I couldn't be responsible for putting another boy in the hospital.

My attacker jumped to his feet, fast for a man his size. With his height and bulk, he could have been one of my parents' security guys.

"Somebody, help!" I shouted, but the loud music and laughter inside drowned out my words.

He didn't know how strong my arm was. As much as I hated to rely on it, I had no choice here. I needed to take him off guard, unless I wanted to end up dead or back in the hospital.

I lunged forward and pulled my arm back, aiming for his face. He recovered too quickly, and his large beefy hand collided with my temple.

My head burst into pure pain, and I fell to the ground screaming. Bent over, I clawed at my head. Part of me insisted I needed to be alert. I needed to pay attention to the man trying to kill me, but a louder part cared only that my head was about to explode.

Spots filled my vision. The man stood above me, a hulking mass who blocked out the lights of the house. He reached a hand toward me, and I tried to shrink deeper into the ground and away from him.

But he kept coming. I had to *do* something.

When the man's face came within reach, I swung my left hand forward and struck him across the cheek. He shrieked and stumbled backward. I jumped up and landed on my feet, head still swimming.

Dr. Fisher had told me the arm would read me. It would know what I wanted, so I relaxed and let the programming take over.

I lunged forward, and my metal fist connected with the man's jaw. He howled in pain. I hit him again, this time in his cheekbone. The skin broke and blood spread outward. He crumpled to the grass and tried to crawl away. Without thinking, I struck again.

He threw his hands up to block his face. "No, no, no. Stop." His voice came out a pleading whimper.

I got in one more punch, before I was lifted away from him. My left arm continued to swing once, twice more.

"Lena, stop!" It was Hunter's voice. His arms wrapped around my waist. "It's fine. You got him. You won."

20

THE POLICE AND AN AMBULANCE ARRIVED TEN MINUTES later, and my parents' personal doctor arrived a few minutes after that.

The doctor stitched up a cut in my forehead, just above my temple, where the big man had hit me before I went on the offensive. Afterward, he looked me over briefly, but mostly poked and prodded my arm with fascination.

While the doctor worked, I craned my neck to get a look at the what the medics were doing with Hunter. They bandaged his head and made him lie down. No serious injuries—luckily. My conscience couldn't handle putting another friend in the hospital.

The man who'd attacked us was another story. Two cops accompanied him in the ambulance.

He wasn't in good enough shape to go straight to the police station.

He'd attacked me, not the other way around, but I

watched the ambulance until it rounded the corner and passed out of sight. I'd used my new arm to almost beat a man to death, and I couldn't feel good about that.

But without the arm, maybe I'd be dead right now.

Two detectives stayed behind to get a full account of what happened. A tall, brown-skinned man introduced himself as Detective Brooks, while the shorter man called himself Detective Arnold. My father showed the last of the guests out, while the detectives, my mother, and I remained in the backyard.

"Before we start," my mother said, "I'd like your assurance that the details of events here will not be shared with anyone outside your department. And within your department, only with the people who need to know.

Both detectives nodded, their faces solemn.

"Of course, Mrs. Hayes," Detective Brooks said. "We understand how important discretion is to your family."

She nodded at me to begin my story.

"He hid in those trees." I pointed to the thick greenery at the side of the yard. "He threw Hunter to the ground and then came after me. He was shaking me, shouting about how the spawn of CyberCorp had to die. I pushed him off." I mimed a shoving motion.

"You just pushed him? That's all?"

I nodded and kept going. "He landed on his back. When he got up again, I lunged at him and hit him a few times. Hunter pulled me off him."

"What's Hunter's last name?" Detective Arnold asked.

"I'm not sure. I haven't known him long."

"Shepard," Mom offered. When I cast her a questioning look, she added, "I'm familiar with all of Cyber-Corp's medical cases."

"We'll get his account when we're done with you."

She waved a dismissive hand. "If you must."

"Do you know the man who attacked you? Was he familiar at all?" Arnold asked.

I nodded.

His brows rose in surprise. "Tell me about that."

"Twice before. He's one of the anti-tech protesters at CyberCorp headquarters. The first time I saw him, he was screaming about how technology is evil. He tackled me—almost like tonight actually. But it didn't seem like he was trying to hurt me that time, just trying to make a point."

My mother's lips pursed. "You didn't tell me it was the same man."

I shrugged.

"This man knows where we live, and he's attacked you twice."

"I guess I should also mention he was basically quoting that threatening letter CyberCorp got."

My mother stiffened.

"Letter?" Detective Brooks asked.

"It *was* confidential." She shot me a pointed glance. She pulled her hand-screen from her clutch, opened a digital version of the letter, and passed it to Detective Brooks.

Detective Arnold read it over his shoulder. "Why aren't the police aware of this?"

"My security team is better trained than your officers, and they're also knowledgeable about technology and how we do things. Plus, they're experienced enough with the types of threats we get to know when and when not to react. The last thing we needed is your people bumbling about our property getting in the way. We had it handled."

The detectives exchanged glances with each other in expressions I couldn't read.

My mother paused, then added, "I did, however, inform your chief of police, in light of Harmony Miller's death. He promised to keep it need-to-know—and apparently you didn't need to."

Detective Arnold opened his mouth to respond, but my mom cut him off.

"Would you mind wrapping up this interview? My own security team is going to handle the investigation anyway."

Arnold remained obediently silent, and my top lip curled. Everyone let her get away with saying whatever she wanted to whomever she wanted. I wished the detective would tell her to kiss his ass, but of course, he wouldn't. He'd stand there, bend over, and take it.

"One more thing before we take off?" Detective Brooks said.

My mother gestured for him to continue.

He turned back to me. "There are problems with your story. Even if we believe you managed to shove the man off you, it's hard to swallow that you got in as many as *a few* punches without him hitting you at all. And it's even harder to believe that you did all that damage with only three punches. How much do you weigh?"

"I'm not sure."

"I'd guess that man weighs at least twice what you do. How many times did you hit him?"

I played back the scene in my head. My fist colliding with his face again and again. "Five times," I said after a moment. "Approximately."

Had I overreacted? It was one thing to subdue someone, but I'd pummeled him. I'd made a conscious choice to use the arm, and I'd lost control. I stared down at my hands now, shame washing over me.

Blood covered the knuckles of my left glove. I started to pull it off, but I wasn't sure the metal beneath it would calm my nerves at all.

"Did he hit you at all during that time?"

"Once. I think . . . I think the first punch hurt him a lot, and he wasn't able to react after that."

Detective Brooks raised a skeptical brow.

I glanced at my mom, and she nodded. So I added, "I was in a car accident about a month and a half ago. My left arm didn't survive the crash. CyberCorp replaced it with a cybernetic limb."

"Cybernetic? What does that mean?"

"You wouldn't understand," my mother said, a look of distaste on her face—as if everyone should understand high-tech robotics. "Suffice it to say it's metal. I'll have to talk to her doctors about why it's as strong as it is. It's supposed to imitate a human arm."

"We're going to have to see it to verify your story." He glanced at my mom, his expression apologetic.

When I pulled off the glove, everyone reacted. My mother beamed with pride. Arnold recoiled. Brooks reached out his hand to touch it and then pulled back. That was the thing about technology. It prompted a wide range of reactions, but almost never indifference.

The silence spanned for too long as the two detectives stared. Eventually, my mother cleared her throat. Both men surfaced from the trance and turned toward her.

"I think that will be all," Brooks said.

I grabbed his wrist before he could walk away. "Is that man going to be okay?"

His brow furrowed. "The man who attacked you?"

"He's going to live, right?"

"He'll be fine. He has a concussion and needs to be under observation overnight. Other than that, it's just cuts, bruises, and a broken nose. Those will heal with time."

Some of my stress dissipated. "Am I in trouble?"

"Of course you're not," my mother answered. She rubbed my back and fixed the officer with a stare.

I couldn't help feeling grateful. Despite my mother's overbearing, technology-obsessed, insensitive attitude, she'd defend me just as hard as she annoyed me.

"No, what you did was self-defense," Brooks said. "You've done a great service to this community by helping us capture a murderer."

I wasn't so sure.

After the party cleared and I changed into pajamas, I lay on my bed in my room, staring at the ceiling.

I hadn't gotten a good night's sleep in days. After tonight's excitement, I felt like a shell of myself. Like I was running on automatic and seconds from sputtering to a stop. Despite the multiple cups of coffee I'd drunk today, I could no longer fight the urge to sleep. It was happening, whether I liked it or not.

I needed to do everything I could to avoid another sleepwalking incident. It was looking less and less like I was a killer, but I had no desire to wake on the side of the road regardless.

I squatted to better leverage my weight and shoved one of my two tall dressers until it blocked the door. I pushed the other one in front of the window. It turned out to be easier than I expected, thanks to my arm's strength. I might have been grateful for the thing, if it weren't the cause of all my troubles.

With the furniture in place, I almost climbed under the bedcovers. But that was too easy. If I could move those dressers without breaking a sweat, it would be just as easy for my sleeping self to move them out of my way should sleeping-me feel the need to take a late-night walk.

My desk sat on the other side of my spacious room. With my left arm, I gripped a handhold on its underside and yanked, trying to pull it away from the far wall. With a snap, one of the desk's legs cracked, and one corner of the desk crashed to the floor. My hand-screen and textbooks slid off the surface.

I muttered a curse under my breath and pushed the desk the rest of the way across the room, until it pressed against the dresser in front of the door. Fortunately, I'd managed to keep the two dressers intact.

The desk, on the other hand, would not recover. The two legs on one side had cracks in them, while the two others had split, and the desk surface now slanted deeply to one side. Most likely, it would collapse altogether at some point. If not during the night, then when I moved it in the morning.

Oh well. Maybe the broken desk would keep me inside my room tonight. I toyed with the idea of moving my bed too, but maybe I was being too paranoid.

The relocated furniture did little to ease my mind as I lay in bed. For two hours, I stared at the smooth ivory of my ceiling. One corner held a hairline crack that my mother would freak over if she noticed.

At two o'clock, I was still exhausted and still awake. My mind kept running over last night, and how the man had stood over me but hadn't gone for the kill.

What had he been waiting for?

I swiped my hand-screen off the nightstand and messaged Hunter. *"You asleep?"*

"Nope. Are you?"

"Yes," I wrote back, grinning to myself. *"I'm sleep-texting now too."*

"It wouldn't surprise me." After a pause, another message followed that one. *"You okay?"*

"You mean after being attacked by an anti-tech serial killer and beating him into a bloody pulp with my artificially intelligent arm? I'm totally cool. How are you?"

"Want me to swing by?"

My fingers hovered over the display, tingling with anticipation. I wanted to say yes, but I hated myself for it. *"No, I'm going to try to sleep."*

The response took longer than expected, and for a

moment, I thought the conversation was over. *"Let me rephrase. I'm going to come by. Leave your window open for me."*

I should have told him no, told him I was fine, but I couldn't. *"Sure."* Excitement squirmed inside my chest, but I pushed it back down and locked it in a little box. This was no big deal, just two friends making each other feel better after a traumatic night.

Fifteen minutes later, my hand-screen buzzed with a message from Hunter announcing he was outside.

After suspending our home security alarms, I shoved the dresser away from the window and stuck my head into the chill night air. Because the killer had—supposedly—been captured, security wasn't on high alert tonight. In the dim glow of the streetlamps, Hunter sauntered across the lawn as if he had all the time in the world.

With the remains of his limp, he somehow made that uneven stride look sexy. He handled the tree outside my window so deftly that I was impressed he'd only recently become capable of climbing them, thanks to the new knee.

A moment later, he stood in my room, grinning like a Cheshire cat up to no good. He had changed out of his black catering clothing. Now, he wore a pair of dark jeans. A gray T-shirt clung to his chest, covered only partially by a bomber jacket. He shrugged off the jacket and slumped down into the armchair across from my bed.

I felt a twinge of disappointment that he didn't try to sit on the bed next to me. I sucked it up and sat cross-legged, facing him.

He nodded toward the furniture against the door and

quirked an eyebrow at me. "Still concerned about the sleepwalking?"

"Nah. I just did some redecorating. That desk had too many legs."

He chuckled, but then his face went serious. "Get some sleep. I'll stay here and wake you if you try to escape."

"Won't your mom worry if you don't come home?"

"She feels bad that I struggled with my knee for so long. She pretty much lets me do whatever I want now. I'll just let her know I'm at a friend's." He touched his ear and instructed his comm, "Send a message to Mom: I'm staying at a friend's tonight. See you tomorrow."

If I sent a message like that to my mother, she would flip out. All of CyberCorp's security would comb the city for me. It would be a disaster of epic proportions—most likely involving screaming, cursing, and the National Guard.

"So you're all mine until tomorrow?" I asked.

"Or longer." He stared me in the eye when he answered.

Heat climbed over my cheeks and burrowed deep.

"You look exhausted," he said.

"You really know how to flatter a girl."

He chuckled. "It's okay to go to sleep. I promise I'll watch you."

"You don't need to sleep too?"

After a moment of thought, he pulled the chair over to the window and sat down again. "If you try to leave by the door, I'll hear you move that dresser. If you try to leave by the window, you'll have to climb over me. Either way, you'll wake me, and I'll stop you from leaving this room. So we can both sleep. Okay?"

I nodded and grabbed my hand-screen from the night-stand to reenable my home's alarms. Then I climbed under the covers and snuggled into the soft pillows. It had been four days since I got into bed feeling relaxed enough to sleep. Tonight, I was safe.

Tonight, Hunter would watch over me. I wouldn't kill anyone, and no one would kill me.

I emerged from the covers to tell him goodnight and caught him grinning at me. "What?"

"It's kind of like we're sleeping together."

"Shut up and go to sleep." I tried not to smile but failed colossally.

"Okay, okay. And don't worry. Nothing bad's going to happen."

21

In the morning, I woke with a pit of dread growing in my stomach, but it dissipated with my first glance around the room.

The dresser and broken desk still sat against the door. Hunter sat in the chair under the window, his body sprawled out into almost a lying position, his mouth hanging open.

I grabbed a throw pillow from the floor and lobbed it at him. It hit him square in the face. True to his word about being able to watch over me even while sleeping, Hunter leapt to his feet, arms up in a ready stance. I cracked up laughing.

The tension fell from his face when he spotted the pillow on the floor beside him. "This is what I get for being your knight in shining armor." He slumped back into the chair.

"I don't need a knight in shining armor." I pointed at my left arm. "I literally *am* in shining armor. But I did need someone to have my back last night, and you did that. Even knights need backup every once in a while."

He held up his hands in surrender. "My mistake."

A fist pounded on the door to my room. "I've told you a hundred times not to lock your door, Lena," my mother called. "Your father and I have to head to the office. How are you feeling after last night?"

"Crap," I muttered. It was a good thing I'd locked it. Otherwise, she would have asked why I had a dresser and a desk in front of my door, and that would have been harder to explain. I tumbled out of bed and ran into the bathroom.

"What are you doing?" Hunter called after me in a loud whisper.

I turned the shower on full blast. The sound of water battering tile filled the room. A few seconds later, my mother's footsteps receded down the hall.

"She's not going to expect me to unlock the door if she thinks I'm in the shower," I said. "Like I said, I'm my own knight in shining armor."

He gave an appreciative nod, and then pointed toward my bedroom door. "I should head out before she gets back. You want some help moving that furniture?"

"Sure."

Hunter helped me move the dresser and desk—or what was left of it—back into their regular places. When we finished, he headed toward my window.

I stopped him by wrapping my arms around his neck and pulling him into a hug. "Thank you for hanging out with me overnight."

"Anytime." His voice came out low. It vibrated through his chest and into mine.

His arms clasped around my waist, and I leaned into his chest, inhaling the scent of him. Now familiar, the fresh soapy-minty smell that lived on his skin filled up my nose and my head. Reluctantly, I pulled back—just as his face came forward to where mine just was.

His face flushed deep red, and he released my waist so abruptly that my knees collapsed under me.

"Oh, I'm sorry." Hunter gripped me by the forearm and pulled upward while I pushed off with one leg, sending me reeling into his chest. "Oh, God." He stumbled away from me, one hand covering his eyes. As if not looking at the awkwardness of this moment could make it go away.

Despite trying my best to hold it in, laughter burst from my chest like soda no longer under pressure. It felt so good that I let it roll through until my whole body shook.

Hunter stared at me, a scowl curling his lips downward.

"I'm so sorry." But as soon as I spoke, another wave of laughter came. When he didn't laugh, I inhaled a long breath and held it until I composed myself. "Were you trying to kiss me?"

"Um . . ."

"It's okay if you were."

He grabbed the back of his neck and pulled his lips tightly together. "It's okay. We don't have—"

"Shut up." I pressed my lips against his.

His lips were warm and soft. He didn't press the moment, just held me while I enjoyed the feeling of closeness. When I opened my lips, he did too. And he tasted like he smelled—sweet and perfect, like peppermint hot chocolate at just the right temperature.

"You should go," I whispered. My lips brushed against his with each word, and my spine tingled with heat that threatened to light my whole body on fire.

"I'll see you later," he whispered against my lips.

I nodded. When I realized I still clutched his shirt, I released my grip, each finger uncurling one at a time, extending this moment for as long as possible.

Hunter pulled away and climbed out the window. He waved from the branches of the tree outside before climbing down and out of view.

My heart still fluttered like crazy. My thoughts swam with both delight and guilt. Pleasure and heartache. I shook my head hard, then took advantage of the already running shower.

Forty minutes later, I joined Marcy and Allie in the kitchen. Marcy was putting clean dishes away, while Allie worked on a bowl of cereal at the table. I pulled up a chair next to Allie and set my hand-screen on the table in front of me.

My parents had already left for work, despite the fact that it was Saturday. Otherwise, they would have demanded Marcy turn the vid-screen off. My mother had this thing against watching it while eating. She found it undignified.

On the screen, the same emotionless blonde news-woman who had reported Harmony's death sat behind her desk at the television station. Beside her face, a still image showed the man who'd attacked me last night entering the police station in handcuffs. His mouth, half open, was twisted in the midst of shouting something.

One of the few bonuses of being part of CyberCorp's first family was that the press didn't have the nerve to flood the front of our home like they'd done to the Millers. The entire town did its best to stay on the good side of Mr. and Mrs. CyberCorp.

Unfortunately, they still had to report the news, and in this case, they couldn't keep my name out of it.

"A suspect was apprehended last night while trying to kill a third victim, Lena Hayes, daughter of CyberCorp founders Thomas and Marissa Hayes . . ."

Allie let out a choked gasp and stared at me open-mouthed.

"I'm fine."

Her gaze scanned me from my hair down to my feet. She nodded when she'd satisfied herself that I was still in one piece, and then went back to her bowl of cereal with marshmallows.

She'd eaten most of the marshmallows already. Now, she squinted in concentration as she fished through her bowl with the spoon, trying to capture the few that remained. She scooped two out with a triumphant flourish and sucked them off the spoon.

"Is it good?" I asked her, laughing.

She fished out another marshmallow and thrust the spoon at me. "Last one. Want it?"

"No, but thank you. You eat it, little one."

She scrunched up her nose at the nickname, then slurped down the last marshmallow. "Finished!" she announced to Marcy.

Marcy craned her neck to get a view of the bowl. "Eat the rest of it, Allie."

"I'm full."

Marcy gave her a stern glare.

"I'm gonna eat it," Allie muttered.

My hand-screen buzzed, vibrating the kitchen table. I swiped it up and checked the display—a call from Claire. The last time I talked to her was that horrible day in the cafeteria—and then Harmony died.

My chest constricted. I squeezed my eyes shut to block out the memory of me twisting her arm, of her hating me only hours before she died.

I sent the call to voicemail and returned my attention to the vid-screen.

The newswoman was still talking about last night. "The suspect has been revealed as Adam Pollock."

My mouth fell open.

"The Pollocks are an affluent family of philanthropists known for their anti-robotic stance. In recent years, they've provided a large amount of funds to assist Cyber-Corp competitors in non-robotic research and development, in hopes of displacing CyberCorp as the top tech company in the industry. In the past, however, there's been no evidence of ill will between the Pollocks and the Hayeses."

I had heard the name Adam Pollock before, but I wouldn't have imagined he was the outspoken protester I kept encountering—and the man who'd attacked me last night.

If I squinted at the image of Adam and imagined him with darker hair and without the scruffy facial hair, his features almost matched those of his brother Philip. Apparently, although the two had similar values, Philip was the more reserved and deliberate of the two.

The image beside the woman's face jumped into motion and became a video of Adam being hauled into the police station.

His voice filled the room. "I didn't kill those kids. I'm innocent!" The video froze, once again leaving Adam's mouth twisted.

"The police appear to agree with his statement of innocence," the reporter continued. "Pollock was released just two hours ago. We join him now for a press conference."

"They released him?" I asked Marcy.

She frowned. "It's news to me too."

How could they have released him? I'd had my doubts about his ability to pull off the crimes. Two murders that required getting past insane security. I couldn't see those being planned by a man who could barely string a sentence together.

But the fact that he was a Pollock made his guilt more likely. As a member of that family, he had the resources to get past any security he wanted to.

The image on the vid-screen changed, and an outdoor press conference replaced the news studio. Adam Pollock trudged up to a podium, urged along by a man in a perfectly tailored suit. The suited man stood too far from the camera for me to see his face clearly.

Reporters crowded in front of the podium. Pollock reached the microphone in the center and faced the group of about fifteen people. He glanced over at the guy I assumed was his lawyer. The man nodded his encouragement.

Pollock himself was the most astonishing thing about the scene. He'd cut his hair short, so it no longer brushed across his shoulders in a stringy mess. It looked neatly washed and combed out of his face. He, too, wore a perfectly tailored suit in deep gray. Between the hair and the suit, he looked more like a stockbroker than a lunatic protester.

The most shocking thing about his appearance was the injuries to his face. I cringed as he turned toward his audience and the camera. A swollen mess of red and purple covered the right side of his face, with the colored parts mostly centered around his eye, cheekbone, and nose. His left side hadn't come out of the battle unscathed either, and a series of scrapes marred the area near the eye.

For a moment, I glanced down at the floor, too guilty to look at the damage I'd done. But my curiosity won out, and my attention returned to the screen.

"I want to apologize for my behavior over the past couple weeks." Pollock's voice boomed, amplified by the microphone. He stepped back and licked his lips, clearly nervous. "My family wants to assure the public that, although androids threaten our society as a whole, we do not condone violence against humans in the protesting of robotic development."

A reporter in the crowd shouted, "Why did you attack Lena Hayes?"

Pollock glanced at the lawyer-type again, who nodded. "I offer my sincere apologies to Miss Hayes and her family. I've been medicated for psychological issues for a long time, and I briefly went off my meds. I was not in my right mind when I attacked Miss Hayes. That is not who I am or what my family represents."

The words sounded practiced. I might have thought them insincere, if the man didn't look so completely sorry. His lip even trembled a bit.

"Did you kill Harmony Miller and Kevin Rodriguez?" another reporter shouted.

Before Pollock could answer, the lawyer guy strode toward the stage and gestured for Pollock to step aside, which he did, his head obediently dipped.

Up close, the lawyer's facial features became clear, and I recognized him as my idol Philip Pollock. I leaned closer to the screen.

"Adam Pollock did not kill anyone, which is why he was released," Philip said. "During both murders, Mr. Pollock was at his home, sleeping. His house's extensive security records, as well as the house staff, confirm his presence there. The police have verified this alibi. No more questions." He led Adam from the stage.

Marcy stared down at me, brow crinkled.

"What's up?" I asked.

"If the murderer is still out there, perhaps your parents should consider putting your bodyguard back on duty."

"Shh," I hissed. My parents had long since left for the office, but still, I didn't want that thought out there in the universe. That was exactly the sort of thing my mother would do. "The only places I go these days are school and home, and Lionel escorts me. No one's going to murder me on a crowded campus, and no one's getting in here to kill me."

"They got past the Millers' security."

"Then the Millers must have a flaw in their system."

Marcy raised a skeptical brow.

But that wasn't my largest concern right now. Pollock wasn't some deranged lunatic who enjoyed attacking people. He was just a guy who had gone off his meds and lost control. I could empathize with that—losing control. I'd twisted Harmony's arm and beaten Adam Pollock into submission. I couldn't blame Pollock for losing it himself every now and then.

Me, on the other hand—I was another story. I despised CyberCorp almost as much as the Pollocks, and unlike Adam, I had no alibi for Harmony's and Kevin's murders. In fact, I had the opposite of an alibi. An anti-alibi—if that was a thing.

I was sleepwalking and had no idea where I was. Plus, I'd been upset with Harmony when she died. Adam Pollock trailed far behind me when it came to number-one suspects for these murders.

His family could have modified their own security

system to make it look like he was home, even instructed the staff to lie for him. But still, without an ID chip, it was easier for me to get past the Millers' system than it was for him.

I looked guilty as hell.

22

Before heading for the school's front steps on Monday morning, I locked the doors of my new car and ran my fingers along the shiny red hood. Full of curves and angles, it held so much more personality than the sweeping, impersonal shape of more modern vehicles.

My mother had been trying to make a point when she chose this particular model. I guessed she wanted to prove I'd miss the technology—the automatic locks keyed to ID chips, auto-drive, ultra-adjustable seats. I didn't. Instead, I felt like I finally had a car that suited me.

My bodyguard Owen exited the vehicle next to mine and strode behind me until I stopped at the school's front steps. When Adam Pollock had been released, Owen returned to my side once again. I'd had one bodyguard-free night and morning, and now he was back.

I scowled and shuffled away to put more distance between us. The last thing I needed was the additional attention I'd get from toting the oversized bodyguard around.

"I need you to get me a phone number," I said into my hand-screen. I'd called Ron as I was parking my car.

"Whose?" Ron asked.

"Adam Pollock." The best way to discover for myself whether he was guilty—and whether I was innocent—was to talk to the man one-on-one.

Silence on the other end of the line.

"Ron? You still there?"

"Yeah, I'm here. Why do want to talk to the guy whose face you beat into a bloody pulp?"

I'd mapped out the various paths the conversation could take, but nowhere in my map did I expect Ron to use the term *bloody pulp*. I did, however, have an answer to why I wanted to talk to Pollock. "I want to formally accept the apology he offered me at the press conference, and offer him one in return."

"I don't think that's a good idea."

"Can you get the number or not?"

"I'll see what I can do."

We disconnected the call, and a second later, I felt a tap on my shoulder. I turned to find Hunter smiling down at me.

As usual, his body tilted slightly to one side when he stood still, favoring his bad leg. He gave me the same crooked smile that had caught me off guard when we first met. His humble confidence made him so different from Jackson and so different from me.

I threw my arms around him and squeezed.

"Hey," he said when I pulled back. "You okay?"

I wanted to confess everything on my mind—that I needed Adam Pollock to be a murderer because otherwise I might be one. I had gone against my own judgment and not demanded another surgery to remove the arm. I should have insisted harder, even refused to leave CyberCorp until I got what I wanted. But I hadn't, and now this was my punishment.

To top it off, I couldn't stop thinking about Hunter—when I should have been camped out at Jackson's bedside. Because even if Harmony and Kevin weren't my fault—even if I was innocent of that—Jackson's fate rested squarely on my conscience.

Still gripped in my metal fist, my hand-screen vibrated. For a moment, I had a surreal, out-of-body feeling as I realized my skin wasn't touching the device at all, but still, I could somehow *feel* the vibration.

It was freaky.

The small display on the side informed me it was Ron calling. I accepted the call and placed the device to my ear.

"That was quick."

"The Pollocks aren't exactly hard to find," Ron said. "Their family is almost as high profile as yours." He rattled off the number.

My hand-screen captured the number during the call, and when I disconnected, it asked if I wanted to call it. I confirmed, and the device placed my call to Adam Pollock.

A man answered on the fourth ring, just as I was about to give up. "Hello. Philip Pollock speaking."

I went mute, taken aback that this apparently was not a

direct line to Adam's micro-comm—and doubly taken aback that I'd just reached *the* Philip Pollock. The same Philip Pollock whose audio programs I listened to religiously.

I would keep it together. I would not be some starstruck teenager. Not right now.

"I was trying to reach Adam Pollock. Please." I added that last part as an afterthought. "Is this not his micro?"

"Adam doesn't have a micro." It was a little disturbing how much this potential murderer had in common with me. "And, regardless, we have no comment about the events of the last few days. As we've said before, Mr. Pollock did not kill anyone, which is why he was released."

"I'm not the press," I said, before he could disconnect. "I'm Lena Hayes."

Silence on the other end, and then, "What can I do for you, Miss Hayes?"

"I'd like to speak to Adam please. If you ask him, I'm sure he'll agree to talk to me." It was worth a shot. After all, Adam had apologized to me during the press conference, and he'd looked sincere when he did it. If he meant his words, he would want to relay them in person.

After a pause, Philip said, "I'll tell him you called. Unfortunately, he's under medical care at the moment and not available to talk."

"Do you know when he'll be available?"

"Later today, perhaps. Goodbye, Miss Hayes."

"Wait!" I shouted into the hand-screen before my idol could end the call.

"Yes, Miss Hayes." Annoyance laced his words.

"I'm sorry, but I just have to tell you. I listen to your audios. They're fantastic."

"Are you mocking me, Miss *Hayes?*" This time, when he said my name, he emphasized it hard—as if I needed a reminder of who I was. "CyberCorp is a blight upon humanity. Humans are the ones that need celebrating, not inanimate objects—and certainly not ones masquerading as humans with *artificial* intelligence. Our complex brains make us unique in this world. We cannot be duplicated by machines."

"I know that. I—"

"Machines are not companions or employees or protectors. Neither your parents nor any other human being should make intelligence artificial. In the end, we can rely only on ourselves—on humans—to guarantee our future existence. In the end, there is—"

"In the end, there is only us," I said, concluding with the catch phrase he often used to wrap up his audio programs.

"Yes. Only us." Hints of fury bubbled at the surface of his words. I could hear him fighting to keep them contained. I couldn't tell whether that anger was because he still thought I was mocking him or because he was simply passionate about his beliefs.

"I'll tell my brother you called."

The line went silent, leaving just the sound of me breathing staccato breaths into the receiver. My right hand felt warm, and I looked down to find it gripping Hunter's, my knuckles bright with the pressure. I uncurled my fingers, mumbling an apology too low for him to possibly hear.

I was both devastated at not having been able to talk to Adam and thrilled that I'd just talked to my idol. My disloyal heart still raced with excitement, despite my silently informing it that I was in the midst of some serious shit, and now was not the time to be starstruck.

I needed to talk to Adam Pollock to find out whether he was telling the truth about his alibi. These ultra-modern security systems were flawed, just like the older ones they replaced. They assumed people had ID chips, and anyone without a chip could potentially beat them.

For all I knew, Adam Pollock—who spent his days decrying technology outside the CyberCorp building—had no chip. His family could afford to hire a doctor willing to remove it.

Adam's alibi could be bogus, and I *needed* him to be guilty.

Hunter waved to get my attention, and I realized I'd been staring off into space.

"Sorry," I said.

"Why did you just call Adam Pollock?"

I turned to face Owen. "I need to speak to my friend in private for a minute. Can you give us some space please?"

He scanned the area around us and then nodded. "Stay where I can see you."

I grabbed Hunter's hand and pulled him away from the nearby students, until I felt confident we stood out of anyone's earshot. "They're saying Adam Pollock didn't kill Harmony and Kevin."

"We've been over this already. You didn't kill them."

"But the sleepwalking—"

He cut me off. "I don't know what I was doing in my sleep on those nights either. But neither of us killed them."

"How do you know?"

"You're not a killer. You don't break into people's houses and strangle them. You didn't even know Kevin. Why would you kill him?"

"I don't know!" I shouted, and then regretted it when nearby students glanced at us.

Now that they'd seen me—the girl with the robotic arm—they continued to stare. I grabbed Hunter's hand and moved him to the far end of the school building. Owen followed behind us but still left enough room for us to talk in private. When I loosened my grasp to drop Hunter's hand, he gripped me tighter. His hand felt warm around mine. I leaned into him until my shoulder touched his chest, and stayed there.

"I don't know why I'd kill him," I said, more calmly this time. My insides felt all twisted, but Hunter's nearness helped quell the panic. "Maybe to intimidate CyberCorp into scrapping the Model One rollout."

"In that case, wouldn't it be easier to just kill your parents?"

My mouth dropped open, and I tried to pull away from him.

"I'm not suggesting you do that. I'm just saying, if you're the killer, your plan is illogical. You live in the house with CyberCorp's owners. It's a privately owned company. If its owners die, don't you inherit the whole thing?"

My brow scrunched up. "I assume."

"Except, if you were a murderer, you *would* have thought about it. Instead of this convoluted plan to kill CyberCorp kids to convince their parents to call off the rollout, you would have killed your parents and canceled the thing yourself. Or dismantled the whole damn company."

"Maybe I'm not that bright when I'm sleepwalking."

"You'd have to be bright to get past the security in Harmony's and Kevin's homes."

I patted Hunter on the shoulder to let him know I understood his point. "So basically, I'd have to be dumb or crazy to kill Harmony and Kevin, and I *couldn't* have killed them if I was dumb or crazy."

"Feel better?" he asked.

"A little." And I did. The weight that had pressed down on me since Harmony's death felt a little lighter. "But I still don't know why I'm sleepwalk . . ." I turned when I noticed him staring at something behind me.

A police car had just parked in front of the school. Out of it climbed two plain-clothed detectives. A tall, broad-shouldered man and a woman of medium height, her dark hair pulled back into a tight ponytail. Both had perfect posture as they strode toward the front steps.

"You think they're investigating the murders?" I asked.

"Probably," Hunter said. "Kevin and Harmony both went to school here. It was only a matter of time before they started questioning students."

"Yeah, I guess." I checked the time on my hand-screen. "We should head inside. Class in five minutes."

Owen rejoined us and we hurried into the school building. Inside, Hunter and I went our separate ways toward our lockers.

A redheaded girl stood by the bank of lockers my friends and I shared, her back toward me. Claire stood with her, leaning against her own locker and quietly tracking the girl's movements.

Harmony?

No, Melody. Of course, it was Melody. And Claire was watching her closely because she'd lost her twin sister. Harmony had left for good.

Melody seemed shorter than usual today, her hair pulled into a messy ponytail, her shoulders slumped. I itched to run up to her, hug her, and tell her how much I missed her sister too.

I reached out a hand to tap her on the shoulder. She turned a split second before I made contact. She shrieked and jerked to the side to avoid me.

"What are you doing?" Her voice rang out across the hallway, shrill.

"I was just . . . I wanted to see how you're doing." I cringed even as the words were coming out. *How she was doing?* Her twin sister died last week. She was feeling like crap. "I was hoping we could talk."

Claire grabbed her hand and tugged it toward herself, away from me, mumbling something too low for me to hear. Melody didn't budge.

Melody stuck her hands on her hips. "What would we talk about—how you murdered my sister? What happened to you?" Her eyes did that blinking-rapidly thing people did when they were trying not to cry.

"Let's go," Claire said, more loudly this time. To me, she mouthed words that looked like an apology.

"Harmony never liked you," Melody continued. "Mostly she hung out with you because Claire and I did, and because you're a Hayes. She thought you were weird, the way you insist on using old tech. She always said Jackson could do better."

"Why are you telling me this?" My voice caught in my throat.

Claire tugged on her arm again, and Melody yanked her hand back.

She looked me straight in the eye. "You killed my sister. Maybe *because* she didn't like you—or because of what happened that day—I don't know why. But you're a monster."

Her words stabbed me in the gut and twisted, and I doubled over with the pain. Harmony was my friend. If she had thought otherwise, I didn't want to hear about it. I didn't want to know.

When I opened my mouth, all that came out was a gasp, and my whole body felt liquid. Unstable. Claire hurried toward me and held me up until Melody grabbed her arm and dragged her back.

Something behind me caught Melody's attention, and her gaze shifted to look over my shoulder. I turned.

The two detectives from outside strode toward us. In front of them walked Debbie, who was one of the principal's student assistants.

I never spoke to her except about schoolwork, but I sometimes saw her at CyberCorp family affairs, since her mother worked for my parents. Debbie pointed at me as they approached.

Since the cops had Melody's attention, I took the reprieve to inhale a few sharp breaths. Melody was lying. Harmony and I were friends—best friends—and I didn't kill her.

"Lena Hayes?" the female detective asked.

I nodded, still fighting to push Melody's words out of my brain. Still fighting not to burst into a sobbing mess in the middle of the hallway.

"I'm Detective Garrett, and this is my partner, Detective Johnson. We'd like a few minutes of your time."

Melody stepped forward. "Is this about Harmony's murder?"

"Miss Miller." The detective's face softened. "We're doing everything we can to find your sister's killer."

"She's right there." Melody jabbed a finger at me. "Lena did it."

"We're exploring all options, but we need to speak to Miss Hayes alone." She shifted, placing her body partly in front of Melody's to remove her from the conversation, and gestured for me to follow.

Debbie dismissed herself, and I let the two detectives lead me to an empty classroom. Melody and Claire watched us go. I felt their gazes on us until the detectives pulled the classroom door closed, with the three of us inside and them outside.

I sat down hard on the surface of the teacher's desk,

the closest seat to the door. "Am I a suspect in Harmony's murder?"

"We need to officially eliminate you as one," Johnson said. It was the first time I'd heard him speak, and he had just the kind of low, authoritative voice I would have expected of a law enforcement professional. "We want to make sure we understand your side of the story. Tell us about your fight with Harmony last Monday."

His words thrummed around me like an echo. Far away. Melody's face still glared at me from behind my eyelids. Or was it Harmony's?

"Miss Hayes?"

"We were friends." My thoughts jumbled together, but that part I knew. Or I thought I did. I shook my head and stood up, back straight, narrowing my focus in on the detectives. "When I saw her that morning, we were in a good place. Happy, getting along. She wanted to get to class early, so she left Melody and me alone. That's when I told Melody about my new arm. I'd hidden it up to that point."

"Your new arm?" Johnson nodded down at my metal hand. "Tell us about that."

"I lost my original arm in a car accident a month and a half ago. Last Monday was my first day back at school. I thought Melody would understand and accept it, but she didn't. The next time I saw her was at lunch, and Harmony was there too. I told everyone about my arm, and they were okay with it at first."

"At first?" Detective Garrett's left eyebrow started an upward march.

"Harmony tried to comfort me by touching my shoulder, which isn't healed yet. The pain made me react without thinking."

Both detectives now leaned forward, their faces expectant. They knew I was leaving something out. They probably already knew all about the fight and just needed to hear it from my point of view.

"I grabbed her arm and yanked it around behind her back." The words tumbled out in a rush, as if saying them quickly would give the detectives less time to realize what they meant. "She shouldn't have touched me. It wouldn't have happened if she hadn't."

"You blame Harmony for the physical altercation?" Garrett said.

"No . . . I don't know. I just wish it hadn't happened. I realized what I did—that I made a mistake—and I left the cafeteria. That was the last time I saw Harmony."

They were quiet for a span of several seconds, and I shifted from foot to foot as I waited. My father told me once that being silent was a good way to make other people talk. Others felt awkward in silence and tried to fill up the space.

I had a feeling the officers were doing that now, waiting for me to volunteer information. I pressed my lips together and willed myself to stay silent.

I could have told them the fight wasn't my fault at all. The arm had reacted. But I knew from Ron and Simon's lectures that I controlled the arm. If it reacted, it did because I wanted it to. Suggesting I wasn't in complete control would make me look *more* like a murderer, not less.

Detective Johnson took over the questioning again. "Where were you last Monday and Tuesday nights?" He asked the question casually, as if it were a mere formality and not a subject of great concern—more like *panic*—on my part.

"I went to bed around 10:30 both nights." That was the truth—not the whole truth of course, but as close as they needed to know right now. Until *I* knew exactly what I'd been doing on those nights, I didn't want the police looking into it. If I was going to end up in jail, it would be on my own terms.

"Can anyone confirm that?"

"My parents and housekeeper can confirm about Monday. For Tuesday, there's also my nighttime bodyguard." I tilted my head toward Owen. "Not him. There's another guy. He sat outside my bedroom door all night. Walt something-or-other. My parents can give you his full name."

"Good. That's all we need for now," Detective Garrett said. "Thank you for your time, Miss Hayes."

Even though these cops didn't know it, I was invested in this investigation. If the police found the killer, I was off the hook. And if I ever wanted to get a good night's sleep again, I needed to be off the hook.

"Wait." I grabbed her arm to stop her from leaving. By instinct, I used my left hand. Instead of shaking me off, Garrett stared at the hand, her expression fascinated. I yanked it back. "Do you have any suspects?"

"We're not at liberty to say." She turned to walk away again, but I slid in front of her.

"Greg Miller has a lot of enemies. You should track them down. Start with Dr. Athena Fisher. He fired her son and blackballed him with other tech companies. Also, check out Mark Hoffman and Kyle Lowry. Miller fired them on Christmas Eve, and one of them raised a stink on his way out. And don't forget about Adam Pollock. He's probably the one."

"We've spoken to all four of them," Garrett said. "Anything else?"

Since I had no intention of offering myself as a suspect, I shook my head.

"Thank you, Miss Hayes. We'll let you know if we have any more questions. In the meantime, stay safe." She pointed at my bodyguard, who nodded at the detectives. "Keep this guy nearby."

Maybe Owen could protect me if the murderer came after me. But if I turned out to be the killer, could he protect everyone else?

23

As planned, when my morning classes dismissed for lunch on Monday, I visited Ron and Simon to handle my sleepwalking.

A twinge of disappointment nagged me when I walked through the CyberCorp lobby. The windows looked like new. They'd been replaced, and not a shard of glass remained on the floor. CyberCorp was invincible.

Ron and Simon led me up to a large corner office. A plaque beside the door informed me that the space belonged to Dr. Fisher.

I pointed at the nameplate as we stepped into the room. "Is she going to join us?"

Simon shook his head. "She's busy with the Model Ones."

"We don't have offices of our own. Just cubicles." Ron pointed at an array of cubicles nearby. "She said it was okay to use hers for this. How are you feeling, by the way? I heard about the little incident at your folks' party after I left."

"Just a little weirded out."

"Lucky you had the arm. I heard it saved your life. Who knows whether you would have been able to defend yourself without it?"

Yeah. Lucky me. "I guess. They're saying there's no way the man who attacked me—Adam Pollock—could have killed Harmony and Kevin."

"And you think it's Fisher," Ron said, with more than a hint of amusement.

"I didn't say that."

"No, but you're not as subtle as you think. The only reason she didn't realize you were grilling her Friday night was that she was drunk. I, on the other hand, was not. She didn't do it."

"What makes you so sure?"

"Fisher is an academic. If she wanted someone out of her way, she'd make it happen with this." He tapped his temple. "Not with brute force."

I had to admit his assessment of Fisher seemed accurate. I couldn't imagine her breaking into the Millers' home and strangling Harmony in her bed. Fisher was tightly strung, but she wasn't a killer.

If I needed any more evidence of Dr. Fisher's dedication to the Model Ones, her office gave it to me. An oversized vid-screen acted as the far wall, and it currently displayed life-size versions of three Model Ones, the first turned to its right, making its left profile visible, one faced forward, and the other turned to its left.

In digital ink, Dr. Fisher had scrawled notes all over the vid-screen, some with arrows pointing to different parts of the Model Ones. No one that dedicated would work against CyberCorp by killing its employees' kids.

The wall to my left held stacks of cubbies, each holding metal parts and wires, and each with a neat label underneath. An android's head sat on the edge of her desk surface. Its metal eyelids were open, and its red eyes stared at us as we stepped deeper into the room.

It reminded me of the broken android skull I left in my wake the night I'd pulled an unwitting Hunter into my destruction of the lobby.

It seemed a waste to have the attention of two Cyber-Corp employees and not ask them what they knew about the vandalism. I'd been so worried about the murders—which I might not have committed—that I'd ignored the crime I *had* committed.

It would be nice to know whether anyone suspected it was me. Then I could do some damage control. Maybe I could confess to my parents before they found out from their security team.

"I overheard my dad saying something about a break-in in the lobby." I tried to keep my voice casual, like I was asking out of curiosity. "What happened?"

"We're not sure." Ron gestured for me to sit in one of the two leather guest chairs in front of Dr. Fisher's large desk. "Probably one of those crazies who hang out on the sidewalk. The security team is doing a complete overhaul. There's talk of upgrading all the equipment now. It's never been necessary in the past, because ID chips are so reliable.

No one gets past the lobby without an authorized chip, and our scanners all over the building tell us who's been where."

"Didn't the scanners record who was in the lobby during the break-in?"

"That's the problem," Ron said. "According to the security personnel, there were two intruders. One stayed outside the whole time, so our chip scanners couldn't get a read on him, and the cameras didn't get a good view. The other guy was inside, but he kept his face hidden." He cast me a look with narrowed eyes. "He was in full view of our chip scanners, but they didn't read an ID chip."

Did he suspect me? He was among the few people who knew I had no ID chip.

"Security replaced all the scanners in that section of the main floor," Simon added, before Ron could say more. "At least one of them should have caught a reading, so we're scrapping all of them."

Ron grabbed a cable from one of the cubbies against the wall and removed his hand-screen from his pocket. Pulling the sides of the hand-screen apart, he extended the screen in one direction and then the other, until it was almost as large as a piece of paper. Then he used the cable to connect the hand-screen to the plug in my arm.

"Let us concentrate for a few minutes," Simon said. "Okay?"

I nodded and kept silent.

He and Ron spent the next ten minutes looking through the files that made up the program for my arm. They flipped through one file after the next, muttering to each other about the contents. All the while, the fingertips of my right hand played a quickening rhythm against the underside of my chair. Eventually, Simon grabbed my hand to stop me.

"Your code looks fine," Ron said. "It hasn't been tampered with, and it looks like it's running the way it's supposed to."

Simon nodded his agreement.

I tried to peer at the hand-screen over their shoulders. "So nothing's wrong?" There had to be *something*. If the code wasn't the cause of my sleepwalking, then I had no idea how to stop it.

"We're still looking," Ron said. "Give us a bit longer."

A few minutes later, Simon squinted at the display. "Are you seeing this?"

Ron pushed his face closer to the screen. "It's hard to miss."

"What are you guys looking at?" I asked.

Simon ignored me, his gaze glued to the hand-screen.

"Remember how we told you your arm is artificially intelligent?" Ron said.

"I wish I could forget it, but unfortunately, it's melded to my flesh."

"That means it's a learning machine, based on the Model Two actually. Its software has both code and data. The code tells it how to interpret the data, which is everything it has encountered while interacting with the world. It learns from those interactions."

"So what?"

"So this file represents your data—everything your arm has learned since we powered it up two weeks ago."

"That's a lot."

"That's the problem," Simon said. "We expected a lot of data, but this is a *lot* of data. Too much for the time period the arm's been active."

"What has it learned?" I asked.

"It's hard to tell from a quick look," Ron said. "We're going to have to go through it line by line and figure out what it means when combined together. It'll take a while."

"But the timing of the data is interesting." Simon pointed at the display on the hand-screen. Each item in the list included a timestamp. "Looks like you're doing a lot of learning late at night, which is odd because we'd expect you to do almost no learning while you're asleep. That's probably a result of the sleepwalking." For the first time, he dragged his gaze from the screen to me. "You sleepwalk every night?"

I shook my head. "It's only happened a couple times." I didn't mention that those times lined up with the murders.

"Your arm learns a lot every night, so the sleepwalking isn't the only cause of that. We need time to weed through it. We might need to delete some of this data if the arm has picked up some bad habits."

"Why don't you just delete all of it?"

"That'll take you back to square one. You'll have to start over with your physical therapy, which means you'll have to move back in here again."

As horrid as that sounded, if I were back here at Cyber-Corp, I wouldn't have to worry about murdering people in my sleep. Plus, I'd be too weak to hurt anyone. "I'd rather do that than the sleepwalking. I've been exhausted for a week and a half, afraid I'll wake up on the side of the road somewhere—or worse."

"Let's save that as a last resort," Simon said. "At least until after the Model One rollout. Dr. Fisher is going to flip if she's pulled off that project to oversee your case full time again." He unplugged my arm from the hand-screen. "Go home. We'll let you know when we figure out what's going on."

I trudged from the room, head hung low. I had hoped this little session would tell me why I was sleepwalking, and maybe even fix the problem. Instead, we'd discovered that not only was my head connected to a machine.

But we had no idea what that machine was doing.

24

WHILE I WAS IN THE BUILDING, I FIGURED I OUGHT TO visit Jackson. This time, I didn't ask Ron or Simon's permission to see him. Instead, I persuaded one of the engineers I passed to direct the elevator to his floor for me. I would have needed an ID chip to do it myself.

I dragged my feet to Jackson's room, prepared to sit by his bedside like a dutiful girlfriend—or ex-girlfriend. I still couldn't be sure what our status was.

I knocked when I reached his door and then opened it without waiting for an answer. If he was alone in there, I couldn't exactly expect his unconscious body to invite me inside.

But he wasn't unconscious.

His blue eyes were wide open, and he sat up in bed, scarfing down what looked like multiple portions of scrambled eggs. He was working on one bowl full of the stuff, and an empty bowl sat on the cart next to him.

My shoulders lightened at finding him intact, smiling, and *alive*. For a moment, I didn't care that we were in the middle of an epic fight, or that his metal parts outnumbered his flesh ones. I ran to his bedside and threw myself on top of him.

Laughing, he squeezed me back, lifted me from my feet, and rolled me over him to the other side of the bed until I lay next to him.

I laid my head on his shoulder. "You're awake," I said.

He grinned at me. "And you say obvious things."

"How long have you been conscious?"

"Not long. Since yesterday."

"Why didn't you call me? I would have come over."

"We broke up." He said it so matter-of-factly that I felt like a fool for wondering whether we'd made a clean break.

A few seconds before, everything had been perfect. I fit perfectly in the crook of his shoulder, and the world had righted itself after having tilted this way and that over the past few days. This was home . . . except it wasn't anymore. We'd broken up, and I didn't know how to feel about that.

Jackson pushed a lock of curly hair out of my face and leaned close to whisper. "But you came anyway. That means something."

My heart skipped. Everything had changed. My life had been tipped upside down, but this one thing—Jackson and me—this was something I could fix.

This could go back to the way it was supposed to be. And if this could be good again, maybe everything could be. Safe and comfortable.

"I know you didn't mean it when you said I don't listen to you."

My smile wavered.

He continued, oblivious to the fact that I had shifted farther away from him and was now nearly falling off the bed. "I'm on your side, but I don't think you're being fair. We'll have a great life."

I slid off the bed and changed the subject. "How are you feeling?" He looked a little *too* well. The last time I saw him, he'd looked barely alive, pale with a sickening mix of metal and flesh. I squinted at him now but found no signs of injury.

A wide smile stretched across his face. "I'm perfect. Better than ever." He pointed at his left arm. "This arm is awesome." Then he pointed to his collarbone and the left side of his rib cage. "These are awesome." He pointed down at his pelvis, his left leg, and then his right. "All awesome."

My mouth dropped open. "They replaced all of that?"

He nodded. "This is actually the second time I woke up. The first time was three weeks ago, when they'd only replaced the left arm and leg. Those were unsalvageable. The other body parts were a mess though. They told me all about the years of physical therapy I'd have to endure, and *maybe* someday I'd be able to pee on my own. I told them to replace everything they had to." He pointed at his pelvis. "I died on the table twice while they were replacing this one."

I couldn't respond to that. Whether I wanted to be with him was still unclear. But Jackson was one of my oldest friends. I'd known him longer than I'd known Liv—even longer than I'd known Allie. I couldn't imagine waking up each morning to a world where he didn't exist. The thought of him lying dead on that table broke my heart.

But I didn't know whether *this* life was much better—a life controlled by machines.

"I'm glad you're okay," I whispered.

"I'm better than okay." His face lit up with excitement when he spoke. "I never knew my body could feel like this. Powerful. Invincible."

"You're not invincible, Jacks. You almost died."

"If I were in that same accident again, I could step out of the car with nothing but flesh wounds." He grabbed a pen from his nightstand and rammed it into his left forearm.

I shrieked and pressed my hands to the wound to staunch the flow of blood. He laughed and waved me away.

He wasn't bleeding.

It looked like real flesh, but the gash revealed metal beneath. No red liquid leaked from the cut. Thin threads of flesh reached out from both sides of the wound, stretching toward each other.

The threads twisted together and pulled the two sides toward each other like a cavern gradually becoming a small crack. The flesh stitched itself back together, until all that remained was a thin scar. A moment later, even that disappeared.

My stomach lurched, and I tasted bile in my mouth.

Still chuckling, Jackson reached out to touch my chin and shut it. "Now tell me again how I'm not invincible."

"You're not."

I'd been fooled by how perfect Jackson looked. Skin covered his metal, but that didn't make it human. Just machines masquerading as a boy. Jackson had a chip in his head just like I did—but he wanted it.

He loved everything I hated. Underneath the perfect smile and the perfect skin, he *was* everything I hated.

I inched farther away from him.

Jackson grabbed my wrist, his expression solemn. "It's keeping me alive."

I softened.

He tugged my wrist, and I stepped closer.

"How'd you get them to install all your skin already? They keep saying I'm not healed enough yet."

"They've been tinkering with my hardware every day for the past month and a half. Plus, they put me in the healing tube multiple times per day when I was unconscious. They're done tinkering, and I'm healed."

"No more pain?" I asked.

"Not much. A little when I pushed myself too hard in physical therapy." He gestured toward my left arm. "What are they waiting on with you?"

I grimaced. "Headaches."

"Bummer." His face suddenly became serious. "Can we get back to our other conversation—the one about us?"

I knew this was coming, but I didn't know what I wanted to say—which was the worst-case scenario. I didn't want Jackson convincing me that his way was the right way.

He continued, even though I hadn't given him a response. "I love you, Lena. I don't want to stay broken up. I want to fix this."

"I can't—"

Jackson folded my metal hand in one of his flesh-covered ones. "Is this because I want us to take over CyberCorp?"

He shifted to sit up straighter, and the move was so effortless—like half his body hadn't been replaced with robotics. The smile shone the same as always, even the dimple on his cheek had survived. Despite our sitting in a hospital room in CyberCorp, the familiarity of the moment set my head spinning.

The car accident had done more than crush my arm into a pulpy mess. That silver car flying at me out of the darkness shattered not only my arm—but also the perfect portrait of my life. It left pieces scattered all over the inter-section.

Deep in my gut, I yearned to sort through the muck for each piece, dust it off, and fit it back into place. But some-times, when things get broken, no amount of spit and glue would save them.

I couldn't unwind the seams of time and put all the pieces back together.

That was a fantasy.

"We want different things. We're not the same—like we used to be."

A nurse popped her head into the room. She was clean

faced, no makeup, with her hair pulled back into a tight ponytail. "You need anything, hon?" Her brows rose when she saw me, and she stepped fully into the room. "Miss Hayes?"

"Don't mind me."

She hesitated for a couple seconds before shifting her attention back to Jackson. "Ready for lunch yet?"

He flashed her a smile, and she seemed to relax again despite my presence. She looked a bit younger than my parents, maybe in her early thirties, but even an older woman couldn't resist a Jackson Watts thousand-watt smile.

"I've got it right here." She stepped out of the room and returned several seconds later with a tray of food. It held what looked like meatloaf, broccoli salad, and a pudding cup.

"Would it be all right if I get a different flavor?" He pointed at the clear bottom of the prepackaged pudding cup, which clearly showed it was chocolate.

"What would you like?"

"Anything except chocolate. Strawberry maybe?"

"No problem." She plucked the pudding cup off the tray, swept up the empty bowl from the cart beside Jackson's bed, and set everything else in its place. "I'll be right back." She disappeared through the doorway, leaving Jackson and me alone again.

Jackson and I stared at each other in silence before he spoke again. "You think I don't care what you want?" he asked, his voice more hushed than before. "You're wrong. I just want the best for you."

I didn't answer because I didn't need to. We both knew that's who he was. He was still holding my hand, and when I tried to tug it away, he held on tighter.

"We don't have to be your parents," he continued.

"I've told you a thousand times I don't want to run CyberCorp. You don't listen."

"And I've told *you* a thousand times I don't expect you to. You get to *own* it."

"I don't want—"

"When you own your parents' company, you can kill the artificial intelligence research. You can amp up the medical research. You can even sell the company in tiny little bits and pieces until nothing left of it exists, and then donate the profits to non-profit STEM programs for minority kids."

My mouth gaped open.

"Or whatever you want—because CyberCorp will be fully and entirely yours."

"What?" All this time, he never wanted to be a Cyber-Corp mogul?

"It's good money, Lena. I admit that I'd love to actually run the company, but I know that's not what you want. We don't have to be the bad guys. We don't have to be your parents."

Behind my eyes, I could see the pieces of my life fitting back together. Jackson could help me clean them up, glue them together. It would be perfect.

Was perfection even a thing, or was it lying to myself?

"I don't know," I said.

The nurse picked that moment to return, this time

carrying a strawberry pudding cup. She quietly set it on Jackson's tray, offered a small wave to me, and pulled the door shut when she left.

"You like chocolate." I gestured toward the new pudding on his tray.

Jackson pushed the cup toward me. "You don't."

My stomach chose that moment to growl loudly. "I skipped lunch," I said as I accepted the pudding.

"You don't have to answer right now," Jackson said. "About us, I mean. I don't think I could handle heartbreak while I'm still lying in a hospital bed." His pale-blue eyes pleaded with me.

I loved those eyes. I didn't want to see them sad. The least I could do for him after landing him here—so broken that he now had as many robotic parts as human ones— was to think about it a little more.

"Sure. I'll think about it."

25

BY THE TIME I REACHED THE UNDERGROUND PARKING lot of CyberCorp, I'd made up my mind about one thing— but it had nothing to do with Jackson.

If the Pollocks wouldn't talk to me over the phone, they'd talk to me in person. Before starting my car, I placed a call to Ron. He answered on the first ring.

"I wasn't expecting to hear from you so soon," he said.

"Could you get me Adam Pollock's address? I'm sure CyberCorp has it on file somewhere."

"You realize this state has anti-stalking laws, right?"

"Can you get it or not?"

"Hold on." There was silence on the line. Then Ron returned and gave me the address.

I repeated the information aloud for my car's navigator, and its display screen showed me a map to the Pollocks' house. Adam lived thirty minutes east of downtown.

I couldn't remember the last time I'd driven a distance

that far manually the entire way. I didn't mind though. I even rolled down the driver-side window and let the chill breeze whip through the car. With the exception of the night of the accident, I couldn't remember the last time I'd done that either.

"You have arrived at your destination," the navigator chirped when I drove past the driveway of the Pollocks' grand home. I parked on the side of the road, one block up, then got out and walked back to the house.

Cypress trees surrounded the grand property. The only gap in the greenery made way for a tall, wrought-iron gate. The house beyond the gate oozed old-fashioned charm. Its brick façade rose two stories, with a white entryway and a red door and shutters. My home's white, marble, and glass seemed cold in comparison.

An intercom and security camera sat on the fence to one side of the gate. It made sense that the Pollocks would avoid modern forms of surveillance and opt for old-style cameras instead.

For most people, that might make bypassing security easier. After all, cameras had been replaced by chip scanners because camera footage was too easy to modify and fake, and cameras were too easy to obstruct. But in my case, having no ID chip, I could beat high-tech security systems in my sleep—maybe literally.

If Philip caught me here, he'd block me from seeing Adam. And I couldn't have that.

I stepped to the side until I was confident the camera couldn't see me. At the nearest two cypress trunks, I pushed aside the thick, prickly leaves. Behind the trees stood more of the wrought-iron fence, extending from the gate to wrap around the property. The vertical rungs didn't provide any kind of footing for me to climb over, but I wasn't giving up that easily. I'd come all this way, and I intended to talk to Adam.

I gripped one dark rung with my metal hand and pulled it away from the one beside it. It buckled, enlarging the space between them. I grinned and bent the other rung as well, before I squeezed through.

Two cameras stared down from the front corners of the roof. I ran toward the side of the house. Since the cameras pointed away from the structure, I would have a better chance of avoiding detection if I stayed close to the walls.

Six large windows marked the second floor at the back of the house, and I figured they were bedrooms. I scooped up a handful of pebbles from the landscaping and tossed one at the leftmost window. An older woman pushed aside the heavy drapes and peered into the yard. I pressed myself against the house, waited for her to close the window, and then moved on.

At the side of the house, I chucked a pebble at the first window there. About ten seconds later, it slid upward, and Adam Pollock stuck his head out. Jackpot!

"Adam," I hissed up at him. He must not have heard me because the window began to slide shut, so I shouted. "Adam!"

It rose again, and he searched the yard. I stepped into view and waved up at him. "It's Lena Hayes," I said. "Can we talk?"

When he spotted me, his brows shot upward. "Meet me at the back door."

I returned to the rear of the house. A few minutes later, the door opened, and Adam Pollock emerged.

Today, his appearance fell somewhere between that of the last two times I'd seen him. Still short, his hair now hung out of place, uncombed and oily. Stubble camouflaged his swollen jaw. Red rimmed his tired eyes. Most of the dark bruises I'd given him had dulled to a sickly yellow, and the swelling had come down a bit.

He was talking even before the door shut behind him. "I'm so sorry about Friday." He made a praying motion with his hands, both palms pressed together. "I was off my medication. I would never put an innocent life at risk otherwise."

I gave him a weak smile that I hoped looked real. Seeing Adam like this—so contrite and harmless—made me doubt more and more that he was the murderer, which made me look guilty. This man with the sad, pleading eyes didn't strike me as a serial killer.

On the other hand, the screaming, unkempt mess of a man who'd attacked me twice had proven unpredictable, and that was who this man had been before his arrest.

"Did you kill Harmony Miller and Kevin Rodriguez?"

Adam's shoulders slumped, and he let out a long stream of air like a popped balloon. "Why would I do that? I had nothing against those kids." I couldn't tell whether his posture suggested guilt at murdering two people—or sadness at being suspected.

"Do you have something against *me*?"

"Of course not. I'm so sorry for Friday."

"And last week Sunday?"

His eyes narrowed. "What happened last Sunday?"

"I was leaving the CyberCorp building. You were protesting the Model One rollout. You broke through security and tackled me, screaming about how artificial intelligence would lead to doom and destruction and whatnot."

"That was you?"

After our most recent encounter, I'd assumed I was a target, chosen because of my closeness to CyberCorp. Now, his reaction suggested our first encounter was a coincidence.

I pulled my hand-screen from the pocket of my leather jacket, opened it, and brought up the threatening letter my mother had shown me. "Did you write this?" I passed it to Adam.

He glanced at it for only a second, cringed, and then passed the device back to me. "Yes. But again, I was off my meds."

"You were off your meds when Harmony and Kevin were killed too."

"I didn't kill them!" he shouted. He shot a glance at the house behind him and lowered his voice. "What would it prove?"

"I don't know about proving anything, but it would discourage CyberCorp employees from continuing work on the Model Ones. After the murders, some employees quit, and others bowed out of the project."

"Really?" His face brightened. The slightest smile danced there and then fell again.

My eyes narrowed. He denied being the killer, yet he seemed happy about the result of the killings. Adam Pollock was an odd man, hard to figure out.

"Are you happy they're dead?" I asked.

Adam's gaze shifted to the left for a moment, before returning to my face. "Their deaths serve a purpose. When we die, that's the best we can hope for. Isn't it?"

"The best we can hope for is to live long happy lives and die as old people in our sleep. I would never want to die for someone else's cause." I shook my head hard. "Don't get me wrong. I object to the Model Ones too." Harmony's face hovered in my mind. "But this isn't the way to get the attention we need. Our cause needs positive attention, not negative. We need—"

Adam cut me off. "What do you know about it? You walk around in your giant house full of luxuries paid for by CyberCorp, and you have the nerve to decide what's best for our cause." Although he was calmer than at other times I'd seen him, now—with his tight jaw and wild eyes—I saw the ghost of the man who'd attacked me only a few days ago.

I brought my volume down a notch and smoothed out the roughness in my voice, hoping Adam would take a cue from me. "I care about stopping CyberCorp as much as—"

"I think these murders are exactly what we need." His voice trembled with intensity.

Stunned, I said nothing for a moment. And then, "You killed Harmony and Kevin."

The silence spanned so many seconds that I wondered if he heard me at all.

"You killed them."

He nodded, his back straightening. "Maybe I did."

I took a large step away from him. I'd wanted a confession, and this was as good as one. In hindsight, the whole idea of coming here seemed ludicrous. I had gone out of my way for an audience with a possible killer, and maybe I'd found one.

I was now alone with him on his property. He could attack me, again, and kill me this time.

I spun away from him, almost slipping on the slick grass, and ran back toward the front of the house. I squeezed through the bars of the fence, jumped into my car, and drove away from the Pollocks' home as fast as I could.

26

MY HAND-SCREEN VIBRATED AS I LEFT THE POLLOCKS' neighborhood. I removed it from my pocket to check the display. Jackson was calling.

I couldn't stomach the thought of having another discussion with him about our relationship—or lack of relationship. Plus, a murderer had almost confessed to me, and that took priority. I waited for my voicemail to pick up and then started a new call.

"Call Fuller County police," I said to the hand-screen. The sound of ringing filled the vehicle. I reached into my glove compartment and grabbed the bag of gummy candies I'd stashed there before school this morning.

The ringing stopped abruptly, and a man answered. "Fuller Police Department."

"I have information about Adam Pollock's involvement in the murders of Harmony Miller and Kevin Rodriguez," I said, chewing on a red gummy.

The line went quiet, and I thought the man had hung up. But then a woman said, "This is Detective Garrett." It was the female detective I'd spoken to at school.

"Hi. This is Lena Hayes. I have information about Harmony's murder."

"Tell me."

"I just left Adam Pollock's house—"

She cut me off. "We already cleared Mr. Pollock."

"Yeah, I know. But three minutes ago, he told me the murders were a good thing. He said they serve a purpose. And the way he said it—it was as good as a confession."

"Why would he confess?" Her tone sounded less bored now but still unconvinced.

"I don't think he meant to. He lost his composure."

"Tell me what he said, word for word."

"He said, 'I think these murders are exactly what we need.'"

"Thank you, Lena. We'll bring him in for more questioning." Without another word, the call ended.

Detective Garrett's voice echoed in my head: *Why would he confess?* Adam had already been cleared, so why throw himself back on the mercy of law enforcement by saying too much? I didn't understand it, but his words seemed more like those of a guilty man than an innocent one.

Despite my doubts, my shoulders felt a hundred times lighter. I was not a murderer. Another block of my life fell back into place. I felt almost whole again, almost complete.

The clock in my new car told me the school day had wrapped up, so I placed a second call.

"Hey, Lena," Hunter said when he answered. "How's it going?"

"Fantastic." And I meant it. "I want to see you. Can I pick you up from school?"

"Yeah, sure." The pitch of his voice rose, the way it did when people smiled. "My mom dropped me off today, so I need a ride anyway."

"Great. I'll be there in about twenty-five minutes." I plucked one more gummy candy from my stash before returning the remainder to the glove compartment.

When I arrived at the school parking lot, Hunter was sitting on the front steps, tapping the foot of his good leg in a steady rhythm. Grinning, he pushed himself to his feet. His gaze skimmed over the smooth curves and edges of my car.

"Interesting choice." He slid into the front seat and examined the dash, which had more manual controls than most other vehicles on the road.

I hugged the steering wheel. "I love it, so no jokes. I come with a manual car now. Take it or leave it."

"If those are my options, then I definitely choose taking you."

"You mean *it*."

"Whatever." He grinned and brushed his fingertips over my hand. Warm tingles shot up my arm.

I let him chatter away for the first ten minutes of the drive, while I worked my way up to telling him about Adam. Finally, I braced myself for his lecture.

"I went to see Adam Pollock today."

"What the hell, Lena?" He blew out a long breath. "Why would you visit that guy? He could have killed you."

"He didn't. I'm fine, and I almost got a confession out of him."

"So you didn't just go see a likely murderer. You went to see a one-hundred-percent, honest-to-God, actual murderer. I feel much less freaked out now. Thanks for that."

"You're missing the point. I didn't kill Harmony and Kevin. I have my life back. I don't have to lie awake at night afraid I'm going to strangle someone in my sleep."

"I thought I convinced you it didn't make sense for you to be the killer."

"You convinced me I wasn't necessarily the best suspect. But now, I know. This is good news. I don't want to fight about it. I want you to be happy for me."

"I already knew you weren't a murderer, so this isn't news at all." The anger on his face melted into sympathy. "But I can be happy you got the peace of mind you wanted."

"Thank you."

"What else?"

"What do you mean?"

He pointed at my mouth. "You're making your thinking face."

I didn't know whether it was a good thing or bad that he seemed to know me so well already. "Jackson's awake," I said.

His smile turned stiff. "Did you guys work things out?"

"Not exactly. I mean, I made it clear to him that he and I are over, but I'm not sure he accepted it."

"How do you feel about that?"

"Terrible. I've known him since forever. I hate the idea of us not being on the same page. I don't want to hurt him. Even though we're broken up, it feels wrong that I've been thinking about someone else."

"You better mean me."

I laughed, a full laugh that pushed yet another block of my scattered life back into place. "Yes, you."

He leaned back in his seat and examined my face. "Tell me about him."

"You don't want to hear about Jackson. That would be weird."

"Yeah. But it'll be weirder if you're thinking about him every time we hang out. You clearly need to talk about him if you're going to move on. And it's in my best interest that you move on. So tell me about him."

I paused to sort my thoughts, put them into neat little piles that made some kind of sense. "I love him, but I'm not in love with him. All the greatest memories I have—he's in them. The first time I rode a bike. My first kiss. My sweet-sixteen birthday party. *All* my first days of school. I don't know how to separate him from my life. I don't *want* to separate him. He knows what I'm thinking before I say it—sometimes even before I think it."

"So why aren't you in love with him?"

"How could I be?" I pictured him opening up his arm, just to watch it stitch back together again, and I shuddered. I could barely live with my own arm. The thought of living with Jackson and his gleeful adoration of his metal parts—I didn't see how that could happen. "They ruined him and he loves it. We're opposites."

"You mean the artificial intelligence?"

I nodded.

"Exactly what do you hate about it?"

"It's unnatural. It—"

Hunter held up one hand to cut me off. "Forget everything Philip Pollock has ever said for a second. What do *you* hate about artificial intelligence?"

I hesitated long enough to sort out my thoughts. I'd never taken the time separate my opinions from Pollock's. There had been no reason to. "It scares me," I said, after a while. "I want to feel like I have a special place in the world, as a human being. But if my brain can be duplicated by a machine, if *I* can be duplicated, maybe I'm not special. Maybe I'm nothing more than neurons firing."

"Hmm," was all he said, gaze focused on the windshield in front of us.

"What's that mean?" Now that I'd bared my soul, I expected more than a one-syllable response.

"They're just pretending, you know."

I said nothing.

"Everything artificial intelligence does," he continued, "it's been programmed to do it. It's been programmed to learn. Sure, the programming is more complex, but at the end of the day, it's not real thought. Can't you decide that you're special because you *are*, and refuse to let the existence of a machine that pretends to be intelligent change that?"

At this point, I had little choice. "I'll try."

"Okay, then back to Jackson. You broke up with him before the accident, so I assume his upgrades aren't your only problem."

"We want different things. He looks at his parents and my parents, and he thinks their lives are perfect. He wants me to go to an Ivy League school and then take over CyberCorp, have three kids, and live in a house with a white picket fence."

"You don't want that?"

"I don't know what my future looks like, but I know I don't want it mapped out for me. I want adventure, and I damn sure don't want to run CyberCorp. The whole world is an unknown, and I plan to see every bit of it."

I pulled the car into his driveway. But before he could reach for the door to get out, I grabbed the collar of his shirt and pulled his face toward mine.

Our lips met softly at first—a touch and release. It ended too quickly. He closed the space between our mouths again and, this time, covered my lips with his. We sank deeper into each other. The pressure of his lips was warm and soft. They moved against mine as if we fit together, belonged together.

When he pulled away, I struggled to catch my breath. He'd torn all of mine away. For once, when my head spun, it wasn't because of pain.

"I'll see you tomorrow," he whispered.

And when I crawled into bed later that night, my head barely hurt at all. I looked forward to getting a good night's rest for the first time in almost a week.

27

I awoke disoriented, a familiar sensation by now, followed by a feeling of dread. I wasn't where I was supposed to be—in my room, tangled in lavender sheets. My eyes adjusted to the darkness as I spun a slow circle.

The bed pushed against the far wall told me this was a bedroom. Judging from the size of the room, it was a rich house, but not mine.

I didn't have a window on that side of the room, and the closet and dresser were in the wrong spots.

The longer I examined the place, the more that pile of blankets on the bed looked less like blankets and more like a sleeping person.

Definitely not my room.

I crept toward the bed. Left foot, right, left . . . right. The floor creaked and I froze, waiting for the person to wake and move. No movement. After a couple more steps, I stood over a girl.

Dark hair flowed around the pillow, framing a pale face with huge eyes, wide open. The lips hung apart in a silent scream.

Instinctively, I reached for her. My metal fingers shoved her shoulder, as if that might wake her. I gripped her shoulder and shook, and her head rolled to one side like a broken doll. She remained motionless, unblinking, staring at everything and seeing nothing.

Debbie Carlyle was dead.

And I'd killed her.

All the air must have been sucked from the room, because I couldn't breathe. Hot saliva filled my mouth, bringing with it the taste of my dinner.

I stumbled away from the bed and kept going until my back slammed against a wall. I pressed against it, wishing I could disappear into it and reappear somewhere else, or not reappear at all.

I wanted to fall to the floor and sob until morning came, sob until they found me, sob until my eyes stung and my lungs burst and they dragged me away to prison and stuck a needle in my arm. Because I should be dead.

If I had done this, I should be dead too.

But a small voice in my head yelled at me to move. Move. *Move.*

The wall I'd fallen into turned out to be the bedroom door. I pressed my ear against it and listened for noises on the other side. Nothing. Apparently, I hadn't tripped any alarms on the way in.

In the hallway, a railing hung over a two-story foyer. It was as dark out here as it was in the bedroom. Lucky for me, the house remained deadly quiet. No one came to check on Debbie—which meant I'd managed to kill her without letting her scream.

I should have felt grateful that the police weren't here, and that Debbie's mom wasn't in the hall trying to protect her child. Instead, I felt horrible. I had snuffed out her life so quickly, so quietly, that she hadn't made a sound.

Melody was right.

I was a monster.

As I tiptoed down the stairs, I kept my weight to one side, where the steps would be strongest and less likely to creak. I arrived at the bottom without incident.

A security panel hung on the wall beside the front door. The lit screen displayed the word *DEACTIVATED* in red letters. I would have bet it was activated when the Carlyles went to sleep earlier tonight.

Under the red word, a rectangular area brightened into a keypad. The numbers glowed, so I knew they weren't really there. They were virtual. I was seeing things on the EyeNet again. While I watched, six of the numbers turned from white to red in sequence: *9-4-2-1-7-1*. I rubbed my eyes, and the number sequence repeated: *9-4-2-1-7-1*.

I typed the numbers. The security panel flashed bright blue and emitted a high-pitched beep. The sound startled something deep within my chest, and I fought to keep myself from screaming in surprise. Still, the house remained eerily still.

The screen on the security panel switched from *DEAC-TIVATED* to *ACTIVATED. ARMED. EXIT NOW.*

Obediently, I opened the door, stepped through, and

pulled it shut behind me. My hands trembled, then my arms, and my entire body. Silent sobs ripped through me, and my body went limp on the doorstep. The hard ground caught me, and I curled into a ball.

The small voice was still telling me to run, but I couldn't. They would find me here, and I deserved to be found.

When I squeezed my eyes shut, Debbie lay behind my eyelids, face pale and dead, eyes wide in terror. She'd seen me. What had she thought in those final seconds, being strangled by someone she knew?

I opened my eyes in time to see a figure run toward me across the lawn. It was too dark, my head too cloudy, my vision too blurry through tears to make out the face.

Rough hands yanked me to my feet and dragged me toward a nearby car. I didn't struggle. I deserved anything that happened to me.

I was inside the car before I realized it was Jackson.

The car's digital display spread a dim light through the interior. Jackson stared at me, eyes full of mixed confusion and concern.

I swallowed my sobs and fought for control of the moment. "Let's go," I hissed at him.

"What happened? You're a mess."

"Drive!" I shouted. Tears streamed down my face, and I sucked in huge gulps of air. "Please."

He pulled the car away from the curb. Debbie and I lived in the same neighborhood, but Jackson took an indirect route around the outskirts of the subdivision.

"Explain," he said after he'd been driving for a few minutes and I stopped whimpering.

"I don't know how." My voice came out as a hoarse whisper.

"Try."

I couldn't just tell him that *I killed Debbie Carlyle*. I didn't plan this. I didn't want this.

"What were you doing in there?" he asked.

I closed my eyes and tried to blot out the memories. But all I saw was Debbie lying there, eyes wide, mouth open.

"Lena?"

I knew I was supposed to respond, supposed to explain what I was doing there—or make up a lie. But fog filled my head. None of my thoughts settled long enough for me to voice them.

Debbie lying dead. Adam supporting the murderer. Jackson sitting beside me. Hunter would be so disappointed in me—and I hated myself for even thinking of him right now. I needed to think about Debbie and her family. I had robbed them of a lifetime together.

"Lena!" Jackson grabbed my face and turned it toward him. "What's going on? What happened in there?"

"I've been sleepwalking ever since I got the new arm," I whispered.

"So see a therapist," he said. "What's that got to do with anything?"

"I'm trying to tell you. This is Debbie's house. Tonight, I was sleepwalking. I woke up in her room. I had . . . I had already . . ." I glanced down at my hands.

"Already what?" Frustration seeped into his voice.

"I strangled her."

He stiffened.

"I strangled her." Now that I'd said it, I couldn't unsay it.

"What are you talking about?"

"I strangled her. In my sleep."

"Stop saying that. People don't commit murder in their sleep."

I stared at him, blinking. I knew I was supposed to respond, but my mind whirred in slow motion. A sob tightened my chest, and the pain doubled me over. Tears flooded down my cheeks, salty where they fell across my lips.

Jackson shook me so hard my teeth clacked together. "Lena, listen to me. You didn't do this. You can't kill someone while sleepwalking."

My answer died in another fit of sobs. But I somehow willed myself to suck in deep, steadying breaths. In. Out. Speak. "Yes." I blew out a long stream of air. "They do. Homicidal somnam—somnambulism. I looked it up."

Jackson stared at me, eyes narrowed. "*When* did you look it up?"

"A few days ago. But I kept hoping it was someone else."

We sat in silence, both watching the wheel of the car turn on its own, thanks to auto-drive.

I managed to control my tears, and now my chest felt hollow. Empty. All the energy had been kicked out of me. Kicked out and stomped into a bloody pulp.

"It's a real thing," I said, when the silence between Jackson and me had stretched too far. "Killing in your sleep, I mean. But usually the killer and the victim live in the same house. Sleepwalkers don't break through security systems to find their victims. Their thinking isn't that complex."

My new arm had to be involved somehow. The chip in my head was still connected to the network, and it had told me how to bypass security. I wouldn't have been able to commit these murders without the help of my new hardware.

CyberCorp did this to me. CyberCorp turned me into a killer.

"Victims—as in more than one? Tell me you're not talking about Harmony and Kevin."

I gave a slow nod. "The nights they were murdered, I was sleepwalking, but I woke up nowhere near their homes. I didn't know for sure. I didn't want to believe it."

The car pulled into my driveway and stopped. For the first time, it occurred to me that I didn't know how Jackson had found me. "What were you doing at Debbie's?" I asked him.

"You weren't answering my calls, and it's Monday."

I was too numb to do anything except blink at him.

"I climb through your window on Monday. Always. But since we broke up, I wasn't sure. I parked my car a few houses over, like usual. And I was just standing outside your house like an idiot when you climbed out the window yourself."

"You followed me?"

"Of course." He said it so matter-of-factly, like following me was a normal thing to do. "Good thing too. We need to work this out."

"*We* don't have to do anything." My voice came out as barely a whisper. "Just me. I have to turn myself in." I didn't want to have this conversation anymore. I wanted to burrow under my covers and sleep, until I woke up tomorrow and discovered all of this was a nightmare. A figment of my imagination.

"Let's talk to your parents first. If the arm is bringing something out in your subconscious, they can figure out how to suppress it again, maybe even pay settlements to Harmony's, Kevin's, and Debbie's families in return for confidentiality agreements."

"Confidentiality? We're talking about murder, Jacks. We can't sweep this under the rug."

He went silent.

Jackson sounded so much like my parents right now. My top lip curled back in disgust, at myself and at him. Mostly at myself.

"I murdered three people." My voice cracked as I stated the full truth of it aloud for the first time. I licked my lips and continued. "And your solution is to throw money at it. I love you, but—"

"I love you too."

"Let me finish." I held up both hands. "I love you, but you and I want different things. I don't want to go to an Ivy League school, marry young, and have babies." My volume increased with each word. "I don't want to be a CyberCorp executive. I don't want any of this." Anger and frustration swelled in my chest.

"I'm sorry." I expected him to say more, but his jaw tightened, lips pressed tightly together. "That's not what you need right now. I'll shut up."

Silence permeated the car, and in the midst of it, Debbie's pale, dead face filled every corner of my mind.

"Keep talking," I whispered.

His mouth opened and then snapped shut, and then opened again. "I'm not sure what the right thing to say is."

"Anything." I let my head drop back against the seat and examined the clear glass of the car's ceiling. Above us, the sky expanded gray in all directions, lit up by the street-lights around us. "Just make noise."

Jackson inhaled a long breath. "Things are a mess right now. I know." He motioned toward my robotic arm. "Our lives have changed. And thanks to CyberCorp, we'll get through this after things settle down."

"*Thanks* to CyberCorp?" My voice burned with acid. I was wrong. Talking was not better than silence. "Thanks to CyberCorp for controlling my life since the day I was born? For ripping my arm off and making me a murderer?" By the time I finished, I was shouting. The words shredded my throat, still raw from crying.

"Calm down." His voice had that annoying soothing quality my mother had mastered.

"I don't want to be my mother," I hissed, more quietly. "That's not going to change when *things settle down*." I pushed all the derision I could muster into those last few words, before opening the car door and scram-bling out. "I don't know what I'm going to do yet, but *I* get to make that decision. Not you and definitely not CyberCorp."

I slammed the car door and stomped around the side of my house to my bedroom window.

Jackson's footsteps followed behind me, but I didn't turn around.

28

By morning, I had to accept I hadn't dreamed the whole thing. It was a nightmare—but real.

And I couldn't escape it. With every blink of my eyelids, there lay Debbie in the dark of my mind. Pale skin, eyes wide, mouth open. Her glaring eyes demanded justice, and I would give it to her—even if it meant a lifetime in jail or a needle in my arm.

My hands had strangled Debbie—and Harmony and Kevin—but maybe that wasn't entirely my fault. If my subconscious was affected by the AI in my chip and arm, I needed to get that fixed now, as in *right* now.

If there was a reason for this, I needed to know it. Debbie deserved that too. Right?

I called Ron.

"Hey, Lena."

"Did you figure out where that data in my head came from?"

"Sorry. Haven't had a chance yet."

He hadn't had a chance yet? Debbie was dead. I had strangled her. And Ron hadn't had a chance to do this one little thing.

I resisted the urge to throw my hand-screen against the wall. "It's really important, Ron. I'm in serious trouble, and I think it has to do with that data."

"The rollout is only—"

"I'm so fucking tired of hearing about the rollout," I snapped. "This is my life. And *other* people's lives."

"What are you talking about?"

Although I wanted to tell Ron the whole truth, I didn't trust him with this. We got along great, but we'd known each other for all of three weeks. I paused to get my tone back under control. "Please, Ron. It's urgent."

"You know I love working on your arm, but it's not up to me. Fisher isn't going to let me take any more time with you without a damn good reason."

"I wasn't exaggerating when I said my life is at stake. Please. Do this for me."

Seconds of silence passed before he spoke again. "Okay. I'll look at it today."

"Thank you. I'll call you later."

I couldn't go to school today. Everyone would know about Debbie's death, and the suspicious stares I'd gotten after Harmony's and Kevin's deaths would start anew. Only this time, I would know I deserved them.

Those whispers and glares wouldn't roll off my back. I couldn't ignore them, not when I had Debbie's blood on my hands.

Even though she hadn't bled when I strangled her, I imagined the red stain on my palms every time I looked at them. For the hundredth time, I rubbed them with soap and water until my right hand—the one that was still flesh—turned red and raw. My eyes stung with tears I couldn't fight. They rolled down my cheeks and clouded my vision.

I left the faucet running and dropped down on the closed toilet seat. Maybe I could stay here forever, with my head in my hands. Maybe I could undo all of it if I just sat here and never moved again.

My hand-screen vibrated on my bed. With a groan, I pushed myself to my feet, shut off the sink, and trudged out to grab it.

It displayed a message from my mother, who wanted me to come downstairs. I wiped the stray tears from my face and dragged myself down the steps. My body felt unreal, distant, like a car on auto-drive.

"In the kitchen, Lena," she called.

When I stepped into the room, I found my mother sitting with Detectives Garrett and Johnson. A teacup rested on the table in front of each of them.

I considered prostrating myself before all of them. I could confess what I'd done and beg them to help me figure out *why* I'd done it. But I restrained myself.

I doubted these police would believe my arm made me do it. I wasn't even sure I believed it.

Up until now, the arm had done only things I'd wanted to do. It reacted to my thoughts, my desires. I'd wanted to hurt Harmony that day in the lunchroom. As much as I tried to blame that on CyberCorp's artificial intelligence, I couldn't.

Now that I knew I'd killed three people, I kept telling myself the arm was a separate entity from me, but history proved otherwise. It did what I wanted it to do. And apparently, I wanted to stop the Model One rollout enough to kill three people.

"What's this?" I asked, instead of the confession I still itched to make. Not that it mattered. It had to be all over my face—written there in bold, block lettering: I'd killed Debbie Carlyle. That was how it went for murderers, right? It got stamped on their souls for everyone to see.

"The police have more questions for you." My mother said this with the same even tone she used when asking Marcy to cook steak for dinner.

An empty chair stood between the two detectives, but I opted to stand. I didn't want to get too relaxed, or I might end up blurting out something without thinking it through. "What questions?"

Detective Garrett glanced down at the empty chair and then back up at me. When I didn't sit, she said, "Your classmate Deborah Carlyle was murdered last night."

I froze and reminded myself to breathe. Breathing was normal; holding my breath was suspicious.

"You sure you don't want to sit? You don't look well."

"No. I'm . . . I'll be okay. Just tired."

The detectives exchanged a look I couldn't read.

"It's come to our attention that you were at Miss Carlyle's house last night," Detective Garrett said.

How did they know that? I started to deny it, but if the

police thought I was at Debbie's, they probably had evidence to back that up. "Yes. Me and my boyf—*ex*-boyfriend—took a drive last night and ended up near her house. It's right around the corner."

"We questioned Miss Carlyle's neighbors. One of them took down the license plate number of Jackson Watts's car. She said he and a young woman caused a commotion on the street, and she wanted the plate number just in case. I understand Mr. Watts is your boyfriend. Is that right?"

"Ex-boyfriend," I corrected.

"What were you arguing about?"

"You were at the Carlyles'?" My mother's grip tightened around her mug.

I waved her aside. Each question exacerbated the ever-present pain in my head, and I could deal with only one of them at a time. "He doesn't accept that we're broken up. He wants to get back together, and I want him to leave me alone." I'd always heard that the best lies are based on truth.

Detective Garrett continued without sparing a glance at my mother, who looked more agitated by the second. "The problem is, Miss Hayes, your mother was kind enough to give us access to your home's security records, thinking it would remove you from our suspect list. The security records show that you were here all night."

Of course, they did. My ID chip was on my nightstand.

"You understand how suspicious that looks, don't you?"

My mother stood and pushed her chair back from the table. "It's time for the two of you to go. I assume you have no warrant for Lena's arrest, or else you'd be executing it right now. So I want you out of my house."

"How is it," Garrett continued, "that you were simultaneously at home and outside the Carlyles' home?" She waited for an answer, but when no one gave it, she continued. "Someone manipulated your home's security system to make it look like you were home, to give you an alibi. Why would you need an alibi unless you were guilty of something?"

"I said *leave*." My mother's voice stayed even, still as the surface of a deep lake, with a world of monsters beneath it.

The detectives shoved their chairs back and moved toward the doorway.

To me, she added, "Don't say another word until we call our lawyers."

"We'll be back," Johnson said, "with a warrant."

He and his partner stepped into the foyer and out of my view. A moment later, the front door opened and then closed behind them.

"What were you doing at Debbie's last night without your chip?" my mother asked as soon as the cops were safely out of the house. "Do you have any idea how suspicious this looks?"

Not nearly as suspicious as it looked when I woke in Debbie's room over her dead body. But still pretty bad, I imagined.

I slumped into the nearest chair. My breathing—almost calm a moment ago—broke into short, deep pants. I'd managed to block Debbie's face from my mind for only a few minutes, but now she returned with full force. Still staring. Still accusing.

"I . . . I haven't kept my chip on me since I came home from the hospital." I pulled in a long breath. "It stays on my nightstand. No one can force me to carry it. It's unconstitutional, and I choose not to . . . I choose not to . . ." I'd given this chips-are-evil speech before, but now I couldn't recall how it went.

"Yes, yes, I know." My mother gave a half-shake of her head, but it suggested a full amount of annoyance. "But it's not socially acceptable not to have one. Don't you . . ." For the first time, she seemed to notice that I was on the verge of a panic attack. "Lena?"

"It's . . . invasion of my privacy . . . It's . . . Nobody can make me—"

"Lena, stop." She placed a hand on my back and rubbed in a slow circle. "Breathe, honey. What's going on?"

"Debbie . . . Debbie . . ."

Pale skin, eyes wide, mouth open.

"Don't say another word." Her hand stilled on my back. "I'm calling our lawyers and our public-relations people. We'll spend the day figuring this out. I'll call your school to let them know you're home sick, and your father to let him know we need him here today."

Before I could respond, she'd already touched her ear and opened her mouth to give instructions to her micro-comm. Her hand started rubbing my back again in long, slow circles.

I gathered my breath and managed a shout. "Marissa!"

She touched her ear again to put the device back on

standby and stared at me, brows raised. "We don't have time to waste here, Lena. Whatever's on your mind should be said to the lawyers. Not to me. I can be subpoenaed."

"I need to tell you. I need to tell someone *now*." I spit it all out. "I've been sleepwalking ever since I got the new arm. Last night, I woke up in Debbie's bedroom."

"Okay." She moved her hand from my back and dropped into the nearest kitchen chair. Her eyes closed for a few seconds and then reopened. "What are you saying?"

She knew exactly what I was saying, but she wasn't going to believe it unless I used the actual words. "I didn't plan to, but I killed Harmony, Kevin, and Debbie. In my sleep."

She dropped her face into her hands. When she looked up again, her eyes looked tired, and her face lacked its usual poise. "I'm going to call your dad, and the lawyers, and the PR people. And we need to get you to CyberCorp to reprogram your AI chip."

"Shouldn't we remove it altogether?"

She shook her head. "Unfortunately, that's not an option. We can't remove the chip now that it's embedded in your brain—at least, not without risking your life, and definitely not before you've healed properly from your other surgeries." She pressed her lips together. "Can I ask you some questions? Since I know the truth, it can't hurt for me to get a few more details."

I nodded.

"Did you touch anything while you were at the Carlyles?"

"No, not with my right hand anyway, and I don't think

the left would leave any evidence behind. No DNA, no fingerprints."

She nodded. "Why was Jackson there? He wasn't . . . helping you, was he?"

"God, no. He followed me."

"How much does he know?"

"Everything. I was a mess when he found me. I told him everything."

"How much do you trust him?"

If she had asked me that two months ago, I'd have told her I trusted him with my life. But things had changed since then. "I don't know. We broke up."

"Last night?"

"No, the night of the accident. He was there last night because I wasn't taking his calls."

"Is he upset enough to tell the police what he knows?"

I shrugged.

She chewed on her lower lip. "It's your word against his. Things will go easier if you take him back."

"I don't want to be with him anymore."

"You don't love him?"

"I don't want to be with him anymore." This time, I pushed more emphasis into each word.

"I see. You'd rather be in jail?"

"Yes."

"Yes?"

"Yes!" I jumped up from my chair. "I'd rather be in jail. You didn't see her, staring at me with those eyes. She saw me. Before she died, she watched me strangle her. And now she's gone and . . . and we're not just going to cover this up."

She raised both her hands and gestured for me to sit back down. "Breathe, Lena. Try to stay calm."

I did as she asked and sat back down—not at all calm, but making a decent show of it.

"Cover it up?" my mother asked. "It sounds so distasteful when you say it like that."

"Is that your plan though? Because I don't want that. Debbie deserves better."

"I haven't decided. Right now, I want to give our lawyers as much information as possible, so they're armed to handle the situation. We'll decide as a family what our next step is."

"The lawyers aren't part of our family."

She glared at me. "Now is not the time, Lena."

"Fine," I muttered. "You haven't asked me yet if I *wanted* to kill Debbie. Aren't you curious about whether I'm a premeditated killer? Do you even care, or is it more important that I don't tarnish your good name?"

"Do you think so little of me?" She brushed her fingers against my face. "I know who you are. You're a lot of things, but killer is not one of them."

Tears threatened to break the dam of my eyelids— desperate tears. Because I wished I had as much faith in myself as my mom did. Until last night, I would have agreed with her.

But waking over a dead body had changed everything.

29

By afternoon, my mother had doped me up on a sedative.

I still saw Debbie every time I closed my eyes. But it left only a dull ache in my stomach now—rather than a burning need to claw my belly open and spill my guts onto the floor just to have something else to think about.

Six lawyers filled the living room. They took up the couch, a few armchairs, and a couple spots on the floor. The stress of their questions wreaked havoc on my head, and no amount of pain medication and sedatives made the lawyers disappear.

I'd managed to find a spot on the last available armchair, where my mother had insisted I sit in case they had questions for me—and they had a lot of them.

I had never felt my blood pressure rising before, but I could feel it now. Tension increasing second by second, shoulders stiffening. Inside, a small voice grew louder and louder, urging me to escape this room, this house, this arm.

But I couldn't outrun what I'd done last night. Everywhere I looked, the image of Debbie's body ghosted over everything else. Inescapable.

And I didn't deserve to escape it. If she haunted me, it was no more than I deserved.

When I couldn't stand it a minute longer, I pushed to my feet and smoothed my clothing. Paper stopped rustling, phone calls paused, and every eye turned to me.

My mother was the one to speak. "Where are you going?"

I didn't have the heart to come back with a snappy remark—something about how I didn't need a horde of people watching over me. Unfortunately, last night had proved otherwise. I needed all the watchers I could get. But right now, I wanted my little sister. "Bathroom."

Thankfully, she didn't question me when I raced past the guest bathroom and up the stairs. Allie's door stood closed, which meant she was probably napping. I opened it and slipped inside.

Cocooned in pastel-pink blankets, my sister lay in her bed. Through the window, the sun cut a stripe of light across the darkened room and across Allie. Her face was turned toward the window, as if to soak up every ray. Her lips were parted in an unconscious half smile, and with each breath, her chest rose and fell. And of course, she was snoring loudly enough to rouse a hibernating bear.

I didn't want to wake her, and more than that, I didn't trust myself to touch her after last night. It was better that she was asleep, and I didn't have to explain any of this to her.

I slid to the floor and hugged my knees, my back against the inside of the door. Allie's snoring calmed me. Comfortable, predictable, safe. I closed my eyes and willed myself to relax. For a second—less than a second—it worked.

Then I slipped into silent sobs that quaked through my body.

I must have cried myself to sleep because when I opened my eyes again, the light in the room had shifted. I needed to get back downstairs before my mother sent the troops for me. After rubbing the sleep from my eyes, I pushed off the floor and to my feet.

My fingers left a streak of red on the carpet. I stooped and examined it. Dark and wet. Was that blood? I leaned closer and inhaled the earthy, acrid scent of it.

Definitely blood. Allie's?

Panic ripped through my gut, leaving a sickening, empty feeling in its wake.

The sun no longer fell across Allie's face. In the darkened room, I couldn't tell whether she was smiling anymore, whether she was moving, whether she was breathing. And for the first time, I realized she wasn't snoring.

With my heart pounding in triple time, I ran to Allie's bed. Maybe—*maybe*—I could live with having killed three of my classmates. Although it would shatter my soul every day to think of it, I might survive.

But if I had hurt Allie . . . if I had hurt my sister, I

couldn't live with that. I would not wake up every day for the rest of my life to a world where my sister didn't exist.

I'd rather not wake up at all.

Was this Debbie's justice? A life for a life. I had taken hers, and my sister would pay the price? I deserved no better, but Allie was innocent.

Not my sister. Anything else. Anyone else.

The trip to Allie's side took infinite time in only an instant. During it, nothing existed except the terror of what I would find.

I'd barely touched her when she sat bolt upright in bed and shoved me away. "What? Stop shaking me."

A dam broke inside me again. Tears flooded over my cheeks, and I did nothing to stop them.

Allie leaped to her feet on her bed, face level with mine. "Don't cry. Why? Don't cry." She petted my cheeks.

My emotions were bigger than me. I could no longer fit them inside. I'd killed three people, but Allie was okay. Allie was fine. And still, I'd killed three people. "You weren't snoring." Tears continued to drown my cheeks, unchecked.

"I woke up." After a pause, she added, "I don't snore." She pointed at my forehead. "Bleeding."

I touched my face where she'd pointed, and my fingertips came away red. One of my stitches had popped. Allie was not bleeding. I was.

I lifted her off the bed and cradled her against my body, burying my face in her hair. She smelled of strawberry-scented conditioner. I breathed deeply and tried to memorize the smell, memorize the sensation of her hair against my skin, memorize the feel of her in my arms.

Perhaps sensing that I was too overwhelmed to explain it to her, Allie said nothing, just allowed herself to be pressed against me. Eventually, I set her back in her bed. She stared up at me with solemn, huge brown eyes. I kissed her on the forehead and left the room.

Although I hadn't hurt Allie, I could no longer trust myself around her. And that meant I couldn't stay here. I had to leave.

In my bedroom, I cleaned the blood from my hands and face. Then I unzipped my school bag, turned it upside down, and shook it until all my books, papers, and pencils tumbled onto the floor. In the empty bag, I stuffed a change of clothes and my pain medication.

I shouldered the bag and headed to the stairs that would lead me back to the foyer. Careful not to make any noise, I tiptoed down the steps. Somehow, my mother heard me anyway.

"Lena, would you come back in here please? They have a few more questions."

If this morning's questioning had been any indication, her definition of *few* would be somewhere around a thousand. I scanned the foyer for a place to stuff my backpack until I could make an escape. Finding none, I ran back upstairs, tossed it in my room, and arrived back downstairs out of breath.

I'd set one foot into the living room, when the doorbell rang. I turned toward the door, but my mother's glare pinned me in place. She pointed to the chair I'd occupied earlier. Head down, I dragged myself to the seat.

The doorbell rang a second time. Marcy hurried from the kitchen and then out of my view as she entered the foyer. A moment later, she led Detectives Garrett and Johnson into the room.

My mother leaped to her feet and ran across the room toward the cops. Her tall heels skimmed over the hardwood floor. She stopped in front of the detectives and blocked them from the rest of the room.

"I believe we've given you enough of our time today," she said. "Lena will come to the station to make a statement when we're ready. Until then, we have nothing more to add."

"That's fine." Detective Johnson dangled a pair of handcuffs, and my chest constricted. "Because she has the right to remain silent." He sidestepped my mother and addressed his next words to me. "You're under arrest for the murders of Harmony Miller, Kevin Rodriguez, and Deborah Carlyle. You have the right to remain silent. Anything you say can and will be used against you . . ."

Johnson grabbed my left wrist and twisted it behind my back, just as I'd done to Harmony. He was still listing my rights, but it all fell to the background, like white noise. My heart rate quickened, and the sound of my pulse rushed past my ears. The pain in my head swelled.

My left forearm jerked loose and came down hard on Johnson's wrist. Metal slapped flesh and bone, and his shriek rang out through the room. He clutched his injured wrist in his other hand, his face twisted in agony.

Garrett reached for her sidearm, but I was already in motion toward her. My left arm grabbed her wrist and snapped it to the side. She shouted and went down.

Screaming filled my ears, and I turned toward it. My mother's mouth hung open mid-wail.

My father's lips moved, making a word over and over again, but I couldn't hear it through my mother's screams and the wail inside my head. From the shape of his mouth, it looked like my name.

Johnson managed to wrestle his sidearm from its holster and pointed it at me. Before he could fire, my mother jumped between us, palms stretched out toward him.

Johnson cursed and lowered his weapon.

I darted from the room.

"Move!" he shouted.

Behind me, my mother grunted, followed by a loud thud as something large hit the floor. A gunshot cut through all other sounds, like a canon.

"Lena, run!" my dad yelled after me.

Footsteps pounded behind me, but I didn't turn to look. The front door stood up ahead, but the detectives were too close. If they shot now, I'd be dead.

I veered to the left and into the kitchen. Something crashed to the floor as the detectives scrambled behind me. I reached the door to the outside, flung it open, and darted into the chilly winter air.

Detective Johnson caught up with me before I got my car door open. For the first time since I'd gotten the gorgeous vehicle, I regretted having to use a key to open it.

He grabbed my right arm. I twisted to face him, ducked low, and slammed the heel of my metal palm into his shin. He cursed as he fell to the ground, and I was in the car before Garrett reached us.

I had no idea where I was going.

A tiny voice in my head screamed at me to stop, to surrender. But it was too late. I had injured two detectives. If they'd had any doubt of my guilt before now, it had disappeared.

30

I pulled out of the driveway and barreled through the neighborhood at seventy miles per hour. My tires squealed around each corner.

One of my neighbors had a driveway that circled to the back of their house. I slowed enough to pull into it and out of view of the street. Less than thirty seconds later, a police siren blared past.

I hadn't intended to run. But my arm had already slammed Johnson's wrist before I realized I was resisting. Now, I had two choices: turn myself in, or figure out whether my AI had somehow caused my actions. If I turned myself in now, I might never know the whole truth.

I needed the truth for Debbie—and for myself.

After waiting another thirty seconds, I pulled back onto the street and navigated through the neighborhood to a main road. I considered slowing to a more reasonable speed, but decided against it.

My new car made a terrible getaway vehicle. Not only was it cherry red and required a key for entry, but it also looked like an antique next to the sleeker vehicles alongside me. I needed to get off the road.

The one thing I had going for me was that, unlike the newer vehicles, mine was made before the safety law requiring that all electric motors make artificial noise. The car coasted along the road in complete silence.

"Message Liv," I told my hand-screen, which had automatically connected to the car's audio system.

"Messaging Liv," it responded through the car speakers. "Speak your message."

"I'm in trouble. Meet me at McCauley Park. I need you."

The hand-screen beeped to confirm. A few seconds later, I received a reply from Liv, who confirmed she was on her way.

I arrived at the park and stopped in a parking space between two family-sized vehicles. If I got lucky, any police car speeding past the park's entrance wouldn't be able to see my compact car between the two much larger vehicles, despite how conspicuous my red beast of a vehicle was.

Just to be safe, though, I got out and sat behind a tree about a hundred feet from the lot.

While I waited, my hand-screen buzzed. I almost sent the call to voicemail. But if I did that, I would have been here alone with my thoughts of Debbie—staring at me, gaping at me. I almost dropped the device as I fumbled to accept the call.

"Hello."

"Miss Hayes, I'm sorry to bother you." It still felt surreal to hear Philip Pollock's voice directed at me after years of listening to his audio programs.

"No. It's no problem at all."

"Actually, there is a problem. It's my understanding you called the police to report my brother's so-called confession. And according to the camera footage of my private home, you did so after trespassing on my property."

I didn't know how to respond to that, so I said nothing.

"As you know, my family enjoys a high level of respect in the community. It's not my intention to discourage you from reporting crimes in general, but in this case, I feel your doing so was . . . imprudent. As I told you, our security system is flawless."

"Look," I said. "I'm sorry about that. I thought it was a confession, and I ran with it—because what innocent man approves of murder?"

"A man who refuses to take his medication unless he's physically restrained. A man who was moved by *your* implication that the murders would garner public attention for an anti-technology point of view."

"But he's always ranting about how the ungodly can't be allowed to live, and about how the spawn of CyberCorp have to die. He came to my house and tried to kill me!"

"The *ungodly* and the *spawn* are not children, Miss Hayes. They're the Model Ones. Those emotionless androids are CyberCorp's spawn, and they were at your house on the day my brother showed up."

My mouth dropped open. That was why Adam hadn't killed me when I was on the ground that night. He hadn't been after me at all. Shame coursed through my gut. I could add Adam Pollock to the growing list of people I had wronged.

"I'm sorry," I whispered. "I shouldn't have shown up at your house like that."

"That's one thing we can agree on. Do not contact me or my brother again." The call ended.

I closed the hand-screen too hard and the metal bent in my left hand. I silently cursed at myself. I'd been so determined to find an alternate suspect that I'd convinced a sick man to support murder. Two months ago, I would have called myself a good person, but now, each moment that passed made me less and less sure of that.

The first bit of luck I'd gotten in months showed up when Liv pulled into the parking lot a moment later. My bent hand-screen buzzed in my lap. Luckily, I could still read the caller ID. It was Liv.

I jogged over to her. She touched her ear as I approached, ending the call. She climbed back into the driver's seat, and I jumped in on the passenger side.

"What's going on?" she asked.

"Drive—anywhere. I want to get as far away from my car as possible." I wanted to get as far away from my *life* as possible, but far away from my car would have to do for now.

She gave me a questioning look but started the motor anyway. "You got it."

Except for occasional concerned glances, Liv left me in peace for the next ten minutes while she drove around town. I spent the time trying to push Debbie's face from my head, and trying to decide how much to tell Liv.

She was bound to hear it eventually, now that a warrant had been issued for my arrest. The least I could do was let her hear it from me. Still, I was in no hurry to do the deed, so I stalled. I stared out the window and pretended not to see Liv's curious glances.

My hand-screen buzzed, and I checked the display. Two messages. Another message from Jackson. I couldn't deal with him right now. I had a more urgent crisis.

I also had an older message from my mother. It had arrived a few minutes ago, but I must not have heard it come in. *"Call me,"* the message said. *"Let us handle this."*

My fingers hovered over the screen. I wanted to thank my mom for the way she'd stood between me and a bullet. But if I called her now, she would take back control of the situation, and so far, that had gotten me nowhere good.

I deleted both messages and stuffed the hand-screen back in my pocket.

"The police are calling me." Liv gestured toward her ear, where she wore her micro-comm. She gave me a pointed look and accepted the call. "Hello." Her eyes narrowed as she listened to whatever was being said. "No, I haven't seen her. Lena would never . . ." She stole a glance at me. "Sorry. I don't know where she is. I'll let you know if I hear from her."

She touched her ear to end the call.

"What did they say?"

"I assume you know you're wanted for the murders?"

I stared down at my hands, which lay twisted together in my lap.

"What the hell is going on? You're not some killer who picks innocent victims to make a point."

Except maybe I was.

"You should turn yourself in. They can't prove you did this because you *didn't*."

I opened my mouth to tell Liv everything. She'd stuck by me through tough times lately, and I owed her the truth. "Liv, I . . ." She wouldn't turn me in. And maybe that was the problem. She could be charged with accessory after the fact or obstruction of justice—or something—for keeping her mouth shut. If I told her the truth, she would be guilty of helping someone she knew was a murderer. "I can't stay with you," I said instead.

"What are you talking about?"

"They're going to look for me with you. At your house, wherever you go. They can track you." I pointed to the wrist that held her ID chip. "They're going to assume I'm with you, and they'll find me. And if they find me before I figure this out, I'll always think that I . . ."

Debbie's face squeezed its way back into my thoughts. Pale skin, wide eyes, open mouth.

"I need a little more time," I finished. "That's all."

"What about Hunter? You met him only a few weeks ago. They won't expect you to be with him."

"Fine," I said. "I guess we have a plan."

31

As if in a spy movie, Liv took a long route to Hunter's house. Along the way, she glanced in her rearview mirror almost every minute to make sure no one was following. Despite the somber situation, I almost laughed when she stopped for a yellow light, and then raced through the intersection when it turned red.

"What?" Her jaw stayed locked with firm concentration. "If someone was following us, I wanted them to get stuck at the light."

"Why would anyone follow us?"

"Because . . . Okay, I guess if the police found us, they'd just arrest you." Her face broke into an embarrassed smile. "Give me a break. My life's never this exciting."

My mood went solemn again. "And let's hope it never is again."

Liv continued checking her mirrors, but at least she dispensed with the spy tactics.

A few minutes later, Hunter met me at his front door, waved to Liv, and ushered me up to his room.

His bedroom was exactly what I would have expected. Shades of blue and yellow filled the room. Yellow pillows topped a blue bedspread. In one corner, a wooden desk had been painted cobalt and gold in what I guessed, from the dried paint droplets, had been a do-it-yourself project. The carpet held rows and rows of a concentric-squares pattern in numerous shades of blue.

Just like Hunter, the room was full of life and hope, with just a touch of not giving a damn. The best thing about it was that it smelled like him, a mix of mint and springtime soap. I wanted to curl into a ball, forget everything outside these walls, and stay here forever.

He sat on the bed and tapped the space beside him. "How are you?"

I slumped down next to him. "Couldn't be better." I wanted to make a joke to lighten the mood, but all my usual quick words skittered away from me. At least, I didn't have to explain why I was here. Liv had done that when she called him to set this up.

Hunter draped an arm around me and squeezed. Instinctively, I laid my head on his shoulder.

"You going to tell me what's going on?" he asked.

"Liv told you everything."

"Did she?"

"What's that supposed to mean?" I dropped my gaze to the array of blues on the carpet.

"You haven't looked me in the eye since you walked in

this house. That's not the face of someone who's fresh out of secrets."

"I've had a long day. That's all." When I met his green eyes, I saw his skepticism. He knew when I was full of shit, and he was calling me on it. I raised a hand to stop him from contradicting me. "Okay, I'm lying."

I told him the whole story. Almost all of it—from waking up in Debbie's bedroom, to finding Jackson outside her house, to pummeling the detectives earlier today. I left out nothing but the look on Debbie's dead face as she stared up at me.

To Hunter's credit, he listened in complete silence.

"So I'm basically screwed," I finished.

"All this negativity." He swiped at the air with both hands, as if to remove my negative thoughts from it. "Let's do something." He jumped up from the bed and pulled me to my feet. "I've spent too much of my life sitting down, and I'm not going to do it right now."

"What are you thinking?"

"We go to CyberCorp, right now, and demand that Dr. Fisher or her assistants work on you. Even if they've heard about your arrest warrant, they wouldn't dare turn you in. They'd lose their jobs."

"It's seven at night. Their office is closed."

"The Model One rollout happens in three days. You think anyone there cares about normal business hours?"

With each word he spoke, a drop of my despair turned into nervous anticipation. "They're going to refuse to see me, or the police are going to catch us on the way there."

"You hate CyberCorp. That's the last place they'll expect you to go."

My head spun when I took a step toward the door, and Hunter caught me under my arm. "Whoa. You okay?"

"My head hurts a little."

"You need your meds." He patted down my jacket pockets. "Where are they?"

I stuffed both hands in my pockets, but came up empty. Then I remembered the bag I'd packed and hadn't had a chance to grab when the cops showed up. "Shit. I left them at home."

"Any chance the pain will go away on its own?"

I shook my head. "It's just going to get worse." Within an hour, it would get so bad that I would think my head might explode into teeny bits of brain and skull.

"They'll have some kind of painkillers at CyberCorp, right?"

"I'd have to get them straight from Dr. Fisher, since they're prescription meds, but she hasn't had time for me ever since she decided I was healthy enough for Ron and Simon to take over. We're not going to be able to drag her away from the Model Ones tonight. We have to stop by my house for the meds."

"Is that a good idea?"

"It's a terrible idea, but the alternative is to continue feeling like rats are chewing through my brain matter."

That brought a sympathetic smile to his face. "We don't want that."

"Maybe I should just turn myself in," I said.

"No way. We're going to CyberCorp."

"I should warn you. There may be nothing they can do for me. They can't shut down my AI without killing me or turning me into a vegetable—at least not yet."

Hunter held up a hand to stop me. "What's the alternative? You turn yourself in, and maybe—if you're lucky—you end up in prison or a mental institution for the rest of your life? No. Let's give it until tomorrow to think of something else. Something that doesn't involve you being locked up for crimes you may or may not have wanted to commit."

"Is there really a chance I didn't want to? The arm doesn't think for me. It just reacts to my thoughts."

"Maybe."

"Maybe?"

"But you—" He stopped when a shooting pain caused me to grip my head in both hands. "Maybe we should continue this when you're not hurting. We're going Cyber-Corp. We can get your meds from your doctor there."

"I think I'm going to . . ." My head pulsed. The pain hit me so hard that I couldn't finish the sentence.

Hunter grabbed my shoulders. "That's it. We're going."

"I'm going to—"

This time, the doorbell cut me off. Hunter and I both froze, and silence filled the room. The only sound was the rhythmic pulsing of my head.

Hunter peeked out the window. "It's some boy. Tall, dark hair. I don't know him."

"Lena!" a familiar voice shouted from outside. "I know you're in there."

"Jackson," I murmured.

"Your ex?"

I should have taken his calls. I couldn't deal with this right now, not when my head felt like it would split in two —on top of everything else.

"Lena!" Jackson called again.

I tried to move to the window, but the ache in my skull rose anew. The world tilted toward me, rocked beneath my feet. Hunter caught me and kept me from falling over. He led me back to the bed and sat me down.

I slapped his hands away. "Get out of here!" I shouted.

The noise of my words exploded through my brain, and I screamed. He reached for me again, and I slapped at him a second time.

"Go." I strained to get the words out as the room blurred around me. The pain was too much. "I'm going to pass out." Horrible things happened when I slept, and I didn't want them happening to Hunter.

"Should I call Dr. Fisher?" His voice sounded far away, but I still felt him hovering nearby. "What should I do?"

"Run."

32

A SHOUT WOKE ME FROM UNCONSCIOUSNESS. I HELD A knife in my left hand in a dark room. I loosened my grip, and it clattered to the floor. I squeezed my eyes shut. I didn't want to see. I didn't want to know. But I'd seen enough in that brief moment, even in the darkness.

I was in someone's kitchen—with a knife.

I couldn't stand here all night with my eyes closed. There could be someone here who needed help—someone I'd stabbed. More than anything, I wanted to crawl back into the dark nothingness of sleep, but that was a dangerous place for me.

It was dangerous for everyone, as I'd proven three times already.

"Lena?" Hunter's voice interrupted my swirl of thoughts.

My eyes popped open. Only a few feet in front of me, he sat on the ground, breathless and red-faced. The ripped shoulder of his shirt fell around his upper arm. A bright-red mark marred his right cheekbone. It had already begun to swell. Worst of all, he cradled his right arm to his chest, and blood flowed from a large gash in it. The knife lay on the ground between us.

"Oh, my God. Did I . . ." I pointed at his bleeding wound.

"I tried to stop you from leaving." He grabbed the knife and pushed himself to his feet. "Let's just say that didn't go well. We need to do something about this. *Now.*"

The kitchen table seemed so far away. I wobbled toward it, but my legs collapsed under me. Hunter grabbed me around the waist and led me to a chair.

"Rest for a second."

"I shouldn't sit down . . . My head still . . ." But I sat anyway. My body became heavier by the second. My head dipped low.

"I'll be right back." He padded away on bare feet. "Do *not* fall asleep again," he shouted over his shoulder.

Aloud, I counted upward by threes to keep myself conscious. "Three, six, nine, twelve . . ." The pounding in my head hadn't lessened much during my little nap. "Sixty, sixty-three, sixty-six . . ."

He came back with a gray hooded sweatshirt. He set the knife down on the counter to pull the sweatshirt over my head and flip the hood up. "Let's go."

I couldn't stay awake through this pain. I willed my body to stand and move toward the door. But the fog in my head was expanding, blocking out the kitchen. Blocking out Hunter. Blocking out . . . everything.

Hunter stared at me, eyes wide and pleading. "Lena. Lena, look at me. I need you to stay awake."

Focus. I couldn't focus. Pain seared inside my forehead. A small voice in my head screamed at me to *stay awake*. It was important, but my mind was too cloudy to remember why. My eyelids were too heavy.

No. No. *No.*

Hunter was shouting, his voice loud and high-pitched. The sound pierced my eardrums and drilled into my skull.

Glass shattered somewhere in the next room. An instant later, Jackson barreled into the kitchen. He didn't slow and hit me hard in the chest. Air burst from my lungs, and my back screamed in agony as Jackson took me down to the floor.

<hr>

I woke up screaming. The left side of my face felt like it had been hit with a bat, and my back was little better. But worse were the dreams.

I'd dreamed I killed Hunter and Jackson. I'd beaten them to death with my arm, hit them over and over again until their faces looked like twisted bits of flesh.

"Lena, Lena, shh." At the sound of Jackson's voice, I jerked my face toward him and tried to focus on my surroundings.

My head felt clearer. I sat on the floor of Jackson's car, in the empty space between the two rows of seats, slumped against the side of the vehicle. Jackson occupied the driver's seat, rotated to face me, while Hunter sat in the backseat.

I grimaced at Hunter's face. It didn't look quite as bad as Adam Pollock's, but the right side was bright red with a scary looking cut across the chin. Rags were wrapped around his right forearm and left leg, and blood seeped through in both places.

I tried to reach for him, but cringed as rough fibers rubbed against my wrist behind my back. "You tied my hands?"

"You have a bionic arm," Hunter said dryly. "We were protecting ourselves."

"It won't hold me," I said.

"Maybe not, but it'll slow you down if you lose it again."

"Probably a good idea."

Jackson sat with his arms folded across his chest, his expression grim. Unlike Hunter, Jackson looked pristine, which made sense given his newfound invincibility—in his own words. "I gave you some of my pain meds. Does your head feel better?"

"Much. Thank you. It's nice to not feel like my brain is trying to leap from my skull." I turned back to Hunter. "I'm so sorry. I couldn't stop myself."

"It's not your fault. You—"

Jackson cut him off. "We're on our way to CyberCorp. I called ahead and told them you attacked Hunter, that you've been violent ever since you got the arm, and that we think it's their technology's fault. Simon said he'll see you. We're going to get this fixed." He pointed at the side of my face. "Does that hurt?"

I raised my shoulder toward my jaw to test its tenderness, but Jackson grabbed my bicep to stop me.

"That's just going to make it worse," he said. "Sorry about that, by the way."

"You hit me?"

"Twice, but not hard. I heard him shouting from outside. It was either that"—he pointed at my face—"or let you kill him." He glared across the vehicle at Hunter, and by the look on Jackson's face, I suspected he was having second thoughts about his choice.

"Thank you?"

"Any time, babe." He laughed. "I guess my upgrades came in handy, huh?"

I ignored the question.

"No thanks from you?" he asked, raising a brow at Hunter.

Hunter mumbled something unintelligible that could have been a thanks.

"No problem, man," Jackson said, his voice much louder and smugger than necessary. "I did it for Lena. She wouldn't be able to live with herself if she hurt anyone else, and she doesn't deserve that." More quietly, he added, "She's a good person."

The words hung in the air too long, buoyed by their wrongness.

"How did you know I'd be at Hunter's?" I asked, just to fill up the space with something else. Anything else.

"You weren't home or answering your phone, and I was worried." Jackson's tone held a note of accusation. "I called Olivia, and she was super cagey. Then I called Claire. She said you won't return *her* calls either. She also said you seemed pretty chummy with this new guy and I should check him out." He gestured toward Hunter. "So here we are."

"I needed space."

"And look where that got us." He pointed at the right side of Hunter's face, which was still an angry shade of red.

"I was handling it," Hunter growled.

"Really?" Jackson pointedly scanned Hunter's injuries, an edge of his mouth pulling upward.

Hunter jumped up so quickly he banged his head against the ceiling. I shot him a pleading look, and he settled back in his seat, glaring across at Jackson.

When we arrived at CyberCorp, Dr. Fisher, Ron, and Simon met us at the driveway roundabout. They were my last hope to undo whatever was happening to me.

33

FISHER AND HER ASSISTANTS USHERED THE THREE OF US upstairs to a large room. A vid-screen covered one wall, and small piles of parts were scattered over the floor. An unidentifiable device sat in the middle of the room, its wires and circuit boards exposed.

Simon moved the device to a corner and dragged a chair into its old spot. Fisher untied my hands and cut off my shirt sleeve over the robotic arm, while Ron plugged me up to the nearest hand-screen.

My data flooded the hand-screen as well as the huge vid-screen on the wall. Having my arm's code scroll across the giant display felt a little like being flayed open for the world to view my insides. Instinctively, I crossed my arms over my chest to cover myself.

Simon escorted Hunter and Jackson from the room. When he returned a moment later without them, I raised a questioning brow.

"One of our colleagues is patching up Hunter's wounds and checking Jackson for injuries," Simon said. "They'll be back."

Ron poked and prodded my arm, checking and rechecking the joints and the connection to my shoulder. I cringed as he moved down to my spine. Now that my last dose of pain meds was dwindling, my back felt the result of that impact with the floor after Jackson hit me.

Dr. Fisher examined the odd lines of data Ron and Simon had discovered the day before.

"Where the hell did all this come from?" she asked. "The arm's been up and running for only a few weeks. This has to be a year's worth of data."

"Can't you read it?" I flinched as Ron touched my back again.

"Of course, we can read it," Fisher snapped. "But there's just so *much* of it."

"I noticed." I screeched as Ron prodded the base of my neck, near where the chip was embedded.

"Okay, okay," he said. "I'm done. All the connections look okay from the outside."

"We can't be sure unless we open her up though," Simon said to him, "and we may need to do that anyway if she's having a problem with impulse control. We'd need to troubleshoot the hardware."

I was definitely having a problem with impulse control. "Do it. I've got nothing left to lose."

"You have your life to lose," Ron said. "The chip is in your brain, and now it's adapted. We take a risk every time we tamper with it."

I looked to Simon, who shrugged. I guessed that meant he agreed.

"I can't go around attacking people all the time. Rip the thing out, and I'll take my chances." If I died, then at least Harmony and Kevin and Debbie would have some company.

"Let's leave that as a last resort," Fisher said, gaze still locked on the data displayed on the oversized vid-screen.

"It looks like the chip received some files every night over the past week or so." Simon pointed at a collection of file names scattered throughout the data. "You mind if I look at these?"

"Help yourself." Fisher touched something on the hand-screen. The larger display split into two halves, both showing the same information.

Fisher took control of the left-hand side, continuing to scroll through the data. Simon approached the right side of the giant screen and touched one of the file names.

A video filled the right side of the display. I gasped as the images played. It was a series of three-second clips, each one displaying someone strangling someone else. A man choking a woman on the ground in a dark alley. A man pressing a smaller person against the wall, hands clenched around his neck. Clip after clip of strangulations.

Fisher's side of the screen stopped scrolling, and she stared open-mouthed at the gruesome images. "What the . . ."

Simon shut down the video and touched a different file name. Half of the display filled with images of headline after headline proclaiming that some murder or other had gone unsolved. The next video he selected contained clips of anti-tech speeches, including audio:

"Another small business closed its doors today, thanks to CyberCorp . . ."

"It is inevitable that artificial intelligence, if allowed to grow unchecked, will displace humanity . . ."

"Human interaction has decreased four percent over the past year . . ."

"Oh my God," I said. "This is what you've been feeding my head while I sleep? Is this why I ki—" I started to say *killed three people*, but then realized I hadn't told them that yet. "Is this why I've been so violent?"

"We're not feeding you anything," Simon said. "I have no idea where this came from, but it would definitely increase your level of aggression—especially toward Cyber-Corp personnel."

"The goddamn network," Fisher muttered. "The chip must have received all of this over the EyeNet."

"But Ron and Simon turned off my network connection."

"No." She waved a dismissive hand. "We can't turn it off without modifying the chip. They just disabled the output to your eyes. You've been networked the whole time, and that's where this data came from."

"Who sent it?"

"Hell if I know." She sounded as dumbfounded as I felt. "You can't just *send* data over the EyeNet. There are security protocols. Only approved providers can upload data, and all their data is tagged with provider identifiers."

"There are no tags here," Simon added.

"Yes," Fisher said, irritation coating the word, "which means it didn't come from an approved provider. It came from a hacker, and it would cost a fortune to assemble a machine that could hack the EyeNet."

"This explains why your headaches are still bad," Simon said. "Ever since you started receiving this data, your subconscious has been fighting against your programming." He placed a hand on my shoulder. "Any aggression you've been acting on isn't your fault. The data forced you. You tried to fight it off, but you couldn't."

I shook his arm off. "This doesn't prove anything except that I was influenced, but my actions are still my own." I looked to Fisher for confirmation. "Aren't they?"

Dr. Fisher's mouth twisted to the side while she considered this. "Ron, grab me a Model Two prototype, would you?"

He didn't move an inch. "What are you going to do?"

"Just get the damn robot."

Ron hesitated long enough that I thought he might object. Instead, he trudged from the room. In his absence, Fisher went back to muttering under her breath as she read my lines of data. Simon joined her and did the same, without the muttering.

A few minutes later, Ron returned. A fully functional Model Two glided into the room behind him, its metal feet graceful despite their weight. It stopped in front of Fisher and Simon.

"Identify yourself," Dr. Fisher said.

"Android M2A12," it said. Its lips moved just like a human's, shaping each word. The effect was surreal. For a split second, I forgot it was a machine, and that just made me hate the thing more.

"Grab a chair, A12, and have a seat."

The android dragged a chair from the back of the room and sat. Again, it was hard for me not to marvel at how much my arm looked like the Model Two's, and I didn't appreciate the likeness.

Ron's gaze darted back and forth between the Model Two and the door. Without instruction from Dr. Fisher, Simon connected the android to another hand-screen. He seemed to have caught on to what she had in mind, or at least, he was humoring her.

"What are you doing?" I asked him.

"Your hardware comes almost entirely from a Model Two," Simon answered. "Your arm, your chip, and the connection between them—they're all based on the same design. You're even using a modified version of the Model Two software, with your main program calling the same set of functions. The difference is that your brain plays a role in determining when the functions are called, while the android brain is entirely artificial."

I understood most of that, but I nodded and pretended I understood every word.

"Basically," he continued, "we're substituting A12's learned data with your data to see how he reacts to it."

"If he doesn't turn into a violent anti-tech enthusiast," Fisher said, "then we have to assume you are to blame for your own actions. But if he behaves similarly to you, when given the same data, it's most likely the common AI that's becoming violent and controlling you through the chip in your head."

On the left side of the giant vid-screen, a dialog box popped up with the words *UPDATING DATA* and a progress bar beneath them. The lights in A12's eyes went out, leaving dull, dark-red orbs. The android's head slumped.

"This is going to take a few minutes," Simon said. "There's a lot of data he needs to learn."

Ron snatched the hand-screen from Simon. "This isn't a good idea." He touched the screen, and on the oversized vid-screen, the progress bar froze at sixty-two percent. The words *UPDATING DATA* changed to *REVERTING*, and the bar inched back in the other direction, toward zero.

Dr. Fisher crossed her arms over her chest. "What's the problem, Ron? We all have places we'd rather be. The sooner we try this, the sooner we can cross it off our list of options of things to try."

"I'm concerned about false positives," he said. "You know, when a test gives a positive result even though it shouldn't."

"We know what a false positive is," Dr. Fisher said. "Explain how it applies to this situation."

"If A12 goes crazy, we won't know if it's the data that's causing it, or if it's the result of a bad reaction between the data and his other programming. We never tested Lena's original code on a full Model Two, only on an isolated arm."

She snatched the hand-screen from him, and a moment later, the large vid-screen's display changed back to

UPDATING DATA. Ron's gaze locked on the hand-screen, and for a moment, I thought he might grab it back.

"You okay?" I asked him.

"Yeah," he muttered. "Perfect."

While the data updated on the Model Two, Fisher approached the large vid-screen. It still showed rows and rows of information. She crossed her arms over her chest, her foot tapping a steady rhythm as she contemplated it. I didn't understand a word, but that data controlled my arm —part of me.

Several minutes later, the vid-screen beeped, and android A12's posture straightened. Its head turned left to right as the android scanned the room. Metal eyelids clicked shut and then opened again, but the rest of its body remained motionless. My hopes plummeted to the floor.

The android leaped into motion. It barreled across the space between it and Dr. Fisher.

"Shut it down," she screamed as the thing struck with its left arm. The hand-screen fell from her fingers. The impact lifted her into the air and slammed her against the wall.

34

FISHER GROANED AND WENT LIMP.

Terror froze me in place. The android turned toward Simon. Without a second's hesitation, he spun and darted toward the door.

The android bounded after him, its steps more like giant leaps devouring the space between them. The hand-screen bounced across the floor after it, still attached by the cable.

I would have thought a humanoid made mostly of metal would be slow, but this Model Two proved me wrong.

It moved like a wild animal, quick and predatory and lethal. With a final leap, it grabbed Simon around the waist before the fleeing boy reached the door.

Simon went down face-first. His arms shot out to save him, but even from across the room, I heard his teeth clack together as he hit the floor.

Facedown, Simon threw his hands behind his head to block whatever was coming. I told my self-preservation to fuck off and ran to his aid.

But the android's reaction was faster. It grabbed him around the neck and squeezed. When Simon thrashed, trying to flip over to face the thing, the android slammed his head downward. Simon's face hit the floor again and again, leaving a red splotch against the gray surface.

I jumped on the android's back. That at least seemed to distract it from pulverizing Simon's face. Its arm reached behind it and locked onto my left shoulder. I screamed as metal fingers dug into flesh that was still healing, but I didn't let go.

A12 yanked me forward, like I was no more than a doll, and tossed me off its back. I skidded across the floor.

The hand-screen lay on the floor next to the android, still connected by a cable. Pain blossomed through my body as I stretched toward it.

My hopes soared when Ron sauntered over to the device. The android eyed him but didn't attack. Ron swiped up the hand-screen and casually tossed it to A12. The android crushed it as if it were nothing more than a paper cup. Broken metal pieces fell from its fingers and clattered to the floor.

"Ron," I shouted. "What the hell are you doing?"

"Continuing what I started."

"What you . . ." I was so baffled by his statement that I didn't know how to finish my question.

"This company doesn't deserve the power to decide

who lives and who dies." His words contained no hint of anger, just quiet resolve. He waved a quick goodbye and turned for the doorway.

There was no way he was leaving this room without explaining.

With a groan, I pushed off the ground. Dark blood dripped into my eyes. I wiped it away and dove toward Ron. We tumbled to the ground in the doorway, and I raised my left arm to pin him down. Pain ripped upward from the base of my neck. I clutched my head and screamed.

Over the past weeks, I'd thought my headaches were bad, but this reached a new level of pain—like a fire had started at the base of my skull, and it burned hotter by the second.

Ron tossed me off him. "Don't fight the programming."

Programming? What the hell was he talking about?

"You think I'd let my own weapon be used against me?"

"I'm not a weapon." I squeezed the words out through gritted teeth.

"Aren't you? I know three people who would disagree—except they're dead now."

The pain subsided, and with a grunt, I pushed myself to my feet. I lunged toward Ron again, but the pain came back like a bat to my skull.

"Stop fighting it, Lena!"

I let my body go slack, and the pain disappeared.

"See," Ron continued. "I'm not trying to hurt you. Believe it or not, I consider you a friend."

"You programmed me to kill three people, and you think that's not hurting me?" Despite the evidence in front of me, I refused to believe it. I needed to hear him say it. "Harmony. Kevin. Debbie. They did nothing to you." I gestured toward Simon without glancing at him—I couldn't stand to see him motionless on the floor. "Simon's your friend!"

"He's a colleague—one who works for the company that convinced my mother to get that surgery for her cancer. She would have died anyway—I know that. But my dad would have lived."

I could have sworn Ron's father was alive. "Your dad's dead?"

"Not yet, but soon. Cirrhosis caused by alcoholism. He started drinking when CyberCorp's so-called cure failed my mother. They should have left my mother to die. He had made his peace with it. Then your mom showed up, wearing her fancy suits and swearing up and down that she could save the day. She gave him hope. That's what made him turn to alcohol when she died anyway."

My body tensed up with each word, and I stood with hands fisted at my sides. "My classmates had nothing to do with that. *Harmony* had nothing to do with that."

"Her dad did. All of their parents. Miller designed the nanobots. Dr. Carlyle adapted them for medical use and implanted them in my mom. And Rodriguez—he's the worst of all of them. He sat at my mother's bedside with my dad and pitched the treatment, smiling and encouraging every step of the way. They needed to feel what I feel." Ron gestured toward Simon's and Fisher's still forms.

"Anyone else who works here is just as much to blame for supporting a company that cares about nothing but their bottom line."

"You killed three people—made *me* kill three people."

For a second, he looked regretful. "I didn't know you when I started this, or I might not have done it this way. When your folks brought you in for surgery, it was like a gift. It was perfect—using the daughter of the people who destroyed my family to destroy their company."

So I'd been nothing but a convenient pawn—right time, right place. He'd destroyed my life out of convenience. Without thinking, I lunged at Ron—and then screamed as agony tore through my skull.

"Temper. Temper." Ron clicked his tongue.

I didn't care if I died in the process. I was going to smash his face in.

I gritted my teeth and swung my left arm forward. Ron's eyes went wide, and he jerked to the side—but not fast enough. The two of us screamed in tandem as my fist clipped his cheek. I dropped and curled into a fetal position. My head burned. Ringing filled my ears and vibrated through my teeth.

"Bitch." Ron spat blood and tried to scramble to his feet.

Pushing through the fire in my head, I rolled on top of him. My knees pinned his hands to his sides. I felt him shift his weight, getting ready to heave me off. But I raised my metal hand, threatening.

He froze.

"I swear," I said, "if you move, I will break your face."

The pain had dissipated some, now that I wasn't actively attacking him, but I was prepared for it. I knew the cost of hitting him, and it would be *so* worth it.

Ron had caused all the trauma I'd been through after the accident. More than that, three murders rested as much on his shoulders as on mine.

His face screwed up, and for a second, I thought he would beg for my mercy. Instead, he laughed, so loud and full that his chest shook.

"What?" I growled down at him.

"You're just like them. How do you not see that?"

I should have smashed his skull already. I was a murderer. Why not add one more to my tally? "I'm like *who*?"

"Your parents."

I leaned down until our noses almost touched. "You really want to piss me off right now?"

"You're so high and mighty. Sitting on your high horse in judgment of everyone around you. But you need technology as much as the next guy. Your hand-screen? You couldn't get through a physical-therapy session without it. Useful, isn't it?"

I said nothing.

"You can't even deny it." Ron nodded toward my arm, still poised to strike down at him. "And you need that arm. You need it to keep on with life as usual. Most of all . . ." He laughed again. "You think I wouldn't have thrown you off me already if you weren't threatening me with it?"

I'd blamed my parents and CyberCorp for everything wrong with my life, because they'd attached this arm to me.

But the arm worked beautifully, just like my old one except for the bad data Ron had fed it. *Ron* was the problem. He'd used it to commit murder.

And now I was about to use it to kill him? How did that make me better?

I dropped the arm to my side and took a long breath to steady myself. "I'm not going to hit you. But you're going to jail."

Ron shot up and tipped me off him. Before I could stand, he was on his feet and standing in the doorway. I cursed and stepped after him, but a noise behind me caught my attention.

I turned to find Dr. Fisher wobbling to her feet. She looked unscathed, except for the vacant expression.

"Oh, thank God." Tears of relief swam in my lower eyelids. She was alive.

"Lena?" Fisher scanned the room until her gaze landed on Simon, still bloody and motionless. She let out a high wail and ran toward him.

Android A12 hadn't moved through my conversation with Ron, but now, its eyelids clicked as Fisher ran across its field of view. Its head rotated to follow her.

"Oh, this is the good part." Ron leaned against the doorframe and grinned—which could only be bad.

"Dr. Fisher!" I lunged toward the android.

A12 was faster. It darted toward her, its face expressionless, serene. I leaped before I reached it and pulled back my left arm. I put everything I had into the punch and struck A12 across the side of its jaw.

Metal crunched, and my fist left a dent in the android's

face. It turned toward me, eyes glaring red. My second swing hit the same spot, and the dent deepened. My metal fingers came away crushed together.

A12's arm rose, but mine was already moving toward its face again, and I couldn't stop the momentum. My fist clanged against the android's palm. A12 squeezed, and my metal hand crunched, fingers crumpled and pressed into the palm. I yanked free with a screech of metal and swung my mangled fist toward the thing's face again.

The android dodged and countered. Metal glanced across my face. It barely made contact, but the room spun, lit with bright white spots. I slumped to the ground. My shoulder hit the floor first, but that pain barely registered over the throbbing in my cheekbone.

While I groaned on the floor, A12 bounded after Dr. Fisher, who had almost made it to Ron and the door.

Jackson stepped around Ron and through the doorway, hands stuffed in his pockets. It took him only a second to spot Simon face down on the floor, me bleeding and crumpled, and Dr. Fisher fleeing toward him. He shoved Fisher behind him.

She careened directly into Ron, knocking them both to the floor.

The android slowed, and its gaze shifted from Fisher to Jackson, and back to Fisher. It didn't seem interested in Jackson, except for the fact that he stood between it and Fisher. Now that I thought about it, the android hadn't seemed interested in me either, until I tried to stop it from killing Simon and Fisher.

Its hand shot out and gripped Jackson around the wrist. It tugged, but Jackson's arm didn't move. He stood firm. When it came to arm strength, he had two arms on the same playing field as the Model Two's, where I had only one.

When I spared a glance for Dr. Fisher, she was *sitting* on Ron in the hall just outside the door. At least that was covered.

Jackson rolled his wrist from the android's grip and clasped his fingers around its arm. He twisted, and the sound of groaning, creaking metal filled the room.

A12 slammed its other hand into Jackson's face. He dodged, and the blow skimmed its target. Skin tore off Jackson's cheek, and metal shone through underneath. Jackson released the android's arm, which hung limp at its side, connected by wires now visible.

A small smirk played on Jackson's lips as the skin on his face knitted closed. The boy who loved technology—who had *become* technology—had found a worthy toy to play with. He lunged at the android, and the two of them hit the floor grappling.

While the Model Two shoved at his shoulders and tried to release itself from Jackson's grip, Jackson grabbed the loose arm and pulled, teeth gritted with the effort. Metal screamed and sparks flew as the arm tore free of the android's shoulder, leaving wires hanging loose from the ruptured socket.

Jackson lifted his head to grin at me. The android took advantage of the distraction and rolled Jackson onto his back. Its knee dug into his stomach, while the other leg pinned his wrist. The smile washed from Jackson's face, and his mouth twisted in pain.

I scanned the room for something—anything—that could help us shut down the Model Two.

The hand-screen we'd used to load my software onto it was a small, twisted piece of metal. I had another hand-screen in my jacket pocket, but I didn't know how to remove the data we'd just loaded onto the android. And even if I could manage that, the larger problem was getting the device connected to A12.

The android rained down punches on Jackson, who wrenched his captured wrist free. He held both arms over his head to block. I cringed at the blunt sound of each strike. Jackson wouldn't be able to hold the android off for long. He thought he was invincible. A12 might prove him wrong.

"An EMP gun!" Dr. Fisher shouted from the hall, where she was lying spread-eagle on top of a struggling Ron. "Check those drawers."

Her words shocked me into motion

I ran to a metal organizer along the far wall. It had eight drawers, four stacked atop one another on the left and four on the right. I started with the top right.

It contained nothing but tools. Wrenches and screw-drivers, and other things that looked tool-like but I didn't recognize.

I shifted the items around, but the drawer was so packed with metal objects that I couldn't be sure I was seeing everything. The EMP gun Dr. Kim had shown me was no bigger than some of these and similarly shaped. One could easily be hiding under all this junk.

The *thump, thump, thump* of blows between the android and Jackson continued behind me, now mixed with Jackson's grunts.

"Hurry up!" he shouted.

"Screw it." I yanked the drawer upward and out of its frame, bending the frame in the process, and dumped the contents upside down. I shifted through the items on the floor for only a few seconds before deciding there was no EMP gun there.

The sound of Jackson taking blow after blow assaulted me. I cringed at every impact. The best way I could help him was to find the EMP gun, but I had to look. His arms were starting to wear. The android's one-armed punches had broken past the skin on his arms, and the metal shone through, dented and bent but so far still holding. The clank of metal against metal sounded at each strike.

I didn't bother shifting the items around inside the second drawer, just yanked it out of the frame and dumped its contents on the floor. This one had been filled with a few cables but mostly small devices with out-of-date technologies. Hand-screens that couldn't be resized. Too-large micro-comms.

In the third drawer, the EMP gun sat right on top.

"Found it!"

"It's coded to my ID chip." Dr. Fisher beckoned me toward her.

I snatched it up and ran halfway back to the door before chucking it the rest of the way.

She caught it smoothly and pointed the device toward Jackson. It looked just like the one Dr. Kim had for testing the Model Ones. Hadn't she said they worked on *all* electronics?

"Wait!" I shouted.

"Don't wait. Shoot." Jackson's words came out staccato, as he braced for each blow from the android still on top of him.

"You'll kill him. Half his body is cybernetic."

Reacting to my words, Jackson dropped his arms for a split second. A12's next punch struck his eye, and he howled in pain. "Just fucking shoot it," he shouted, as another punch skimmed his mouth. His lip split, and blood gushed down his chin. "Don't miss!"

Fisher's eyes narrowed, and she pulled the trigger.

I screamed.

The muzzle lit up bright blue, sputtered, and then died.

Oh crap.

I threw myself at the android. Air burst from my lungs as I slammed into the solid metal. The two of us rolled across the floor. Jackson darted after us and yanked the android to its feet. He wrenched its remaining arm behind its back.

"Its power supply!" Fisher shouted. "In the chest cavity."

Ron finally gave up struggling under her considerable bulk and went limp, his eyes glaring.

The android faced me, Jackson still holding its arm behind it. I leaped toward the thing's torso, but it kicked out. Its foot nailed me in the chest. I sank down to my knees, gasping for air. Another leg shot out toward me, but I dropped to the side to avoid it.

I jumped back to my feet and threw my left arm forward. The android kicked again, but I dodged and slammed my fist into its chest. The metal panel bent at the impact and hung awkwardly in its frame.

With my right hand, I grabbed a protruding edge of the loose chest panel and yanked. Metal creaked, and the panel ripped free. I stumbled backward, panel in hand.

Inside, an array of wires and unrecognizable parts greeted me. The Model Two finally ripped its arm free of Jackson and punched him in the chest. Jackson stumbled backward. The android's arm shot out, and fingers closed around my neck.

It lifted me from the ground, and I kicked empty air. Its wrist blocked my view downward to the parts inside the open chest. Blind, my right hand fumbled in the chest cavity. Wires, more wires.

"Lower," Fisher shouted.

Jackson yanked at the android's arm that held me, but A12 was immovable.

My lungs screamed for air, and I fought to remain conscious. Darkness inched in around me. Each time I blinked, I yearned to keep my eyelids closed, to drift off to sleep. Off to a place where my chest didn't feel like it was on fire.

My right hand touched a warm piece of metal inside the android's chest.

"There!" Fisher shouted.

I pulled. Cables snapped, and a smooth metal disk came off in my hand.

The android's bright red eyes flickered and died. The metal fingers around my neck loosened, and I dropped. My legs buckled beneath me. I sank to the floor, beaten, bruised, but still alive.

35

I LAY IN ONE OF CYBERCORP'S HOSPITAL ROOMS. THE doctor standing over me wasn't Dr. Fisher, but like her, he wore the glaring red CyberCorp logo on the pocket of his white jacket.

I closed my eyes briefly and wished I were in a normal hospital, one without murderous, psychopathic androids.

"It's good to see you awake, Miss Hayes." The doctor smiled down at me. Above the CyberCorp logo, his name appeared in red thread: Dr. Morris. He gestured to the opposite side of my bed. "Your father's been worried."

This was the second time in the span of a few weeks that I'd woken in a hospital bed with my father at my side. His chair sat right next to the bed, one hand clutched loosely around my right one. The other arm cradled a sleeping Allie, who snored with her head tucked in the hollow between his neck and shoulder.

Marcy leaned against the wall in the far corner. She gave me a warm smile.

"I want to go to a hospital," I said.

My father shook his head. "You're not going to one of those any time soon, not with that arm." He released my hand and pointed at my head. "And not with that chip in your head."

I let out a long stream of breath.

"There's no way to get it out without risking your life."

"Which is exactly why someone should have asked me before putting it in there."

"You're right."

I jerked upright, and then groaned as aches rocketed through my body. I couldn't recall ever hearing him say that to me—or to anyone. "Ugh. Can you save shocking revelations like that until after I've recovered?"

His full laugh showed off perfect teeth and a wide, beautiful smile. He squeezed my hand tighter.

"It's fine," I said. "It's going to have to be." I'd spent all this time sulking about having an artificially intelligent limb. But without it, Jackson and I wouldn't have been able to take down that Model Two. The arm was never the problem. *Ron* was the problem. "As long as Ron's out of my head."

"He is. We removed all his programming from your chip." My dad's face went serious. "And he's squealing like a pig. We knew he needed a serious financial backer to pull off the stuff with the EyeNet. He's negotiating a lighter sentence in return for giving up Philip Pollock."

My instinct was to defend my former idol, but I no longer had it in me.

If life was fair, they would both spend the rest of their lives in jail. And Pollock's cell would be fitted with extra tech—the best artificial intelligence in the security field—just to make him squirm.

"Good. Where's Mom?" The last time I'd seen her, she'd been standing between me and a gun.

"Your mother's fine. She said she was going for a bathroom break." He leaned forward and lowered his voice to a loud whisper. "But I think she really went to boss around some of the doctors and nurses. She's worried about you." He nodded toward a guard blocking the door from the inside. "Some friends are here to see you."

The guard opened the door, and in flew Liv, followed by Hunter. I gave them a wide smile, which fell the slightest bit when I saw Jackson wasn't with them.

Liv squeezed me in a long embrace and then wiped the wetness from her eyes.

"You're such a sap," I told her.

Hunter shot a glance at my dad before giving me a one-armed hug.

My dad pushed up from his chair and stepped away to give us space. Standing, he repositioned Allie to sit on his hip, her head leaning on his shoulder. She mumbled something in half-sleep.

Liv and Hunter both sat on the edge of my bed, with Liv closer to my head.

"How are you feeling?" she asked. She chewed her lip, the way she did when she was nervous.

I inventoried my body. My back still throbbed from when Jackson had thrown me to the floor, as did my cheek where both Jackson and the Model Two hit me with their large—and very metal—fists. My throat felt raw and dry. But I was alive and in one piece.

My left arm had been replaced with a brand-new one, thanks to A12 having mangled the old one's hand. I wished I could have my original one back—the one made of flesh and bone—but this would have to do.

I could get used to it. Someday.

"I'm fine. A little tired, but I'll survive." I gave Liv a tired smile.

She didn't return it.

"I said I'm fine. I promise." I grabbed her hand and squeezed it, but her expression remained worried.

My father touched his ear to take a call. He listened for a moment, then said, "I'm in my daughter's hospital room right now, so give me a moment to step out." He pointed to the door to let me know he was leaving.

Marcy followed and smoothly relieved him of Allie, setting my sister on her hip instead.

With those three out of the room, Liv surrendered her position close to my head. She stood, and Hunter shifted into her spot.

My hand fit perfectly into his. When he leaned over and touched his forehead to mine, I threaded my fingers into his dark hair, still damp from a recent shower. The soft rhythm of his breathing and the spring scent of his shampoo calmed me.

The door opened, and Hunter jumped away. My father

looked back and forth between us, and then to Liv standing several feet away. He'd never seen me with any boy except Jackson. I didn't look forward to the interrogation I'd get about Hunter once things settled down.

I scrambled to fill the silence. "How's Jackson?"

The edges of Hunter's mouth twitched downward.

"He's here too," my dad said, "but the doctors are still working on him. He's awake, and he'll be fine. He's been asking for you." He shot another glance at Hunter.

Jackson had been there last night only because he followed me after I broke up with him. But without him, I'd have more dead bodies on my conscience, or I would be dead too. I owed him a conversation.

More importantly, I *wanted* to have that conversation. I'd been able to count on him for most of my life, and last night, when we were as far apart as we'd ever been, he'd leaped in and stood beside me.

"I want to know when he's available."

"I'll make sure you do."

I took a deep breath. "And . . . Simon?" The image stained the inside of my eyelids—A12 slamming his head into the floor over and over. Blood leaking from poor Simon's face.

My father's shoulders slumped. He didn't need to answer.

"Thought so." Tears stung my eyes, and I let them fall. Unlike the others, Simon hadn't died by my hands. But he'd died trying to help me, and that hurt my soul almost as much.

"But you saved Dr. Fisher's life. You and Jackson both."

I offered him a weak smile.

"Dr. Fisher is so grateful for your intervention that she's prepared to testify on your behalf about the three murders. She doesn't know all the details, just that you're a suspect. We'll go down to the police station and make an official statement as soon as we can. Fisher and Jackson will come with us, and I hope that will be enough witnesses to back our story that you weren't really to blame for the murders."

"Are we sure about that?" I asked. "The arm was designed to follow my instructions, even the ones I didn't know my brain was giving."

He brushed my hair away from my face. "You're not responsible. The Model Two's reaction to your data proves that. It got aggressive because of the same data that made you do those things. The AI was in control, and Ron was in control of *it*."

"What about Jackson? He had a lot more replaced than I did, but he seemed fine. Doesn't that prove there was something about my brain that made me act that way?"

"No." My father's jaw worked as he ground his teeth together. "Apparently, Ron chose to target only you. We discovered a while back that the Model Ones and Twos were vulnerable to the EyeNet, but we patched the issue. Jackson got the correct software, patch included. You had the correct software initially—your mom oversaw the original installation—but Ron must have removed the patch at some point."

"During physical therapy." I groaned as I recalled how he'd deleted some code from my software when he adjusted my arm strength. That was when he'd done it. Even before I left the hospital, I'd been under his control.

"Hey. It's okay." My dad reached for my right hand, which I had balled into a fist. "Everything will be fine. It's all over now. I promise."

The warmth of his hand in mine quieted my thoughts, and a massive weight rose from my chest.

"They've removed all the data your chip learned in the last week and a half, and they added code to destroy any data coming in from the EyeNet. You should be back to your old self now."

I wasn't sure I knew what that was anymore.

"I'm not a murderer." I tested the words in my mouth. The explanation was logical, but the words tasted like a lie. When my eyes closed, even when I blinked, I saw Debbie's lifeless body sprawled across her mattress.

It had been less than two weeks since I woke from the coma with this arm, and in that time, I'd taken three lives and saved one. The math didn't add up.

But that last one—the saving—I did that by choice. I embraced having the arm, and I saved a life with it.

For now, I would try to take comfort in that.

36

They kept me under observation for another day. The next morning, I went through the familiar process of checking out of what I'd come to think of as CyberCorp Hospital. I didn't have a suitcase this time, only a small backpack and the change of clothes Liv had brought me this morning.

Liv zipped yesterday's clothing into the bag and threw it over her shoulder. "Ready to go?"

"You have no idea."

They'd just given me a large dose of meds, so I was pain free and ready to get the hell out of there. I restrained myself from running out the door.

In the hallway, images of Philip Pollock and his vital stats flashed across the walls as we glided by on the moving walkway: *Six-foot-two, 180 pounds, brown hair, brown eyes. Suspected of multiple counts of murder and attempted murder. Last seen unarmed, but the suspect has unlimited resources. Do not approach. Call CyberCorp security immediately on sight.*

I stepped off the moving walkway to get a closer look, and Liv followed close behind.

So much had happened in the past day that I'd had little time to think about Philip—how he'd tried to make me believe all this was my fault—how he preached hatred for technology and then used it as a weapon against innocent teens like Debbie.

The image of his face zoomed out until the screen displayed his whole body. Then the screen blanked, and the information began again on a loop.

"Why do you think he did it?" I asked.

Liv was trembling, her hands fisted at her sides.

"What's going on with you?" I asked. "And don't tell me it's nothing."

Sad eyes stared at Philip's image on the vid-screen. "Ron is my boyfriend," she whispered.

My mouth dropped open. "He's the older guy you're dating?"

She nodded, chewing her lip.

"He asked me to make sure you didn't press the issue about changing your arm's programming," she blurted out. "I didn't know why. He just said your arm was important to his job. I was trying to help him out. I swear I didn't know what he was doing. And I definitely didn't know he was working with that crazy Pollock dude."

"But I introduced you guys when we toured CyberCorp."

"No. He didn't want you to know about us—said something about not wanting special treatment from his employers because of having a personal connection to you." She flushed bright red and stared down at her toes. "I didn't question it much. I should have."

I buried the anger trying to boil to the surface. I'd strangled three people because of Ron, and Liv had helped him. But also, Liv had stood by me through everything. The least I could do was forgive this.

"Are you mad?"

I threw an arm over her shoulders and squeezed. "I made my own choices. He duped both of us."

Tension drained from Liv's face. "I don't know why he did it, though. He's got nothing against AI. He thinks the androids will make life easier for everyone."

"He said his dad has cirrhosis because he started drinking after the treatment for his mom failed. He blames CyberCorp for his dad's health."

Liv nodded in understanding. "I should have seen it."

"How could you?"

"He's so angry about his father. He gets all twitchy every time the subject comes up, but I figured he was mad *at* his dad for drinking."

"I guess he picked a different target to be pissed at. He must have reached out to Philip to help him. Dr. Kim and Dr. Fisher both said it would take a super-expensive computer to bypass security on the EyeNet."

"Or maybe Philip reached out to him. Either way, they're both evil."

According to my father, they'd removed the bad data from my system and modified my code to destroy anything else received from the EyeNet. If anyone else wanted to commit murder over CyberCorp, at least next time they would have to do it without my help.

We stepped back on the moving walkway and headed down to the parking garage.

We'd almost reached Liv's car when a set of service elevator doors opened across the lot. Two men rolled out a flatbed cart supporting twelve Model One androids. The men hauled the cart toward the back of a large truck with the CyberCorp logo splashed across the side in huge letters. Under it, in smaller letters, were the words *Home Delivery*.

I stopped walking and called my father.

He answered on the first ring, faster than he'd ever answered my calls in my entire life. "Hel—"

"Why are Model Ones being put on a delivery truck?" I asked, before he could get the whole word out.

He paused before saying, "I feel like this is a trick question. Isn't the answer obvious?"

"What about the EyeNet bug?" I'd seen firsthand what a bug in CyberCorp's AI could do, and I had no desire to see it a second time, regardless of whether it involved me.

"I told you it's been resolved. We handled that bug three weeks ago. These machines are all patched up."

"They are?"

"Yes. The only reason you had an issue is that Ron made sure you got the old software, the version without the patch."

"Don't you want to be sure? You know, take some time to double-check them?"

He gave me an exasperated sigh. "Lena, we've double-checked, triple-checked, and quadruple-checked those androids. Believe it or not, I know what I'm doing. I've managed to run this business for twenty-one years without your assistance."

"Yeah, okay. Sorry. I'm still shaken up about the whole thing."

His voice softened. "Why don't you go home and rest? I'll have Marcy cook whatever you want for dinner, and your mom and I will both be home around six."

"Everything okay?" Liv asked when the call ended.

I cocked an eyebrow at her.

She laughed. "You're right. That was a stupid question. But what did your dad say?"

"They handled the bug weeks ago. The androids are all patched up." I repeated the words back mechanically.

"You don't believe him?"

"He's got no reason to lie to me." Even as I said those words, I stomped across the parking lot to the home-delivery truck. The two men had already loaded up the Model Ones and were walking around to the front of the vehicle.

I waved to get their attention. "Hi. Can I ask you a question?"

"We're on a schedule," the one on the passenger side said, as he climbed into his seat. His glance landed on me as he reached for his seat belt. "Miss Hayes?"

"Have these androids been updated with the latest software?"

The man's posture straightened. "I don't know anything about an update. All we do is pick up and deliver. You can take a look if you want."

"Thanks. It's important."

"You got it."

He jumped out of the seat, circled to the back of the truck, and rolled the door open. Inside, twelve Model Ones stood on their pallet, ready to go. He interlocked his fingers and let me use them as a step into the back of the truck.

I squeezed between the first and second rows of androids, chose one, and opened the small panel on its lower back. When I pressed the power button, the android hummed to life. A screen inside the panel displayed information about the machine, including its identification number and software version.

The software was dated last week—which meant they had the patch.

I jumped down to the ground and thanked the man for his time.

"What did you find out?" Liv asked, after the truck pulled away.

"It's fine." Tension leaked out of me as if a valve had opened. More than anything, I just wanted to curl up in a ball and sleep for the next week. "Everything is fine."

Liv climbed into the driver's seat of her car, and I slid in next to her on the passenger side. The auto-drive took us out of the parking garage and onto the main street.

As we rode, in the rearview mirror, CyberCorp Tower receded into the distance. It became smaller each second, but still ever present.

Technology was part of my life now, like it or not. I just hoped the rest of the world was ready for that too.

ACKNOWLEDGMENTS

There are so many people who helped and inspired me to complete this book, and it wouldn't exist without them.

Thanks to my parents and to Victor for being a constant source of support.

Thank you to Susan Jessen, Rachel Lauderdale, Kelly, Sonja Griffing, and Kristin Potchynok for being amazing beta readers. Seriously, guys, I am so grateful.

Thanks to Dani across the pond for believing in this book and for insisting that I change the title. That original title was *not* good.

Lastly, thank you to my readers. Your time is valuable, and I appreciate that you took a chance on me. I have a ton of new stories in the pipeline, so please stick around. My contact links are on the next page.

ABOUT THE AUTHOR

I decided to write books about ten minutes before graduating from law school.

Now, I'm an Atlanta attorney moonlighting as an author, electronics junkie, and secret superhero. With degrees in computer science and a healthy diet of fiction, I love all things high-tech and unreal.

I write mysteries, sometimes for young adults and sometimes in fantasy and science fiction settings.

Now you know where to find me:
www.writeralicia.com

Sign up for my newsletter to keep in touch:
www.writeralicia.com/newsletter

amazon.com/author/writeralicia

bookbub.com/authors/alicia-ellis

facebook.com/writeralicia

instagram.com/writeralicia

twitter.com/writeralicia

goodreads.com/writeralicia

patreon.com/writeralicia

www.ingramcontent.com/pod-product-compliance
Lightning Source LLC
Chambersburg PA
CBHW061042190726
48286CB00006B/1569